The Uninvited Caller

The Domestic Thriller Collection

Ramona Light

The Uninvited Caller

© 2023 by Ramona Light

All rights reserved.

No part of this book may be reproduced or transmitted in any form or by any means, electronic or mechanical, including information storage and retrieval systems, without express written permission by the author, except for the use of brief quotations in a book review.

This book is a work of fiction. Names, characters, incidents, and places are either products of the author's imagination or used fictitiously and are not to be construed as real. None of the characters in the book are based on actual persons. Any resemblance to persons living or dead is entirely and unintentionally coincidental.

Contents

Part 1: Lilith	1
Chapter 1	3
Chapter 2	9
Chapter 3	15
Chapter 4	19
Chapter 5	23
Chapter 6	27
Chapter 7	31
Chapter 8	37
Chapter 9	41
Chapter 10	45
Chapter 11	51
Chapter 12	55
Chapter 13	59
Chapter 14	63
Chapter 15	69
Chapter 16	73
Chapter 17	79

Chapter 18	83
Chapter 19	89
Chapter 20	95
Chapter 21	101
Chapter 22	105
Chapter 23	109
Chapter 24	113
Chapter 25	119
Chapter 26	125
Chapter 27	131
Chapter 28	137
Part 2: Virginia	143
Chapter 29	145
Chapter 30	151
Chapter 31	155
Chapter 32	159
Chapter 33	163
Chapter 34	169
Chapter 35	173
Chapter 36	177
Chapter 37	183
Chapter 38	189
Chapter 39	193
Chapter 40	197

Chapter 41	201
Chapter 42	205
Chapter 43	209
Chapter 44	213
Chapter 45	219
Chapter 46	223
Chapter 47	227
Chapter 48	231
Part 3: Lilith & Virginia	237
Chapter 49: Lilith	239
Chapter 50: Virginia	243
Chapter 51: Lilith	249
Chapter 52: Virginia	255
Chapter 53: Lilith	259
Chapter 54: Virginia	263
Chapter 55: Lilith	267
Chapter 56: Virginia	271
Chapter 57: Lilith	275
Chapter 58: Virginia	279
Chapter 59: Lilith	285
Chapter 60: Virginia	289
Chapter 61: Lilith	295
Chapter 62: Virginia	299
Chapter 63: Lilith	303

Chapter 64: Virginia	307
Chapter 65: Lilith	313
Chapter 66: Virginia	319
Chapter 67: Lilith	323
Chapter 68: Virginia	327
Chapter 69: Lilith	331
Chapter 70: Virginia	335
Chapter 71: Lilith	339
Chapter 72: Virginia	343
Epilogue: Virginia	349
Also By Ramona Light	355

Part 1: Lilith

Chapter 1

In the twelve years since my husband died, everything in my life has become easier. I know that might seem cruel to some, but living with Fletcher DuBose was hell. Of course, there were pleasant moments also, but they were far fewer than the nasty ones.

Still, I sometimes feel like I'm simply going through the motions, but I suppose that's just what a quiet life entails, really.

Our house on Beacon Hill is too big for my daughter and me. Even though Mom is always here, it is still too spacious. The four bedrooms, living room, dining room, kitchen, large den, and office have always felt wasteful. We have a view of the Boston Common and its sprawling trees and lake. It has been our house for five years, but it will probably never feel like a home.

"Eat your food," Mom says through a mouthful of meat and vegetables. She nods at my plate and creases her brow, making me feel nine years old instead of thirty-nine. "I went to a lot of trouble to make that."

I fork an extra-large pile into my mouth and smile dramatically through it. She laughs, then instantly covers her mouth when she catches herself. Astrid chuckles, too, shaking her head as she looks at her grandmother. Mom rolls her eyes, but she is still smiling.

"You see what I have to put up with?" she says to Astrid. "Your mother has always been a cheeky one."

There is no meanness in her voice, only playfulness. Virginia Townsend *does* have a playful side. It can be shy in coming out and the seriousness that is her default personality can be a little overwhelming to those who don't know her. I know a lot of adults wouldn't want their mothers practically living with them for so long, but most of them haven't gone through the things we have.

"It's lovely, Mom," I tell her, and I mean it. My mother has always been a good cook. Well, she has *become* one. Growing up, not so much.

"Yeah, it's great," Astrid confirms.

My little girl is not so little anymore. In fact, she'll be off to college next year. It looks like she'll follow her heart and study biology. When she was small, I'd hoped I'd influence her to opt for English literature, but that was never my choice to make. Astrid DuBose is a strong, independent young woman who will always decide for herself what path she is going to take.

Her long black hair—the same color and length as mine—is tied up expertly in a cool ponytail. Although I think she is wearing makeup, she has it so scantily applied that it is hard to tell. Her big green eyes—so like her father's—show an alertness that never seems to leave them. At five-two, she has an inch on me, but Astrid holds herself much taller. She is a proud young woman, and I'm an even prouder mother because of it.

Like everything else in this house, the large table we are sitting at in the spacious dining room feels like it is too much. It probably is, but when Fletcher's life insurance came through five years ago, I thought we deserved a little grandeur after the seven years of struggle that preceded it. Mom had been insistent that I use the money for some good. As she put it at the time, "no amount of money could make up for the bruises and scars he gave you."

That's the thing with my mother—she only saw the damage Fletcher left behind. Yes, sometimes he scared me, but he was still my husband. And it hadn't always been that bad, at least in the early years. Yet when he died, I felt a twinge of such relief that I cried with guilt more so than pain for the first few days. Should I have experienced that initial emotion upon hearing of his accident? Probably, as Fletcher had made my life a living hell for a long time. Still, he was a good father when he wasn't in that dark place, and he probably deserved a better fate than being swallowed up by the Gauley River.

"Ma?" Astrid says. "You okay?"

"Yeah." I nod and take another forkful of my dinner. "Just thinking about work."

I don't enjoy lying to my daughter, but she doesn't need to know the things that are currently running through my head. Working part-time as an English Lit teacher doesn't usually take up much of my thoughts. I love the job, of course, but it has become monotonous over the last few years. Mom thought I should have retired once the insurance money came in, but I'd miss the kids too much. Witnessing those rare occasions when one of them lights up over a passage in *Huckleberry Finn* or something by Hemingway means the world to me.

Astrid and her grandmother have fallen into a conversation I'm only partly listening to, and I let their words become the background to my thoughts. I like it when dinner melts into a pleasant experience like this, when I don't feel the need to fill every silent moment with my words. I suppose I've always wanted to do everything I could to make Astrid's childhood as normal as possible, which has sometimes caused me to overdo it.

Growing up without a dad can be tough. I know because I lost my own when I was sixteen. But Astrid's father died when she was only five, and her memories of him are spotty. That is probably a good thing, as Fletcher DuBose wasn't a very pleasant man to be around, mostly.

I take another bite of food and swallow. It really is wonderful, and I wish I had more of an appetite. Something has been off with me recently, and I can't quite put my finger on it. I have been thinking about Fletcher more than usual, so that might have something to do with it. I don't often reminisce about the past—at least, I don't think I do—but bumping into Robert two days ago brought it all flooding back.

My so-called father-in-law had been as snarky as ever. I rarely see him these days, and it could go a year without me even hearing his voice. We have nothing left to say to each other, and we run in completely different circles. Robert DuBose is one of the most successful men in Boston, and his construction company has raised most of the major buildings in the whole of Massachusetts. I'm just a part-time teacher who fell in love with his only son twenty-three years ago.

"That's great, Nana," Astrid is saying. "I'm happy for you."

There was something about the way Robert spoke to me the other day. It wasn't so much in his tone—he only has one—but that he talked to me at all. In fact, he actually crossed the hotel lobby to speak to me. I had only been there for lunch with a friend, and the Galileo Hotel isn't exactly of the class Robert would usually be seen in. But he had stopped me on the way out.

Hearing him mentioning Fletcher had brought it all back to me, and Robert had seemed overly concerned about how I was doing. In the twelve years since Fletcher died, I don't recall Robert ever asking about how I was holding up.

Have you ever asked him? I ask myself, making me wince inside.

Probably not, but we weren't even on speaking terms for years. It took the courts seven years to declare Fletcher legally dead, and in all that time, I think Robert was holding on to the belief that his son might still be alive. Add to that his unwavering belief that I should be held responsible for Fletcher even being on the river that morning, and you have an angry—

"Lilith," Mom snaps. Her dark brown eyes are narrowed, and the dim lighting in the room has illuminated the streaks of gray in her otherwise jet-black hair. "I asked you a question."

"Sorry, Mom. What is it?"

"Do you want a glass of wine?"

"Sure," I reply. I don't even want one. Then again, it might help me shake this incessant feeling that something is wrong.

Or am I simply trying to create some excitement in my life that isn't really there?

Chapter 2

The house has always felt too big, but it's ten times worse when I'm alone like I am tonight. Astrid is studying at Rachael's place this evening, and Mom told me at breakfast that she wouldn't be around until tomorrow. She hasn't gone out; I can see her silver Ford Focus parked outside next to the small house we had built for her when we moved in. The lights are burning inside, and I can see the constantly shifting glow of the TV shining through the curtains. She must have just wanted a night to herself, which has been happening a lot more recently.

I take another look at the handwritten thesis of William Golding's *Lord of the Flies* and toss it back onto the coffee table. The words have refused to stick, and I still have a full pile to read next to the one I've just discarded. After sitting here for over an hour, I've spent more time looking out the window at Mom's place than I have marking my students' work. I don't think I'll get any more done tonight, so I may as well forget about it until tomorrow.

I take a sip of the glass of club soda in front of me. The ice has melted, but it is still cold and refreshing. A massive flat-screen TV looks down blankly at me from the wall over the mantle. On either side are my prized possessions—two tall, tightly packed bookcases. First editions hold pride of place on the top shelves, and they are the only real indulgences I allowed myself when the insurance money came in. Well, those and the large house.

Not for the first time over the last few days, I sigh loudly. I still can't shake the feeling that something is wrong. Is it simply a deep-rooted worry about Astrid finishing high school? I've spent a lot of time recently consciously digging through my emotions to find the reason or reasons for my glum moods. Ironically, all that does is make me feel even more depressed.

Well, "depressed" might be pushing it. In fact, it frustrates me when people claim to be depressed or suffering from anxiety when all that's wrong is that they're having a bad day. When they do this, they dilute the severity of such devastating issues. This leads to genuine sufferers getting dismissed as attention-seekers or drama queens simply because all the empathy has been sucked out of the room by the actual attention-seekers and drama queens.

I need to stop thinking so negatively. If I can't pinpoint the reason I feel so anxious, then there is probably nothing to worry about. I hate when my thoughts turn negative like this.

I take another sip of my drink and place the glass back on its coaster. The colors on Mom's window have turned green and stayed that way for a while, which means she is probably watching the game. It makes sense now that she didn't want to be disturbed, as watching the Red Sox is one of the main traditions she carried on after my dad passed away. Seeing them curled up in front of the TV and sharing a six-pack is one of my fondest memories.

My hand instinctively reaches out for the thesis once again, and I stop it. I know I won't be able to concentrate on it fully, and not just because it is so poorly written. When my head gets like this, the only productive thing I can do is ride it out as best I can until it passes. Most people on the outside looking in would point at my beautiful house and recently purchased SUV and wonder just what I have to be anxious about, but acknowledging such stuff does little to bring me relief. It never has.

Truthfully, the whispers—and there were plenty at the time—that I only got with Fletcher because his father was so wealthy used to really hurt. I was sixteen when I met him, and girls that age don't care about such superficial things. Even if they did, Fletcher was gorgeous and charming, so the money was never what attracted me to him.

I slip my feet out from under me and rest them on the plush red carpet. The leather couch groans as I readjust myself. When I sit forward and rest my chin on my hands, I catch myself sighing again.

Am I bored with my life? Is that it? Astrid is old enough now that my working full time wouldn't affect her. She spends so much of her time at school, studying, or hanging out with friends that she is hardly ever at the house. Mom has always been independent. If I hadn't needed her so much in the years following Fletcher's death, she probably would have traveled the world or something exciting like that.

Maybe I need a change in my routine? I find myself staring into space more and more these days. Having money is not the easy ride people think it is, although I'm eternally grateful that it has become something I don't have to worry about. Still, part of me misses the closeness of the three of us working hard and scrimping to get ahead in life. Those seven years after the rafting accident were tough in so many ways, but it was three generations of women against the world. There was something inspiring and passionate about that.

The shriek of the doorbell makes me jump, and I laugh a little at my tingling nerves. Astrid must have forgotten her key again, even though I called after her this morning to remind her. It will always amaze me that my daughter can explain Darwin's theory of evolution or Aristotle's breakthroughs in epistemology, yet she constantly locks herself out of her home!

My back cracks when I stand up, and I rub at it with my hand. The shock of the front hall's cold floorboards on my bare feet after the warmth of the carpet makes me wince, but I'm smiling as I walk toward the door. I think the only time I'm ever truly happy is when I have my baby girl in the house with me. I don't know what I'll do when she goes off to college.

Our front door has both a knob and a slide lock, and I snap the latter to the side. Crime is nearly nil in Beacon Hill, but better safe than sorry.

"I told you to bring your key!" I chime as I twist the knob and open the door. I'm chuckling as I speak. "How many times have I—"

There is a man standing on the porch. He looks to be in his early forties. His shaggy black hair has streaks of gray in it, but it suits him. Under the porch's powerful bulb, I can see his deep tan, and the piercing green eyes looking back at me seem to show recognition.

"Hi, Lilith," he says, his voice husky.

I can't stop looking at those eyes. I know this apparent stranger has just said my name, but I seem unable to accept how he might know me. When he smiles, my resolve breaks, and I feel my vision waver. As my knees buckle, he steps in quickly and catches me in his strong, sinewy arms. He smells of Hugo Boss cologne—just like he always did.

I must have fallen asleep on the couch because this can't be happening. That's it—I'm having a strange dream because of the stress I've been putting myself under. But it feels so real…

My last thought before I faint away is that I'm looking up into the face of the man I fell in love with when I was sixteen. I'm looking up at Fletcher DuBose.

Chapter 3

At first, my surroundings don't feel familiar. Then I tick off the items I recognize—flat-screen TV, bookcases, coffee table, even the stack of students' papers that still need to be graded. I'm in my living room and lying on the couch. Okay, so it was a strange dream. My head is still swimming, and I have to close my eyes and swallow against the wave of nausea that threatens to overwhelm me.

When I open them again, I'm still on the couch, and that's good. The image of Fletcher standing at the front door is vivid, and I shiver. Suddenly, my recent anxious mood and unplaced worry fit. I've been thinking about the past too much, and I've obviously worked myself up. This peculiar dream is just my subconscious telling me to relax and concentrate on the present. But that is easier said than done.

It's funny, but the advice we give to ourselves and others is usually sound, yet it can be so hard to follow more often than not. I know it's been twelve years since I got the phone call to tell me that Fletcher's raft had been found shattered on the banks of the Gauley River. I've had police interviews and even a funeral since, but my mind still throws up crazy images, like my dead husband standing at the door.

Something else that has shocked me is how little I remember of the bad times with Fletcher, and there were many. In fact, the bad far outweighed the good. So why is it that whenever I think back over our time together, I see a young, vibrant Fletcher making me laugh or lifting me up and kissing my lips? Why are the backgrounds shrouded in sunshine and not the grayness of a usual Boston skyline? Does everyone have a tendency to turn those they've lost into saints when they were really demons?

I push myself up on my elbow and wince at the sudden sharp pain in my side. My vision blurs again for a split second, then settles. The glass of club soda I had earlier is still on the coffee table, and I reach an unsteady hand across and bring it to my lips. The liquid feels wonderful as it wets my parched throat.

Another image of Fletcher standing at the front door flashes across my mind. The same piercing green eyes, shaggy hair, sinewy yet strong arms. They had all been there, yet he had aged. There was something so familiar about the phantom who rang the doorbell and something so strange about him too. It had been a re-creation of my dead husband that seemed so real, and I can't help being in awe at the power of the human imagination.

Who knew that we could create such fantastic illusions? All of my dreams and memories of Fletcher to this day have shown him as he was, and usually the younger version. But this time, my thoughts had decided to age him appropriately, which had been the most jarring thing of all. Seeing him as he might have turned out—still handsome, strong, and intense, but refined.

I can hear Astrid in the kitchen as she moves around with care, clearly trying not to wake me. She must have come home while I was asleep. I fumble for my phone and find it tucked underneath my body on the couch. When I check the time, I see that over an hour has passed since my last waking memory. A quick nap hurt no one, but I actually feel more exhausted than I did beforehand.

I hear the click of the kettle from down the hall, then Astrid's muffled footsteps as she tries to find a cup or grab the milk from the refrigerator. I wanted to tell her about my dream, but I promised myself long ago that I would only ever talk about her father whenever she brought him up. Mom will probably roll her eyes at the mention of his name, but I can discuss it with her tomorrow.

I can still see her face that night twelve years ago as she arrived at my house—the porch light of our old place in the suburbs casting long shadows across her concerned and furious face. She had been so angry when she saw the cuts on my forehead and even more enraged at the sight of the bruises on my ribs.

She'd spoken to me through clenched teeth, growling as she demanded to know where Fletcher had gone. I'd told her in between wracking sobs he wasn't in, that he'd left a day early for his rafting trip. Mom had been so, so angry. I'd called her half an hour before then as Fletcher had been pounding on the locked bedroom door, his venomous threats shaking the walls as Astrid shivered in her bed and asked her Ma why Daddy was acting so scary.

To this day, I wonder what would have happened if Mom had arrived ten minutes earlier and caught Fletcher as he stormed out of the house. How would that have played out? It wouldn't have been pretty, that much I know. Probably best not to think about it, though. Fletcher *did* leave before she arrived, and he made it to West Virginia in time to set off on his rafting trip the following morning. How things might have gone is irrelevant.

The house is so silent that I can hear boiling water being poured into a cup. I smile, knowing my baby girl is back home, then sit up straight on the couch and stretch. The resurgence of blood pulsing through my system wakes me up and I actually feel a little better. Maybe this most vivid of dreams was a good thing. I know now that I still need to process what happened, because I never fully did.

Understanding this is a positive step. Maybe some therapy would work better now. Back then, I really didn't want to talk, and I even refused to discuss the bad things Fletcher had done. I felt like he would show up dead if I spoke ill of him. It was irrational and ridiculous, but the grieving mind works in mysterious ways.

It's because you wished him dead so many times before he left for West Virginia, Lilith. That's where the guilt has always stemmed from, right?

"Not tonight," I say, shaking my head in the empty room. "I'm not dealing with that tonight."

Footsteps in the hallway now, moving away from the kitchen.

"Hey, sweetie," I call over my shoulder. When I turn my head to the open door, another sharp pain stings my side. I must have slept awkwardly on it. "I'm up if you want to chat."

"Oh, good," a man says as an enormous shadow fills the doorframe. Then the man who looks so much like Fletcher steps in and smiles, and my heart beats so hard it feels like it will burst through my chest. He is holding two cups with steam billowing out of them. "I made you some tea."

Chapter 4

"You're not Fletcher," I say after what feels like an age. "You can't be."

"I'm sorry," the man replies. He is still standing in the doorway, holding the cups of tea. "I would have called first, but I only had an address."

"How did you... I mean... what?"

He walks over and places the cups down on the coffee table, then sits in the cream-colored armchair facing me. He has aged well, and there is a huge scar on the side of his face. I can see it running up his cheek close to his ear before it disappears under his salt-and-pepper hair.

"You look good," he says, smiling. Something about the gesture doesn't sit right.

I pull my feet up underneath me as if the carpet will swallow me up if I don't. With my arms wrapped around myself, I say, "I don't know who you are, but I want you to leave."

"I know this is hard to understand, Lilith, but it really is me."

He sounds different, and there is something off about the tenderness in his voice, but still...

"Do you think this is funny? Turning up here and playing this sick game? Who put you up to it?"

"Listen," he says, leaning forward and picking up his cup. He takes a sip and smiles. "Drink your tea, Loly. You'll feel better."

I gasp. "What did you just call me?"

Fletcher chuckles. "Loly. I've always called you that."

"How do you know that?"

"It's funny," he says, shaking his head. "I can remember silly things like a cute pet name, yet I can't recall anything at all about our wedding day. Isn't that strange?"

"That's because you weren't there," I snap, but I don't like the lack of conviction in my voice.

"No, Loly. It's because of the amnesia."

"Amnesia?"

"After the rafting accident," he says. He brings his hand up to the deep scar on the left-hand side of his face. "Shit, it took me twelve years to even remember that I *had* a wife and a little girl."

"Stop. Please stop whatever it is you're doing."

"Loly," this man says. I hate him calling me that. Fletcher was the only person who ever referred to me by that name. It made no sense, as it had nothing to do with my real name, but that was probably why it meant so much. It was wholly ours. "I can't explain everything that has happened right now, it would take too long, but I will need you to hear me out in time."

"I just don't understand." My voice sounds like it is coming to me underwater. I can see this man I once loved sitting across from me, but it doesn't feel like reality. Could I still be asleep, having a dream within a dream like some over-the-top episode of *Days of Our Lives*? No, this is happening, and the pain in my side is from when I fainted earlier. My body bent awkwardly before he caught me.

In those strong, sinewy arms, right?

"Listen, Loly—"

"Please don't call me that," I whimper.

"—I know none of this makes sense. It still confuses me. It wasn't until I remembered your name and looked you up on the register that some of it came back to me. Hell, I don't even remember living in this house."

He waves his free hand around the room.

"We moved," I reply, almost like I'm entertaining this nonsense. "Five years ago."

"Where did we live before that?"

"*We* didn't live anywhere before that."

"Sure, okay," he says, still incredibly calm and patient. It's not like him at all. "But humor me, okay?"

Amazingly, I laugh.

"Good, okay," he continues. That gorgeous smile is back, lighting up his tanned face. "So, where did you and your husband live before you moved?"

"South End."

"Oh, wow!" he exclaims, grinning from ear to ear. "Fancy!"

"Does it ring a bell?" What am I doing? Why the hell am I asking such ridiculous questions? "Do you remember now?"

"No, sorry." He clicks his cheek. "I remember some stuff, a little more each day."

"When... I mean, how did you—"

"Start to remember?"

"Yes."

"Ironically, I smacked my head again!"

When he chuckles, I do too. Not much, as I still feel like I could pass out at any moment.

"I still don't understand how—"

"All in good time, Loly," he tells me. Then he stands, picks up my cup of tea, and softly hands it to me. "We have plenty of time to discuss everything."

How can this be happening? How can I get him to leave, and do I really want him to? He seems to think our lives will just go back to the way things were, but none of that would ever be possible, even if this really was Fletcher.

"What do you want?" I ask, holding the hot cup in both hands.

"You, Loly. And Astrid, of course."

"Listen," I say. I can't bring myself to use his name, as that would make his insane claims too real. "I don't know how to tell you this, but I've been seeing someone for over a year."

Chapter 5

Fletcher didn't seem shocked that I told him I've been involved with another man for over a year. In fact, I didn't even register surprise in his demeanor. I know it's been twelve years, but surely hearing me say the words should have had more of a reaction. I mean, I remember one time early in our relationship when we were in a nightclub and he smashed another guy's face into the bar simply because he'd said my hair looked nice. So why has Fletcher been so calm in the half hour since I told him about Reece?

I need to stop thinking of him as Fletcher. Yes, this man does a great impersonation of my dead husband—right down to the knowing smile—but it is impossible that he is who he claims to be.

"I don't even remember the rafting accident," he says. Tall glasses of brandy have replaced the cups of tea on the coffee table. The taste of it makes me want to retch, but the minor relief it has given me from the initial shock is more than welcome. "I woke up in Hagerstown Hospital with no recollection of anything at all."

"How did you know it was a rafting accident, then?"

"I didn't." He shakes his head. "Not until I banged my head a few weeks ago, and the flashes came back."

"Like?"

"Like my wife and daughter, only I couldn't separate the details. I knew I had a wife named Lilith, and a child named Astrid, and I could remember that we lived in Boston, for example." He takes a long drink of his brandy and puts it back on the table. I think I can see a slight shake in his hand. "I was living in a crappy one-bedroom apartment in Pittsburgh, sweeping roads for a living when it started to come back."

"Fletcher DuBose sweeping roads," I say through a tiny laugh. I don't mean it maliciously—I believe all careers are noble when they're done with passion—but the Fletcher I knew wouldn't have picked up a broom if a gun was being held to his head.

"What did I do for a living before... you know?"

"*You*? I couldn't tell you. But my old husband used to work with his father in construction."

"So, manual labor," he says, shrugging. "Not much difference between sweeping the streets and spackling a wall, really."

"Sorry, I wasn't very clear." I take a sip of my drink and grimace at the taste. "Fletcher was in charge of several crews of workers. His fingers never touched a tool his whole life."

"Okay."

There is a not-unpleasant silence for a while. Then I say, "Pittsburgh?"

"Yeah."

"How?"

"I was found miles outside of West Virginia after the accident, and I had no idea where I was or who I was," he tells me. "I was taken to hospital where they patched me up and checked me for everything, but there was no record of me on any files. I was there for months, Loly. I was so scared, but I didn't even know why I was frightened."

I nod. It is all I can think to do. He does the same, then continues.

"After I had been there for a few months and nothing had come back to me, they gave me a new name—Michael Foster—new social security number, new everything. But I had no training or skills, nothing. I didn't mind at first, just took some menial jobs to make ends meet. Over time, I gradually found my way to Pittsburgh and stayed put. I kept thinking that it would all come back to me, but it never did. Still, I kind of always knew in the back of my mind that I had been deeply in love before it all."

This time, I shake my head and snicker. It's mean-spirited, but Fletcher would never have talked like this. "You keep saying you had no recollection of anything from your past, right?"

"Yeah."

"Then how did you know it was a rafting accident? If you were found miles away from where it happened, then how do you know about it?"

"Oh, right," he says, smiling.

"Yeah, sorry to burst your bubble, *Fletcher*."

"I probably should have opened with that," he says. There seems to be no change in his confidence, even though I've just caught him in a lie. Well, there was that slight shake in his hand a moment ago. "I checked online."

"What?"

"When things started to come back to me a few weeks ago, I began to look things up. Like I said earlier, it's really bizarre the details I remember and those that are just out of reach."

"So you remembered the rafting accident?"

"No," he says. His smile is gone. "But the image of a long drive to West Virginia and a certain date kept nagging at me. It was strange. I could almost see the scenery as I drove and smell the smells of the air coming in through the open windows. When I think back now, my mind throws up that date and even what I was wearing. Then it goes black somewhere between Boston and the Gauley River."

"I'm confused."

"How do you think I feel? I checked online for any deaths, accidents, or anything that had happened between the two destinations in the days around that date. When I saw a picture of myself in an old article about a man being presumed dead after going rafting alone, I began to piece more of it together."

"Hmm, very well done."

"Excuse me?"

He looks genuinely hurt, but I don't care. "Tell me. When you're having this pleasant little memory of your road trip, smelling the smells, and seeing the scenery, do you ever recall what happened right before you set out?"

"No," he replies, shaking his head sadly. "I'm afraid not."

"Convenient," I snap, draining my glass.

"What? Why?"

"I want you to get out of my house."

"Loly?"

"Don't call me that." I swipe open my phone and dial 911. "Leave now, or I'm calling the cops."

Chapter 6

"Is everything okay, Lilith?" Reece asks. We are sitting out in the backyard of his place on Rochester Avenue, a small, picturesque suburb just outside of the city.

"Sure," I lie, then take a long sip of the iced tea I don't want. I tied my hair up this morning, but I didn't do a very good job. Stray locks of it keep getting in my eyes every time the light breeze catches it. I blow another one away and add, "I'm fine."

Reece is wearing a dark green sweater vest with embroidered diamonds on it. I would bet I can count on one hand the number of times I've seen him dressed in anything but a sweater vest. He keeps his strawberry blond hair brushed to the side in an attempt to hide his slightly receding hairline, and his sharp jaw is so cleanly shaven it glistens. When he looks at me with his big, brown puppy dog eyes, I feel worse for not telling the truth.

How can I explain what happened yesterday without sounding crazy, though? Do I just come right out and say, "Hey, Reece? You know that husband I had that died twelve years ago? Well, a man showed up at my door yesterday, claiming to be him! And do you want to know the real problem? There is a small part of me that believed him."

"Okay," Reece replies, nodding. His voice is soft—as it always is—and there is deep concern in his expression. "If there is something wrong, you can tell me."

"I know, Reece," I say, keeping my voice as soft as his. When I reach across the patio table and touch his hand, he smiles broadly. "I'm just tired."

I've been seeing Reece McElroy for over a year, but it feels a lot longer. Not in that I-already-know-so-much-about-you way, but more like a book that never seems to get going despite the fact that it could keep a door open if you placed it on the floor. But he is a wonderful man who has never even raised his voice to me, and both Mom and Astrid are crazy about him.

When I arrived at his house an hour ago, the early morning sun had been hidden behind rows of thick white clouds. Now the sky has cleared somewhat, and I have to pull my sunglasses down over my eyes to look at it. Reece's backyard is pristine, with perfectly tended rose bushes, tomato plants, and stucco walls separating everything. It looks like something from Ancient Rome, not the suburbs in Boston.

"How's Mom?" he asks, referring to my mother.

I resist a cringe and say, "She's good. You know how she is."

"Yeah," he replies, nodding and smiling. "She's great."

Every time I closed my eyes last night and tried to sleep, the image of Fletcher at my front door kept playing in my head. Well, not Fletcher, but a man who looks remarkably like him. I can't help thinking that there would be no reason for a stranger who resembles my dead husband to show up at my door, claiming to be him. Yes, I received a decent amount of money from the insurance claim, but it wasn't even in the seven figures department. Anyway, most of it went into the house and the construction of Mom's place next to it.

What makes it even more bizarre is that any news of Fletcher's death would have been twelve years ago. After that, there was nothing. Sure, he was the son of a wealthy man, but Robert DuBose is hardly Jeff Bezos. He has a few million in the bank if I had to guess, but none of that has anything to do with me and never will.

"So," Reece says, breaking my train of thought, "do you want to go out for dinner tonight? There is a new Somalian place in town that is meant to be sublime."

"I can't," I reply, making him visibly wince. "I've got plans for dinner with Astrid."

This is true, at least. I hate lying to Reece—and I don't do it often—but it can be hard to dance around his tender feelings without causing him some sort of anguish. He means well, but I sometimes wonder if his constantly overly concerning nature isn't the same as Fletcher's much more aggressive means of controlling me. I don't think that's what Reece is trying to do precisely, but it can be just as smothering at times.

"Oh, I see," he groans, dropping his head.

I know he is waiting for me to invite him too, but I can't. Usually, I would cave, but I want to spend some quality time with my daughter tonight. I'm not going to tell her what happened last night, and I hope I never have to, either. The man claiming to be Fletcher scribbled his number on a piece of paper and begged me to reconsider before scampering out last night. I hadn't actually called the cops, but I'm glad he believed that I did. Hopefully my insistence on him leaving us alone was enough to convince him that I want no part in his sick game.

Telling Astrid would be hard, but informing Mom would make that seem like a walk in the park. Her hatred of Fletcher ran deep, and she refused to shed a tear in the days following the discovery of his shattered and bloodstained raft. The detectives who came to our old house told us that the blood and hair samples on the wreckage matched Fletcher's DNA records. They also let us know after several days that we should start to accept the fact that he was dead.

"Yeah," I say, my vision slightly blurred from staring at nothing for the last few minutes. I'm still not looking at Reece as I speak. "I just want to be with Astrid tonight."

"Um-hmm." His head is still bowed.

"I hope you understand." My voice is dreamy and distant. Well, it sounds that way to me, anyhow. "We can do something soon, Reece."

I think he mumbles an answer, but I'm too deep in thought to catch it. I guess my big issue lies not with a man claiming to be my deceased husband but with the confusing and conflicting emotions it's bringing with his arrival. Of course, I'm concerned about why someone would go to that much trouble just to mess with my head, but a large slice of my rationality keeps telling me that it just might really be him. The reasons he gave for being gone so long are almost fantastical, but much stranger things have happened in the world. In fact, they happen every day.

No, I think I know why I'm so messed up about the whole thing. It's simply because while he was alive, there were so many times when I wished him dead. Now that he's back—or claiming to be—I can't help feeling that I missed out on something. Even more importantly, so did Astrid. Every little girl deserves to have her daddy in her life.

Chapter 7

Astrid's private school on Brimmer Street is so far removed from the one I went to as a kid that they can't even be compared. Besides buying our lovely house after the insurance money finally kicked in, sending Astrid to Wellington High School was top of my list. Her education before her teens had been public, yet it had made no real difference to her near-perfect grades. Still, I always felt that paying for the best could only do good.

Leaving her friends behind just as high school really kicked in had been hard for her, but the educational aspect had always come first for my little girl. In that respect, she is the same as I was at that age. Granted, my old school, Melville High, was known more for its high crime rate than its grades. I still managed to find my way into Wesley College to study for my BA in English Literature, though.

Fletcher had hated the idea of me going so far out of town for something that he claimed meant nothing. His reasoning was that nobody cared about old books and the saps that wrote them. Also, why was I bothering to learn how to be a teacher when he provided more than enough for both of us? Looking back, I think it just angered him that I was away from home so much and mixing with like-minded people. He was especially pissed that half of them were young men.

"Hey, dreamer," Astrid says behind me, making me jump. When I turn around in my chair, she is smiling down at me. "You were so lost in your little world that I didn't want to disturb you."

I stand up and hug her tightly. Liuxin Restaurant in Arlington is one of the best Chinese places in Boston. The dining area is on the third floor and boasts a fantastic view of the park across the street. From our table, I can see the statue of George Washington, the Garden of Remembrance, and the lake. Although a row of trees blocks it, our place on Beacon sits unseen just beyond it all.

Dusk has started to fall outside, but everything is lit up in that beautiful dying orange hue that predicts more sunshine tomorrow. Astrid is wearing her black wool coat and tight blue jeans that show off her toned legs. Her black hair is down today, and as she sits and brushes some of it behind her ear, I know for certain that I won't tell her about the stranger calling to the door last night.

"What looks good?" she asks, tucking her laptop bag under the table and picking up a menu. "I know I ask that every time."

"Yeah," I say, smiling. "Then you go ahead and order the same thing you always do."

"Hey!" Astrid points her finger at me and shakes it dramatically. "Their chow mein is the best."

"Okay, okay." I raise my hands. "How was school?"

"Great."

"And Ethan?" I ask. The young man in her grade that has clearly fallen head-over-heels in love with my daughter has tried everything imaginable to win her over. So far, nothing seems to have worked.

Astrid rolls her big green eyes. "As persistent as ever."

"And still nothing?"

"Not my type." Astrid shrugs.

"Cute, sweet, romantic. Yeah, those are traits that women hate!"

Astrid laughs through a snort. Then she places her menu down, spreads the fingers of one hand, and counts them off with the other. "Needy, possessive, whiny. Should I go on?"

"Okay, I get it," I say, laughing with her.

The funny thing is, I do get it. What attracted me to Fletcher at first was how dangerous he was. Not in a gun-wielding gangster sort of way, but I never knew what could happen from one minute to the next. We could be sitting around in his apartment bored, then tearing each other's clothes off without so much as a word.

I don't think Astrid is looking for something so similar, but I suppose most young women are to some degree. I just hope she chooses more wisely than I did.

"How was your day?" Astrid asks, her eyes scanning the menu.

"Fine."

"Oh?" she says, looking up. "You sound unsure."

"No, it really was fine. I went over to Reece's, and we sat outside in the sunshine drinking iced tea."

"Well, that *does* sound nice," Astrid tells me. It feels like she is trying to convince me.

"That's what I said."

"Hmm."

"What?"

33

Astrid places her menu back down again. "Is everything okay with you guys?"

"Sure, why wouldn't it be?"

"I don't know, Ma. You've just seemed, well, bored lately."

"Have I?" I ask. I know I've felt that way, but I hadn't thought I was projecting it. And anyway, I think that has more to do with being unchallenged at work than with my relationship with Reece. "Well, I'm not."

"Is it something else?" When I shrug, Astrid's face washes over with concern, and my heart breaks a little. "What is it, Ma?"

"I suppose work *has* been a bit boring recently," I admit. I don't know why, but tears sting the sides of my eyes. I manage to fight them back.

"You mean, for the last five years, right?"

"What?"

"Come on, Ma," Astrid says, reaching across the table and placing her hand on mine. "You need to be working all the time. It's who you are. How much does it kill you to see the low standard of papers you're marking?"

"A lot."

"Exactly. If you were with one class full time, you'd be able to influence that."

Being a part-time teacher is essentially another term for a substitute teacher. The main problem with that is only having a week or two with each class, and sporadically at that. I can be with one set of students for a week in the fall and not see them again for another year. Also, I sub mainly in the less fortunate public schools, so the standard of teacher I'm stepping in for is shoddy at best.

"I know, but—"

"I'm away all the time, Ma," Astrid interrupts. "And you've always wanted to teach full time in the schools that need you more. You'd be well overqualified, and the pay is low, but I know that's what you want."

My daughter knows me better than I know myself, that's for sure. "The pay means nothing to me, and we're set up in that regard. And, yes, I would prefer to make a difference in some kids' lives who have less of a chance."

"Then do it, Ma," Astrid tells me. Before I can argue, she waves the waiter over.

I've always suspected deep down that I need to go back to teaching full time, and hearing it laid out like this has convinced me. Still, with it being mid-December, I'll have to wait until the summer to start applying. I can always start making inquiries now, though.

When Astrid orders the chow mein, I shake my head. She laughs, to the confusion of the waiter, and I ask for the Peking duck. When the waiter takes our drinks order and leaves, I say, "Why do you always study the menu so intently?"

Astrid shrugs. "I suppose it's what people are meant to do, right?"

"Not if they know they'll order the chow mein."

"Ah, well. I guess I'm just eccentric like that."

"I guess so, sweetie."

Astrid is silent for a while as she looks around the room. The hanging paper lanterns and beautifully lit fish tanks everywhere always set a calm, peaceful mood in the place. Outside the large windows, the streets have darkened a little more. Sitting here in this pleasant atmosphere, I can almost convince myself that last night was nothing but a nightmare.

"Oh, I nearly forgot," Astrid says. She leans under the table and pulls an envelope out of her laptop bag. As she slides it over to me, I can see my name scrawled across the front in familiar chicken-scratch writing. "Some guy stopped me outside school and gave me this. Said he knew you from way back."

Chapter 8

Knowing that this imposter—this Michael Foster—has been at Astrid's school is frightening. His letter gave me nothing more than what he had told me when he visited my home, but seeing it in writing brought home just how serious this guy is. He means business, but I can't for the life of me figure out precisely what that means.

One of the students clears their throat, and I look up from my desk. Levinson High School is definitely one of the most poorly funded schools I've subbed in. And since I started here this morning, I've seen nothing to convince me otherwise. The faculty all seem weathered and beaten, and the students radiate anger and frustration. It is everything that is wrong with the American educational system all rolled into one.

A girl that looks far too old to be in the eleventh grade has her hand raised as she loudly chews gum. Her blonde hair has grown out so much that thick black roots show throughout. She looks bored as the rest of the class pretends to silently read chapter seven of *Catcher in the Rye*. I wish J. D. Salinger's so-called classic wasn't still such a staple of the national curriculum, but I suppose it always will be.

"Yes," I say, pointing to the gum chewer.

"I'm done," she says, sighing. "What now?"

Normally the sight of a new classroom full of students I've yet to meet and understand excites me. But ever since my dinner with Astrid yesterday evening, I've been all over the place. I think I held it together enough after she handed me the letter so as not to arouse too much suspicion, but my mind was running at a mile a minute. Before that moment, I'd been able to pretend like my visitor the previous night got the hint and gave up his attempts at playing games with us.

Now all I can think about is what kind of person would go to that much effort? And the scariest part is that I can only come up with one answer: a dangerous one.

"Maybe read the next chapter while you wait for the rest of the class?" I suggest, with little conviction.

"But this book sucks."

I couldn't agree more, but I don't say so. A couple of students giggle at her comment, and she smiles.

"I'm sorry you feel that way, Miss?"

"Alverez. Gigi Alverez."

"Well, Gigi," I say, trying everything in my power to remain professional. These young students don't need to suffer because I'm dealing with stuff. "Maybe we can discuss that in a moment when everyone else is ready?"

"Shit!" Gigi exclaims, chuckling. "A discussion on literature in this school? Good luck, Teach."

"Ms. DuBose," I tell her. "My name is Ms. DuBose, not Teach."

"Right."

"Can you just wait for the rest of the class?"

Gigi doesn't answer and gives me an over-the-top eye roll instead. Her heavily applied baby blue eye shadow makes the gesture all the more prominent. The face that looks back at me is painfully pretty, but there are already signs of the strains of a life that should belong to someone much older beneath it.

Astrid seemed to know there was something up with me when she slid the letter across the table at the restaurant, but she didn't push the matter. Seeing that scrawled handwriting I remember so well shocked me. It looked identical to Fletcher's, and his writing had always been so distinctive. It was childish yet aggressive—like he had been trying to put the nib of the pen through the page.

When I saw my name scratched across the front of the envelope, all of the taste left my mouth. Somehow, it was even more shocking than opening the door to him. It was more real, and it seemed to scream in my head as I looked at it. Waiting until I got home and into my bedroom to open it had been so hard, but then I'd found myself unable to do it for another half hour when I was finally alone.

I know now that I need to see this thing out. If this man is approaching my daughter at her school, then he's gone too far already. If it was just me he was harassing, then I would be able to deal with it. Bringing Astrid into the equation changes everything, and I'm going to have to take action. I just don't know where to start.

Yes, I have his number, and I can call him and ask to meet. But I don't know what he wants, so I can't take the risk. I could call my lawyer, and maybe John can give me some advice on where to go from here. Whatever I decide, I need to get it done before this goes too far. Whoever this man is, he is clearly deranged. Why else would he want to pose as someone's dead husband?

"Ms. Dobbins?"

"DuBose, not Dobbins," I say, looking back up at Gigi.

"Okay."

"What is it?"

"Everyone's ready," Gigi tells me, waving a hand over her classmates like Cleopatra. "Do you want us to have our *discussion* now?"

"Go ahead," I say, forcing a smile. "Why does this book 'suck,' as you put it?"

"This Holden Caulfield," Gigi scoffs. "He's just a spoiled brat with too much time on his hands."

I completely agree, but I say, "How so?"

To my surprise, a couple of other students join in on a semi-organized discussion of *Catcher in the Rye*. As they do, I interact where necessary, but I mostly try not to interrupt the flow. This conversation is for their benefit, not mine.

Hagerstown Hospital, my mind suddenly barks. *The guy said he wound up in Hagerstown Hospital in the days following the rafting accident.*

That's right, he did. And if he is telling the truth, there will be records of him being there. All I have to do is call them and prove him wrong.

Chapter 9

The rest of the school day went better than I ever could have imagined. Once I'd made up my mind to call the hospital and have it confirmed that this man had been lying to me, everything seemed clearer. Of course, I've still been on edge the whole time. And now that I'm sitting in the car with my phone in my hand, I'm suddenly unsure if this is the way to go.

What if they confirm everything he told me? What if they say, "Yes, Ms. DuBose, twelve years ago, a man was found wandering along the highway with blunt force trauma to his head and amnesia." How would I deal with the situation then?

Stop it, I tell myself. *They won't say that because it's not true. And even if they do, it still confirms nothing.*

"Be a hell of a coincidence, though, wouldn't it?" I mumble.

The Levinson High parking lot is empty except for my shiny silver SUV and a rusty Honda. The Boston skyline is dull and almost purple above the bare trees, and faded shadows seem to hang in the air. The hand holding my phone is sweaty, and the finger hovering above the call icon shakes slightly. I picture Fletcher's hand the other night doing the same thing as he reached for his drink, and I shiver.

"That wasn't Fletcher," I croak. "That was some crazy guy playing mind games."

The number for Hagerstown Hospital remains on my screen, but I still can't bring myself to call. I'm not sure what I want them to tell me, and that terrifies me. Surely an end to this crazy situation is all I could wish for, isn't it? To have a doctor confirm that the man who called on my house has been lying. So why is there a part of me hoping his story is true?

Maybe you miss your husband, and you want him back?

Of course, there is some truth to that. Fletcher was aggressive and sometimes violent, but there were times when he was loving. During the last few years of our relationship, his nasty side was prominent much more often. But the man who sat across from me a couple of nights ago seemed kind.

He was manipulating you, Lilith. He always manipulated you when he was trying to win you back.

How many times did he come to me with flowers and a caring smile cut across his face the morning after I wiped his spit off my face? Too many times.

"I still need to know the truth," I tell myself, nodding. But it does no good. The phone's screen has gone black, and I can't bring myself to unlock it again. "Coward."

The parking lot brightens as the headlights of the old Honda on the other side snap on. A thin mist has started to fall, and the beams look faded as the driver maneuvers the car through the double pillars marked EXIT. For some reason, being alone in the lot scares me. I try to shake it away and curse myself for being so weak. I feel like I used to all those years ago when Fletcher would come home smelling of whiskey and cigarettes.

Losing that timid side of me has been one of the biggest achievements in my life. It's only been in the last three or four years that I've felt confident enough to say that I'm becoming who I've always wanted to be. Not so much in terms of my career, but definitely in the way I believe in myself a little more. And in one ring of a doorbell by a man who looks like my ex-husband, I've reverted back into that scared woman I loath so much.

"To hell with this."

I unlock the phone and hit dial before I can stop myself. As it rings, I tap my fingers on the steering wheel. When a woman's voice answers and tells me I've reached Hagerstown Hospital, I close my eyes and swallow hard.

"Hello," I say. It comes out cracked, and I clear my throat. "Hello, I'm calling about a patient you might have had there twelve years ago."

"Twelve years ago?"

"I know. A long time ago, right."

"Sure is," the woman says. She actually sounds pretty curious, which is something, at least. "What can I do for you?"

"It's a strange one," I say, trying to sound professional, yet casual. I should have thought up a reason for calling beforehand—like I'm a reporter or a long-lost sister or something. Oh, well, it's too late now. "I'm calling about a man that was found wandering along the highway."

"Which highway?"

"I'm not sure." Stupid, stupid, stupid. I should have asked him when he told me.

"And it was twelve years ago?"

She sounds suspicious now, and I can feel her guard going up. I clear my throat again and say, "Yes, but it should be an easy enough case to find. He had a head wound and didn't know who he was. He stayed for several months and had to be given a new identity, new social security, new everything."

"And who are you?" the woman asks, clearly annoyed now.

"Me?"

"Yes, you."

"I'm, um, Lilith DuBose. I just need to know if he really stayed there. He said he did."

"And you don't have a name for him?"

"He didn't know his name."

"Look, Mrs. DuBose—"

"Miss."

"—Sorry, Ms. DuBose," she says. "Even if I wanted to help you, we can't just give out information on past patients."

"I thought that might be the case," I reply. I just want to end the call now, and I feel silly. "I just said I'd give it a shot."

"Well, give it a shot on someone else's time, okay," the woman snaps. Then the line goes dead.

I'm about to toss the phone on the passenger seat when it rings in my hand. I almost scream before I see Mom's name flashing on the screen.

I hit answer and say, "Hey, Mom."

"Where are you?" She sounds annoyed.

"Just leaving work. I'll be home in half an hour."

"Okay," Mom says, her voice flat. "We need to talk."

Chapter 10

The fog has really settled now, and I have to keep resisting the urge to speed up. Going at this pace is infuriating, and every possible scenario as to why Mom wants to talk has run through my head a hundred times already. I don't know why because I already know the answer: The man claiming to be Fletcher made contact with her.

I turn off Interstate 90 onto Arlington Street. The traffic is quite sparse despite it being midday. I suppose most people are still in the office or just not stupid enough to try and drive through this weather. A car behind me with its headlights on pulls up too close, and I have to squint against the glare from my rearview mirror.

I hope Fletcher—

It's not Fletcher. It's not him.

—hasn't spoken to Mom. That would not end well. The last time Mom saw him was a few days before he left for his rafting trip, and tensions had been high even then. The night she showed up at my door just after Fletcher had stormed off was the angriest I'd ever seen her. It scared me at the time, but when I imagine Astrid going through what I did that night, I see why my mother was so livid.

I come to a junction on Arlington and slow down. I can see the car behind me clearly for the first time—a white Coupe with tinted windows—as the driver finally lowers their beams. Although I want to get home and find out why Mom sounded so serious on the phone, there is a part of me that's happy the fog is so thick. I know it's only bad news I'm heading toward, so why rush?

Confrontation with Virginia Townsend has never been easy. She is a strong-willed woman who rarely backs down, and I discovered very early in life that the person arguing with her better be 100 percent sure they're right beforehand. It's not that my mom is nasty or cruel—she isn't—she just stands tall when she believes the cause is right.

I realize that the lights have already turned green, and I get the SUV moving again. Behind me, the white car does the same, keeping pace with me as I drive.

I wish I'd thought of a cover story before calling the hospital. They probably wouldn't have given me information on a patient either way, but at least I wouldn't have panicked and given my real name. There has to be a way to get the information I want, though. I have a feeling that finding proof that this man is lying will be the only way to make him stop. Maybe John can advise me on what to do? He is a lawyer, after all.

But telling John is one more person who knows what's happening, and I don't think that's a good idea. I'm not sure why I don't think it's wise, but it just feels right to keep this as close to my chest as possible for now.

The fog is so thick that I can't even see the statue of George Washington on my right. To my left, I can just make out the blurred fluorescent lights that spell out Liuxin Restaurant. Well, I can see the shape, but I can't decipher the letters.

My headlights make no difference to the wall of fog ahead of me. In fact, they seem to be constantly reflecting off it and blinding me. When I look at the speedometer, I see I'm down to 15 mph. The car is basically at a crawl.

A look in the rearview mirror shows me that the white Coupe is still only a few feet behind me. It is so dangerous to get so close in such nasty conditions, but there is no way I'm getting out to tell him.

Him? Really? How do you know it's a man? The windows are tinted.

"I don't," I croak, my eyes constantly flicking rapidly between the mirror and the road ahead of me. "But I kind of do."

I can feel myself slipping back into the old me, which terrifies me even more. That Lilith jumped at shadows and thought everyone was out to get her. In truth, only one man had been out to get me, and his shadow covered everything else in my life.

Then why does a part of you want him to be back? Why do you want Fletcher to be alive?

I don't, do I? Sure, there is a curiosity there. I mean, how couldn't there be? But the idea of him being alive is worse than a nightmare. It would flip everything upside down and destroy all the work that I've done to better myself.

As I wait at the lights to turn onto Beacon Street, I find myself praying that the car behind me won't do the same. His headlights are so bright in my rearview mirror, and even when I shield my eyes, I see nothing but an electric blur. My head is starting to pound, and the hands I'm rapidly drumming on the wheel are slick with sweat. I can feel my heart beating through my chest, and I'm finding it hard to catch my breath.

It's just another car that happens to be going the same way as you, I tell myself.

It does little to relieve me, and I have to concentrate on taking a big gulp of air. What if the guy that claims to be Fletcher is getting out of his white Coupe right now as I wait for the light to turn green? I can't see anything behind me because his beams are so strong and the fog so thick. What if he has a crowbar? What if he slams it into the glass beside my face and drags me out into the street? It's so foggy, and nobody would see it happening!

"NO!" I scream, scaring myself. I follow this with an almost hysterical laugh. Then the light turns green, and I turn onto Beacon.

For a moment, I think he has turned the other way. Then my rearview mirror lights up again, and he's right up to my bumper. It's only a minute to my house, but it feels like it will take forever. What does he want? Did he not tell me everything the other night?

You still don't know if it's him, Lilith. Calm down.

I can just make out Mom's Ford Focus in the driveway, even though I'm only a few feet away and my lights have fallen on it. The silver paintwork meshes with the fog, and it is now just another part of the thick clouds all around me. As I put the SUV in park, I keep my eyes glued to the rearview mirror. I can see the fat beams of the Coupe's headlights as they push through the mist.

When the car stops on the curb by my lawn, I have to bring my hand up to my mouth to suppress a scream. With my engine off, I can hear the low ticking of the Coupe's engine as whoever is driving it sits and watches me. The car stays there for about a minute, then the engine revs, and he pulls away.

As I step out into the fog and walk toward my home, I wipe tears of fear and frustration away from my cheeks.

Chapter 11

"In here," Mom calls from the kitchen at the end of the hall.

I hang my jacket and bag on the hooks by the front door and take several deep breaths. Mom would understand me being upset, but only if I explained why. Again, I don't want to mention the strange man visiting the house until it's unavoidable. Hopefully, that will never be the case.

"Be there in a second," I reply, raising my voice so she can hear me.

When I look in the mirror on the phone table—the one that has never held a phone—I see a middle-aged woman with puffy eyes. The blackness of my hair, which is usually so dark, looks faded, and the tips are frayed. The navy-blue suit I chose this morning feels like it belongs to someone stronger, and the body underneath it looks frail instead of simply slim.

Mom will know something's up, regardless of how much I steady myself before walking into the kitchen. I'm pretty sure she already knows, though. Why else would she call me saying, "We need to talk"?

I take one last look at myself, sigh, and walk down the hall. The kitchen is spotless, as it always is when Mom has been in it. Everything has a polished shine to it, and I can smell scented disinfectant. She is wearing a tight cream hoodie and matching sweatpants that show off her curves. Mom has always had what I'd call a 1920s figure—round where it should be and proud all over.

The table she sits at is set, but I see no pots or pans on the stove. It's not even four thirty yet, though.

Mom must see me looking as she says, "I'll be putting dinner on in a minute."

"I wasn't—"

"It's fine, Lilith." She nods at one of the chairs at the other end of the table. "Sit down."

She definitely knows. My mother is serious by nature, but I've always been able to sense the times when it is something more. As I sit, she brings her hand up to her loosely braided hair—the few gray streaks shining in the light—and readjusts it. I can tell by her silence that something big is coming.

I want to tell her everything—about the man coming to the house and then going to Astrid's school. I want to open up and explain just how scared I was a moment ago when the white Coupe that had followed me the whole way through the fog stopped outside and just watched me as I sat parked in our driveway. I probably should tell her all these things, but I just can't.

"Are you okay?" she asks, pointing at my eyes.

I touch them like I've only just discovered they're there. "Oh, just squinting the whole way in the fog."

Mom looks out the kitchen window and at the clouded grayness beyond. "Wow, it's gotten worse."

"Yeah."

"How was work?"

"What?"

She rolls her eyes. "Work. How was it?"

"It, um, it was better than I expected." My nerves are frayed, and I keep waiting for the axe to fall. I feel like I'm a teenager again, with a mother who knows I snuck out the night before but is making me sweat. Only this time, I don't have Dad here to say, "She's a young woman, Ginny. She's gonna get up to a little mischief."

"Oh, yeah?" Mom says. Her voice is still as flat as it was on the phone. If she had been contacted by that guy, then she surely would have said it the second I got in. I'm not a teenager anymore.

"Yes," I tell her, nodding. "Levinson has a bad rap, but the students I had today seemed sharp. They had a discussion about *Catcher in the Rye* without me pushing for it."

"Oh, wow," Mom says. "That's great. Well, compared to the one you just finished at. What was it called again?"

"Wells."

"That's it."

Wells High had only been a one-week gig, but it hadn't been easy. It was definitely one of the more upper-class schools I've taught in, but the standard was terrible. It wasn't that the kids weren't intelligent; it was just that they didn't care. Of all the papers I marked on *Huckleberry Finn*, maybe two could have been passing grades.

"Have you heard from Astrid?" I ask, taking my phone out and seeing no messages. She has supervised study after school today, so she won't be finished until after six. But the idea of her making her way home in that fog scares me. "I should go pick her up."

"That's what I wanted to talk to you about, honey," Mom says, her tone suddenly softening.

Oh, God, something terrible has happened. That man; he attacked my baby. Why didn't I say something? Why didn't I go to the cops? This is my fault, my fault, MY FAULT.

"What happened, Mom?" I nearly screech. When I stand up sharply, the chair I was sitting on falls backward and clatters to the floor. "Where is she? What did he do to her?"

"Relax!" Mom says, chuckling as she reaches out and touches my hand. "Jeez, Astrid is fine. She said she would get a ride with Rachael's mother after studying. She called me around half an hour ago, just before I called you."

"What? She's okay?" I gasp. My whole body is shaking, and I'm still standing. I must look ridiculous. "Why didn't she call me?"

"She did, Lilith," Mom tells me. "She said your line was busy, so she called me. Just sit back down for a moment."

I do as I'm told. Astrid must have called while I was on the phone with the hospital in Hagerstown. I need to get to the bottom of this whole Fletcher mess, as I'm starting to act crazy. I take a deep breath and say, "So, what about Astrid, then? What did you want to talk about?"

"Her eighteenth birthday is in a few months," Mom says. She pulls a pad and pen out of the pouch of her hoodie. "I think we should start making plans for it, don't you?"

Chapter 12

"John Howerton's office," a woman on the other end of the phone says. Her voice is very cheerful, but it does nothing to make me feel the same way. "How can I help you?"

I'm sitting in the home office upstairs with the door closed. Using the desk phone always feels weird, and I'm still unsure why we ever had a landline installed when we moved in. I suppose because it was simply a part of our Wi-Fi plan, but still, it seems pretty pointless.

Astrid has already left for school, and I'm not due at my new gig for another hour. I haven't seen Mom yet this morning, and I'm glad. I zoned out through her suggestions for Astrid's birthday party yesterday, and I've felt bad about it ever since. I didn't want to be like that, but everything that has happened lately has me rattled.

"Hi," I reply. "This is Lilith DuBose. I'm looking to speak to Mr. Howerton. Is he available?"

"Oh, hi, Ms. DuBose. Mr. Howerton isn't in the office until ten this morning, I'm afraid," the secretary says, and I feel my heart dropping. I don't know if John can do anything to help my situation, but living in the hope that he might was the only thing that allowed me to get even a couple of hours of sleep last night. "Would you like me to give him a message?"

"Yes, I guess. Can you have him call me on my cell? You have my number, right?"

"Sure do," she chirps. "I'll have him call you... oh, wait a sec, Ms. DuBose, Mr. Howerton just walked in." I can hear the phone rustling as she holds the receiver to her chest or arm, then says, "Mr. Howerton will take your call now, Ms. DuBose. I'm just going to patch you through."

There is a moment's pause, then the line clicks, and John Howerton says, "Hello, Lilith. How are you?"

"I'm good," I lie.

"Okay then. What can I do for you?"

Suddenly, this feels like a bad idea. Up until this point, I've done everything I can to keep my strange visitor a secret. Now here I am about to blab about it to my lawyer. Of course, he is obligated to keep my secret, too, but it still feels dangerous somehow.

Dangerous, really?

"I've got kind of a weird request, John," I say, barreling ahead.

"Okay?"

"Would you be able to get your hands on medical records if I needed them?" I feel like I'm in a movie. A bad one, sure, but it is strange talking like this, nonetheless.

"Whose medical records?" John sounds skeptical already.

"That's the thing. I don't have a name," I reply, feeling even more stupid.

"Well, you've officially got my full attention. Can you give me a little more information?"

I take a deep breath and blow it out slowly. What I'm about to tell this man is so bizarre that he'll probably think something in my head has snapped. And could I blame him if he did? I'm on the verge of explaining that a man who looks very much like my dead husband knocked on my door a few nights ago, claiming to in fact be that very presumed-dead husband.

"I had a strange caller at my house three nights ago," I explain. "He is claiming to be Fletcher."

There is a sharp snort of laughter on the other end of the line. "But that is preposterous."

"You're telling me."

"He must just be some nut who thinks you have money or something," John says, the lawyer in him clearly his default mode.

"Yeah, sure."

"You don't sound convinced."

"Here's the thing." I've already told him what happened, so I may as well push on with it. "He really does look like him."

"I see."

"Yeah, I mean, like *really*. But then again, he doesn't either," I say, shaking my head. "What I mean is, he looks more like him than he doesn't, but there was something off about him too."

"Well, listen, Lilith," John says, clearing his throat. "There was no body found. We know that. But still, I hate talking like this—"

"Don't worry about it."

"—but every police officer and detective who saw the wreckage and the, well, the blood and hair agreed that nobody could have survived such an accident."

"I know."

"And even if he did," John says, his voice becoming more and more assured, "where the hell has he been for the last twelve years?"

I explain the apparent amnesia and how this man claiming to be Fletcher said that a second more recent bump on the head jogged his memory. I tell him that this guy told me that ever since then, he has started to remember shards of the past. John says "um-hmm" and "sure, sure" in all the right places, and I actually feel better getting it all out to another human being.

When I'm finished, John says, "I still think it's just some nut."

"I agree." The blinds on the office window are partially cracked, and thin beams of morning light throw bright bars across the plush carpet. I realize I've been drumming my fingers on the oak desk since I called, and I consciously make them stop.

"Still, he has approached your daughter," John says, his voice even more serious now. "So I think we should start looking at a restraining order."

"Okay, John, that sounds good," I say. "There is just one more thing."

"Shoot."

"Those medical records I mentioned. Can you get them for me?"

Chapter 13

"So, Alex tells me he wants to trade Aaron Donald for Trent Williams," Reece tells me, his tone incredulous. I'm not sure how long he has been talking about his office's online fantasy football group, but it feels like hours. "I had to laugh. I mean, really, Alex?"

"That's crazy," I say over a forkful of risotto. I don't know who Aaron Donald or Trent Williams are, but there is no point in telling Reece that. He'd only drop his gaze and give me that scorned puppy look.

The inside of Reece's house on Rochester Avenue is much like the front and back yards—pristine and symmetrical. The glass kitchen table we're sitting at is polished to such a sheen that I can see myself clearly when I lean in to pick up my water. There is always an undercurrent of sandalwood in the air, yet I've never seen an air freshener or a hint of an incense stick.

Reece readjusts his navy sweater vest and places his elbows on the table. He finished his homemade butternut risotto a few minutes ago and pushed the empty plate in front of him with the knife and fork crisscrossed in the middle. He runs a hand through his thinning hair, then rests his chin on his intertwined hands.

"Yep, just crazy," he agrees. "Like I'm going to switch at this stage in the season."

I know for a fact that he has never even set foot inside Gillette Stadium, let alone sat down to watch *Monday Night Football*. Yet give him a format to enjoy the sport through technology, and he can't get enough of it. I'm willing to bet he knows as much about Aaron Donald and Trent Williams as I do.

I force a laugh and shake my head, and Reece falls back into talking about his office. I've met his coworkers a few times, and they're perfectly fine. They are about as exciting as unbuttered toast, but they are harmless. But to hear Reece talk about them, you would swear they were like those guys from that *Jackass* movie Astrid made me watch when she was fourteen.

I let him speak as he's in full flow, and I'm not in the mood to participate in any real way.

John hasn't called me back since this morning, but he did promise to see what he could do to check on Hagerstown Hospital's medical records. He explained that the insurance company would have done all the work for us more than twelve years ago. As he put it, "there is no way in hell that they would leave any stones unturned regarding a six-figure payout."

When Fletcher had been legally declared dead in absentia seven years after the rafting accident on the Gauley River, the insurance company had been left with no other option but to pay out. And according to John, they would have meticulously checked the records of every hospital in the New England area during that period for any signs of a man being brought in with no ID. Anything that could help them avoid giving money out.

If they'd found even a shred of evidence, they'd have pulled the deal.

I've always known that there are shady people in the world, and insurance scams are big business. If anything, the people at Wheeler and Wise would have dug even deeper into the accident than the police did. They had everything to lose and nothing to gain by Fletcher DuBose being dead.

"And Billy," Reece is saying. "You know Billy, right?"

"Yeah, sure, I know Billy," I reply robotically. My risotto has gone cold, and I've barely eaten a thing. Hopefully, Reece doesn't notice because he'll just become overly concerned, and I don't need that right now.

"Right, so Billy says...."

Again, I drift away and let him tell his story. I wish I had the capacity today to contribute to his clear joy at his workday, but I just can't muster it up. My mind is on other things, and I know that the man who handed a letter to my daughter outside her school isn't just going to stop there. People who play such games never do.

When John explained the situation to me, I wasn't sure how I felt about it. If I'm being honest, I still don't. What if it turns out that this man is telling the truth and my husband has been alive and well this whole time, sweeping the roads in a small town in Pittsburgh while his family carried on with their lives in Boston? And what if he is lying? Somehow, that seems even worse, if only because it surely means he has ulterior motives.

My phone vibrates on the breakfast bar across the kitchen. Reece stops talking and looks over at it, and I do the same.

"Are you not going to answer that, babe?" Reece asks.

I can still hear the sharp vibrations, but I can't seem to move. It's nearly seven o'clock, so it surely isn't John calling at this hour. "Sorry, I'll get it now."

I stand up on surprisingly unsteady legs. It's just a phone call, yet it feels like the imminent end of the world. I've been so jumpy lately, and I don't like the feeling. It is too much like the old me, the one I buried with my husband all those years ago.

When I pick up the phone, I can see the name JERK on the screen. Robert DuBose hasn't called me in so long that I presumed his number had got lost in one of my phone upgrades or something over time. I can't even remember changing his name to JERK, but I must have done.

"I'm just going to take this in the living room," I tell Reece, who is still looking at me.

"Sure. Okay," he replies, his gaze dropping like I've just bopped him on the nose with a rolled-up newspaper.

Once I've stepped into the other room and shut the door behind me, I close my eyes and answer the phone.

"Hello?"

"Hi, Lilith," that familiar, growling, domineering voice says. "It's Robert."

There is something else mixed in with his usual cold tone. Something alien to it.

"What can I do for you?" I ask.

"You have to come over here," he says, that weird waver in his voice stronger now.

"Where?"

"My house."

"Why?"

"I can't believe it!" he exclaims, and I realize what it is in his tone that I've never heard before—it's joy. "Oh my God. I just can't believe it. My boy is here. Fletcher is alive, and he's here in my home!"

Chapter 14

I don't know if Robert called me twenty minutes or an hour ago. All I'm sure of is that I left Reece's place in a daze as he fired questions at me and panicked, as is his way. I'll come up with something to tell him another day, but right now, my head is too messed up to even think about it. Reece will just have to understand that something is going on and that we will discuss it at a later date. I couldn't have given him any more than that, even if I'd wanted to, as I'm still so confused myself.

Thankfully, the traffic is almost nonexistent. Out here in the suburbs, it usually is in the evening. I need to talk to Mom about everything when I get home. When I check the clock on the dash, I see it is just coming up to eight. She will probably be at her place, but she could be at our house with Astrid. That won't be good, as I have no intention of telling my daughter about my phone call with Robert DuBose until I absolutely can't avoid it.

Headlights glare in my rearview mirror, and I have visions of a sinister white Coupe before I can even see what type of car is blinding me. When I turn off Storrow Drive, the car behind me follows, and my heart sinks. With everything that has just happened, this is the last thing I need.

The rest of my call with Robert had been a blur. I wonder if that is what it feels like to have someone talking to you when you are deep in a comatose state—hearing the words muffled and jumbled, yet knowing that they are important. I remember him saying that his son is back, that Fletcher is home. After that, I think I just groaned mundane responses and tried not to freak out.

Reece tried his best to find out what had happened when I walked back into the kitchen and grabbed my purse, but he seemed even further away from me than Robert had. I don't know what I'll eventually tell him, but it will have to be soon. He deserves that, at the very least.

When I pass Cheers, I see a load of drunken tourists outside snapping photos. I barely give them a second glance. When I look in the rearview mirror, there is still a piercing set of headlights glaring back at me. They seem less intrusive than the car a moment ago, so it might be a different one. Although I can't be sure, and that's the worst part. Everything spooks me when I feel this way, and I'm constantly on edge.

I make the next turn left, and the car behind me continues north. I let out a huge breath I didn't know I'd been holding in. I keep looking at my phone on the passenger seat, waiting for the screen to light up and the word JERK to appear again. Talking to Robert always made me nervous, even when Fletcher was still alive. But since my husband died, Robert's pure disdain for me became even more obvious.

It wasn't like he tried to hide it when I was married to his son, but he definitely held some of it back for Fletcher's sake. After only a few months following the rafting accident, Robert had basically cut all ties with us. I only really heard from him again five years ago when Fletcher's life insurance was close to kicking in. Even after all that time, he didn't want us to be financially comfortable, despite the fact that it was the insurance company's money and not his that we were set to receive.

As part of Fletcher's will, Astrid will receive a 10 percent shareholding stake in one of Robert's many construction firms, but only once she is legally an adult. It won't amount to much, as it only applies to future earnings and from one of the smaller firms at that. But it should keep her comfortable enough through college. I was as surprised as everyone else that Fletcher had bothered to make a will at all, especially since he was so young.

When I pull the SUV into the driveway of our house, I notice that none of the lights are on downstairs. Although rows of bushes and spattered trees run across the front of Mom's place across the street, they are bare, and I can tell that her living room is lit up.

I still can't believe I'm going to tell her about what has been happening over the last few days. I might keep out the part about the stranger going to Astrid's school with his letter, though. Mom has always been extra protective of her granddaughter, and that would push her over the edge. She never liked Fletcher, even in the beginning. Hearing that this man claiming to be him was harassing Astrid would be too much for her to move past.

I feel the same way, but Robert sounded so damn sure of himself on the phone. He kept asking me to come over to his place right away, but I think I managed to delay him for now. I hope I was convincing enough, but I can't really be sure.

My shoes crunch on the gravel as I pass my house and walk along the small path that leads to Mom's little house. Or is it more of a cottage? Some people call it a granny flat, but I think that might be a British term.

You're procrastinating, Lilith, I tell myself.

I am, and I'm simply trying to distract myself from what is about to happen.

Mom might have always hated Fletcher, but she *despised* Robert. I never fully understood it, as my Dad worked for the man for many years and was paid pretty well. Yes, he died on one of the construction sites, but that was hardly Robert's fault. From what I know, he wasn't even there that day. In fact, Robert is rarely on site. What millionaire construction mogul ever sets foot on the ground floor with the grunts?

Still, telling Mom that Robert DuBose is asking us to visit his home will raise alarm bells, so I can't even imagine what she'll do when I explain the reason why.

I can hear the TV from inside as I approach the front door. My hand comes up to knock, but I can't seem to bring my knuckles down on the cream-painted wood. I can smell honeysuckle in the air, although it feels sickly more than sweet. Above me, an airplane cuts through the night sky, the distant blast of its engines sounding like freedom to me.

It still feels like I'm in a dream. How can I be standing here with my fist frozen in a knocking motion, on the verge of telling my mother that I think my dead husband is actually alive?

My God, I don't think that, do I? Am I saying that I believe this crazy story? Am I starting to think the man who came to my house a few nights ago with a deep, faded scar on the side of his head might actually be Fletcher?

The front door opens before I've knocked, and I let out a sharp scream. Mom grabs her chest and shrieks. Then she laughs nervously and says, "I thought I saw someone pass my window. What are you doing standing out here in the cold?"

"Sorry, Mom," I manage through my own cracked laughter. "I didn't mean to scare you."

"That's okay. What's up, sweetie?"

"Can I come in, Mom?" I ask. "We really need to talk."

Chapter 15

Mom took it about as badly as I thought she would. Her first instinct had been to curse the DuBoses to hell and back for upsetting her daughter. Then she asked a series of questions, most of which revolved around Robert and not the man proclaiming to be Fletcher.

Mom seems to believe that Robert is up to something. I can't see what on Earth he could gain from any of this, but she refused to budge. After I had left her home in the early hours and crunched along the path toward my house, I felt no better than I had before I told her.

We must have talked for five hours, easily. I don't know how many times I had to snatch her phone away as she threatened to call Robert, 911, or our lawyer. None of it would have done any good, and I managed to convince her of that, at least.

"Well," Astrid says, sticking the edge of a full slice of toast in her mouth and holding it there. "I 'ave ew 'et 'owing."

"What?" I ask in a drowsy daze. I don't think I slept at all last night, and I must look awful. Thankfully Astrid has exams today, so she has her mind on other things.

She takes the piece of toast out of her mouth and blushes, her painfully pretty face making my heart ache. "Sorry, that was rude. I said, 'I have to get going.'"

"Sure, okay," I say, trying to smile. I'm still in my bathrobe, even though it's just after eight a.m. "Do you want me to give you a ride to school?"

Astrid looks at what I'm wearing and smiles. "That's okay, Mom. Rachael is picking me up at the end of the street now."

"Oh, okay," I croak. "Be careful."

"I always am. See you, Ma."

"Bye. I love you."

"Love you too!" Astrid calls from behind me. She is already moving down the hallway, and a moment later, I hear the front door slamming shut.

Robert called again last night as I was sitting with Mom, but I ignored it. There was no way I could answer with her in the same room. She would have snatched the phone from me and let Robert have it. Instruction manuals or self-help books for situations like this don't exist. Why would they? Who has ever had to deal with anything even close to this before?

Whenever I try to make any kind of plan, the first step seems like it has been built on quicksand. There is no way to approach this that won't make me go crazy. At least, that is how I feel right now.

When I stand up from the kitchen table, my head swims a little. It's not too bad, and I know I'm just overly tired. Did Mom sleep after I left? I doubt it, as she was seething with anger. But why? If—and I'm still sane enough to know it's a big "if"—this man really is Fletcher, then isn't it a good thing that he's back? Shouldn't Mom be happy that my husband is alive? Wouldn't it be amazing for Astrid to have her father in her life again?

"You've got a short memory"—that's what Mom had told me last night when I raised those questions. Her words had stung, but only because they were true. More than half of my years with Fletcher were hell, but people *can* change. He has been gone for a long, long time. I have to believe that anyone would change their ways if they were given such an impossible second chance at life.

No, I can't think that way. This isn't Fletcher because that's insane. There is no way he could be telling the truth; it's just too fantastical. But stranger things have happened, haven't they?

I remember reading about that German girl, Juliane Koepcke, who fell 3,000 feet from a burning plane while still strapped to her seat and survived. Not only that, but she managed to find her way out of the Amazon rainforest alone after eleven days of wandering. Juliane had been the same age as Astrid is now, and she had gone through all of that. Is the idea of a man smacking his head and forgetting his past any more far-fetched?

I realize I've been standing by the kitchen table for the last five minutes, and I force myself to move. I grab Astrid's empty plate and coffee cup and bring them over to the sink. I should probably eat something myself, but the idea of food is making my stomach lurch.

The woman I see in the reflection from the kitchen window looks older than I remember. I've taken pretty good care of myself over the years—decent diet, plenty of walking, no smoking. Sometimes I catch a glimpse of myself at a certain angle or hear a nice comment, and I actually believe the effort has been worth it. Then I have days like today when I truly see my age, and I feel old and ugly.

I wash the few dishes that need to be done and leave them to dry on the dish drainer. Thankfully, I've no classes today, although the distraction might actually have been welcome. I like the students at Levinson. They're cheeky at times, but they mean well, and they're an intelligent bunch. There is a lot of potential in those rooms, and I just hope they get the support they need to flourish.

A rumbling noise from upstairs startles me. It sounds like the water pipes or something. Then I realize it's my phone vibrating, and I groan loudly. The last thing I want now is to talk to Robert. And what if it's the man who came to see me a few nights ago? God, he looks so much like my ex-husband.

Without realizing it, I'm already marching up the stairs. I've never been able to ignore a ringing phone, not since the day Astrid first went to kindergarten. I see it still vibrating on the dresser and snatch it up. When I spot John Howerton's name on the screen, I take a deep breath and let it out slowly.

"Hello?"

"Hi, Lilith." He sounds morbid, like he is speaking at a wake. "I, um, I called Hagerstown Hospital."

"And?"

"I think you need to come and see me right away."

Chapter 16

John Howerton's office is like something from a TV show. There is far too much faux-leather upholstery, varnish, and fifties throwback decor everywhere. It smells of pine air freshener and cologne, and the large window looking out over the street below is framed by thick red velvet curtains. There is even an antique fountain pen displayed on a small stand, and I can imagine John picturing himself as one of the Founding Fathers as he scrawls his name across the Declaration of Independence.

Mom had insisted on coming with me. In the end, she drove us here. If she hadn't walked into the house as I frantically tried to get myself organized following John's call, she would have never known where I was going. It didn't take her long to get it out of me, but I'm glad she is here. Her skepticism on the ride over here has actually helped, as I need to see that this is all crazy.

Having said that, John hasn't told me anything yet. In fact, all I know is that he wants to talk to me face-to-face. I've created all the worst-case scenarios in my head, which is something I've never needed any help doing.

"Just stay calm," Mom tells me for the twentieth time this morning. She is wearing a slim-fitting blue and white summer dress despite the chill outside and has paired it with white sneakers and a dark green coat. "We know that Fletcher can't be alive, so we can't overreact."

I nod and try to smile. I hate that John has kept us waiting, but as his secretary said, he is in an early morning meeting he couldn't cancel. Given that he called me less than half an hour ago, I suppose he didn't think I'd get here this quick. But I have to know what he wants to talk to me about.

Well, I know what it's concerning. I just have no idea what he could have possibly found that couldn't have been discussed over the phone.

The door swooshes open behind us, and I turn to see John marching into the office. He always moves like he thinks every second lost could mean an innocent man gets the electric chair. Of course, capital punishment is ancient history in the state of Massachusetts, and John specializes in divorce proceedings, child support, and alimony payments. To my knowledge, he has never represented anyone more interesting than angry wives and stressed husbands.

Still, he seems to believe he is on *Law and Order*, which would be quite entertaining on any other day. Right now, I feel like I'll never find anything funny again.

"Sorry to keep you waiting," John says as he sits down in his oversized chair, his expensive blue suit perfectly fitted. He rests his elbows on the desk and links his hands in front of him. Then he looks at Mom and smiles. "Hello, Mrs. Townsend."

"John," Mom replies, giving one sharp nod.

John Howerton has been our lawyer since Fletcher's accident. He was only in his early thirties then, but the twelve years since have been good to him. At least in that he has the money to treat himself to the best cosmetics and vanity laser surgeries. His practice has expanded, and he is seen as one of the best divorce lawyers in Boston. He doesn't come cheap, but apart from the messy business with the insurance company, we haven't really needed him for anything else.

He turns to me and flashes his Hollywood smile again. I could swear he is wearing foundation, but I can't be sure. The morning outside is dull and gray, yet it still seems to cast faded shadows across the room. I can see what little light there is reflecting off John's heavily slicked-back black hair.

"So, I think it's best if I get right to the point," he says after a pause.

"Yes, that sounds good," Mom replies.

"I take it you've been filled in, Mrs. Townsend?"

"Of course," Mom snaps.

"Okay, good," John says, nodding. "So, I put in a few well-placed phone calls, the main one being to Hagerstown Hospital. I told them that I was researching an old case." He brings one manicured finger up to his lips and winks. "But they were still a little defensive."

"Really?" Mom says. "They wouldn't help a lawyer?"

"Getting medical records is harder than you might think, Mrs. Townsend. Especially now that people are suing doctors and surgeons at the drop of a hat. They are afraid that I've got a client who lost his memory and ended up in their care, and now he's suing them for negligence because he thinks they should have done more to find out who he was."

"That's what they said?" I ask, slightly shocked.

"No, sorry," John says, chuckling. "I should have been clearer. That is what they would think after I asked my questions. Hospitals are always shifty when it comes to patient files, especially ones so specific. Any lawyer dreaming of fame would love to get their hands on something like this. If the patient's care has been mishandled in any way, of course."

"And was it?" Mom asks sharply.

"From what I've seen, no," John replies, his patience with her snappy questions never wavering.

"So there *are* records?" I ask. I can feel that strange otherworldliness washing over me again. "Of a man being found?"

"Yes."

"And the dates? Do they match up?"

"Yes."

"Oh, God," I groan. I feel like I might get sick.

"Did this man give you a name?" John asks. He sounds like he's ordering a pizza, not on the verge of obliterating someone's world.

"Yes, he's claiming to be Fletcher," Mom barks.

"Right," John replies, nodding slowly. "But his new identification. What did he say they changed his name to when they couldn't figure out who he was?"

"Michael Foster," I tell him. I'm trying to keep my head together, but it's getting harder to do. "He told me they gave him the name Michael Foster."

For the first time since I met John Howerton, his face pulls back for a split second. I've never seen any expression apart from calm reassurance, and it terrifies me. Then he places a manila folder on the desk in front of me and spins it so I can read it.

"Down in the bottom right-hand corner," he instructs. "The patient's new name is there."

I can hear someone sobbing, and I turn to Mom to comfort her. Then I feel streams of tears running down my face and realize that it's me.

The name is signed in chicken scratch, which would be hard to read if someone didn't know the handwriting. It is also printed right above, and I can't seem to look away. The name MICHAEL FOSTER feels like a dagger through my heart.

Chapter 17

"Just to be clear, this doesn't prove anything," John tells me. His voice is still calm, but I definitely hear a tremor in it somewhere.

The tears have stopped, but I feel so numb. It genuinely feels like a bomb has gone off, and I'm still rattled by the aftershock. Mom is surprisingly quiet and has been staring at the wall behind John for the last five minutes. She has always been a strong sense of reason in my life, but I can see that even she is struggling with this one. Instead of worrying me, it gives me a strange pang of comfort. If someone as strong as Ginny Townsend is finding this hard, then at least I'm not the only one being hysterical right now.

"How can you say that?" I ask. I dab at my face with a tissue I don't remember being given. "How could the names be the same if he's not telling the truth?"

"I'm not saying he isn't this Michael Foster," John tells me. "Or even that his story of being found wandering after smacking his head isn't true, as I'm sure it is. I'm just saying that he might be using it as leverage."

"Why would he do that?" I ask. I'm so confused.

"I'm not sure," John admits. I'm willing to bet it's the first time in his life he's said that phrase out loud. "If I'm being honest, I didn't think the names would match up. I've seen the police reports from the scene at the Gauley River. I saw pictures of what was left of the raft. Fletcher surviving is just an impossibility."

"But it's not," I almost snap.

"Okay, okay," John says. He tries to flash his smile again, but it comes out like a half-grin. "Let's hit the reset button here, okay?"

I take another glance at Mom, who is sitting beside me. She is still staring at the wall, and it is starting to concern me. But I can't deal with that now. I need to get some sort of rational answer—anything at all that won't drive me insane—before I leave this office. Even if it is clearly made up, I don't care. I need one I can grab hold of and try to believe.

"How could he have the same name?" I ask again. "It doesn't make sense."

"Let me think about this," John says. He brings one hand up and scratches his smooth cheek. His dark green eyes looked troubled. I know how he feels.

This is so crazy that I feel like I *have* actually gone insane. I think of the white Coupe and Michael Foster calling me Loly. Being followed through the fog by the car had been terrifying, yet hearing that nickname was so sweet. And wasn't that Fletcher in a nutshell? Loving and caring one minute, then horrible and nasty the next.

Is Michael Foster telling the truth? Why would he lie, and how would he even know what to lie about? It can't all be a coincidence, can it? Or is there even a coincidence here? There would be no benefit to someone pretending to be my dead husband. Yes, we received a good payout from the insurance company, but we're far from wealthy. Anyway, most of that money is gone now.

"Okay," John says, nodding his head. A hint of the old, calm, cocksure lawyer is back in his demeanor. "We have to assume that this man isn't Fletcher."

"Why?"

"Because it's just too crazy," he tells me, like that is the end of the matter because he decided. "So let's look at the facts. A man who claimed to have been injured twelve years ago and brought to Hagerstown Hospital with severe amnesia shows up at your door. He says he is your husband, who died around that time, and he has medical records that show he was given a new identity."

"Look, John," I say, surprised at the firmness in my voice. "The only question we should be asking ourselves is what possible benefit there would be for him pretending to be Fletcher, and the answer is none."

"Sure, but maybe he thinks—"

"No, John," I interrupt. "This isn't a time for a lawyer's outlook. There are some things that just can't be explained."

As I look into his eyes, I think of Juliane Koepcke again. I imagine her stumbling through the Amazon rainforest after falling 3,000 feet from a plane. I need John to know that there are moments in time that defy rhyme or reason. They are usually explained away as fiction, or at best, stuff that just happens to other people. But we might be in the middle of one of those moments right now, and we have to accept that.

"I know this is hard for you to process, Lilith." John has crossed his hands in front of him again. "But I can't believe that Hagerstown couldn't have linked Fletcher's accident to the man they found. There were only a few days between the two incidents. Surely they would have checked for any accidents or car crashes or anything like that in the area when he was admitted to the hospital."

"Maybe they did." I shrug. "And maybe they didn't, John. Maybe they missed it? Who knows. There are a hundred miles between Hagerstown and the Gauley River, so I'm sure it could have easily slipped through the cracks."

"But still, Lilith."

"Also, Fletcher's accident had been reported as a death, not a missing person," I say, and this aspect seems to hit him. I'm glad, as it means I'm making some sort of sense. "Also, there were several states between Maryland and Massachusetts. Why would they even consider he was from so far away? My guess is they wouldn't have even checked."

John screws up his face like he's just tasted something sour. Then he brings his hands up in a whatever-you-say gesture. "I still think you're clutching at straws."

"Yeah, well," I tell him as I stand up. "I have to meet him again and find out for myself."

Chapter 18

I asked Fletcher to choose the restaurant, and he picked our favorite spot, of course. I don't know why I was expecting anything different. With the way everything has been going lately, there was never going to be any other outcome. Had I wanted him to add another reason for me to believe it was him? I'm starting to think that, yes, I had.

Why? Because I did love him once, and not just a little. For the first half of our relationship, I was infatuated with Fletcher DuBose. I would have walked barefoot over hot coals for him, which is why it probably took me so long to realize that cowering in the corner of a bedroom while your husband puts a fist through the drywall isn't okay.

The young waiter at Reginno's hovers as he waits for us to place our order. I keep waiting for Fletcher to belittle the guy or make a scene, but he just places the menu down softly and says, "I'm so sorry, but we haven't really had a chance to decide. Could you give us a few minutes?"

The waiter—I see that his name tag says HARVEY—tells us that this will be no problem. When he is gone, Fletcher smiles at me, and I feel some of the reserve I had before coming here melt away.

We are sitting at the back of Reginno's, in one of the reserved areas. The other seven or so tables around us are unoccupied. When I walked through the rest of the restaurant fifteen minutes earlier, it was quite full. It's just about two o'clock, so I'm not surprised. Reginno's is one of the trendier spots in downtown Boston. Near the end of my marriage, I used to hate coming here, as Fletcher had verbally or physically abused what seemed like every member of staff at one stage or another.

He was already sitting at the table when I was escorted through a quarter of an hour ago by the maître d'. That was a surprise, as I don't remember Fletcher ever being on time before, let alone early. He is wearing a cream sports coat over a tightish black T-shirt that accentuates his firm, sinewy frame. In fact, I think he would be described as "lean" by the Instagram generation, or would it be "shredded"?

Who knows? I've always struggled to keep up with the popular new phrases and crazes, despite having a seventeen-year-old daughter and working with teenage kids.

With the waiter gone, it is just the two of us. I can't believe it was only this morning that I was at John Howerton's office. It feels like another period of my life, yet I can still hear Mom's desperate shouts as I hurried out of the room. She seemed completely devastated when John delivered the shocking news that a man had definitely been found wandering near Hagerstown around the time that Fletcher supposedly died.

She seemed almost hysterical as I walked down the hall and out of our lawyer's office. She has called my phone many times since, but I've let them all go to voicemail. I sent her one firm but loving text to say that I needed some space for the rest of the day and that I'd fill her in later. She replied with several messages of her own, but I haven't checked them yet. They'll only make me feel bad and plant seeds of doubt in my mind.

Fletcher runs two hands through his shaggy black hair and smiles again. Something deep inside me rises in temperature, and I involuntarily shift in my seat. It's not an uncomfortable movement on my part, but rather instinctual and quite pleasant.

"I'm so glad you called," Fletcher says. He takes a sip of the mineral water in front of him. "I was starting to think you had made up your mind about me."

"I had," I admit. "But things changed."

"I'm happy they did."

"This doesn't mean I believe you." I pause awkwardly, and he tilts his head slightly. The gesture seems alien.

"What?" he asks. "What were you going to say?"

"I realized something. Should I call you Michael or Fletcher?"

He leans his head back and laughs. There is no meanness in it, and I smile at his joy.

"I've been struggling with that myself," he says, shrugging. "I've been Michael for twelve years now and only found out my real name a couple of weeks ago."

"I can't imagine how that must feel."

"Sure you can," he replies. "This whole thing is just as shocking for you. Maybe even more so."

"How?"

"Think about it," he says, sitting forward. His piercing green eyes look brighter than I remember, but that could be the lighting in here. Everything in the VIP area at Reginno's is ruby red, even the lampshades. "I just have to accept that my name is different. You have to try and process the fact that the man you thought was dead is actually alive."

I try to smile, but I can't. I don't know what I should be doing at this moment in time. Who would?

"It's okay," he tells me. When he reaches across the table and tries to touch my hand, I snap it away. His expression flickers for a split second, then settles again almost instantly. "Really, it's okay. You don't have to understand all of this right away. All I've wanted since it started coming back to me is that you just try."

The waiter appears through the velvet curtains at the far end of the room, takes one look at us, not even holding our menus, and slips back out again.

Mom will lose her mind when I tell her I met this man for lunch, but I can't deal with that now. I need to figure this thing out on my own. I don't know why that's the case; I just know that it is.

"So," I say. "What name do you want me to use?"

"Well," he replies, dropping his gaze shyly. It's another gesture I've never seen before, but it is exciting in a whole new way. "I would love for you to call me Fletcher. It is my name, after all."

"Okay, Fletcher," I say, nodding. It feels so crazy to be sitting across from him and referring to him in that way. "For now, I will."

"That's all I ask." He picks up his menu and starts to scan it. Without looking up, he adds, "I really am so glad you came, Loly."

"I think I am too. I didn't see your Coupe outside," I say, picking up my own menu. I'm actually quite hungry now.

"Coupe?"

"Yes, the white Coupe."

Fletcher chuckles and looks at me over the top of his menu. The greens of his eyes look like an Irish meadow. "I've never driven a Coupe, Loly."

Chapter 19

Mom comes charging out of the kitchen and down the hallway toward me before I can even get my jacket off. She is still wearing the blue and white summer dress she had on this morning, only now her neatly tied-up hair has come loose in places. It's like she has been nervously pulling at it while I've been gone.

"Look at the time!" she snaps, making me feel like I've been transported back in time.

"Excuse me?" I snort a little laugh, which seems to shock her. "It's not even six yet, Mom. And I'm an adult."

"You know what I mean," she scoffs, waving her hand dismissively. "Tell me you weren't with him."

She verbally spits the last word, and I have to shake my head at her behavior. I understand it, sure, but this is my life. She can't genuinely expect me not to follow up on the information we got from John.

I hang my jacket on one of the hooks and walk past her toward the kitchen. I hear her grunting something as she follows, her footsteps quick and purposeful.

"Don't walk away from me, Lilith," she snaps.

This is crazy. It really does feel like I'm a teenager again. "Come on, Mom. I just went for lunch."

"So you did meet him!" Mom shrieks, making me turn around to face her.

We're standing in the middle of the kitchen with just the length of the table between us. As I look into her eyes, she looks like she has aged ten years since I last saw her. Something hits me, and I say, "Is Astrid here?"

"No, she's out," Mom barks. I'm glad, as I don't want my daughter to hear this stuff. Not yet, anyhow. Mom is still scowling at me as she asks, "What were you thinking, Lilith?"

"Don't you dare, Mom," I snap. "Don't you even dare."

"What?"

"This is my *husband* we're talking about. How am I meant to ignore that?"

Mom snorts sharply out her nose. "You can't be serious? You believe this nonsense?"

"You heard John," I growl. "The hospital has records."

"That a man was found wandering, Lilith, not that this is Fletcher."

"And you don't think that's strange?"

Mom's eyes go as big as saucers. "Strange? Of course it is, but it's not a damn miracle."

I haven't fought with her like this in years, and I don't like it. Why she is so desperately determined to completely dismiss everything, I don't know. She seems incapable of even considering that Fletcher might be telling the truth, and I don't need that sort of negativity right now.

You usually appreciate her skepticism, something inside me insists. *It keeps you grounded. Or is that just when it suits you?*

"Why does it have to be a miracle, Mom?" I ask sharply. "A body was never found."

"Fletcher is *dead*, Lilith."

"Then who did I have lunch with today?"

"An imposter."

The air seems to get sucked out of the room. We are both standing across from each other, breathing heavily. Her pig-headedness is infuriating, but I have to try and see things from her side. This situation is crazy, but it's not the impossible miracle she is claiming it to be. Odd things happen all the time. Just because one of them is happening to us right now doesn't mean it isn't real.

"Why can't you accept that this might be true?" I ask, shaking my head.

"That's not Fletcher," Mom growls through clenched teeth.

"What if it is?"

"It's not."

"My God, Mom," I exclaim, exhaling so hard that I feel lighter. "I think you just don't want it to be him."

"What? Why?"

"Because you hated him from the beginning." It's something I've always known but nothing we've ever discussed. Sure, she admitted her dislike when the violence started, but she was off with Fletcher from the moment she met him.

"I did not," she snaps, but some of the conviction has left her voice. Not much, but enough that I notice. Mom seems to recognize this and straightens her back. "I hated him when he started smacking you around, Lilith."

Her words sting, mainly because they make me realize how crazy I just might be to be letting this man back into my life. Do people change? I must have believed they did at some stage.

Why else would I have stuck it out for so long? By the end, that belief had become more of a wish, but still...

"I remember, Mom," I hiss. "But I remember the first time I told you about him too."

"What are you talking about?" she scoffs, waving her hand like a Pharaoh dismissing the help.

"You hated him, Mom. You never gave him a chance."

"I hated the DuBoses, Lilith." Her voice is so full of venom that I recoil a little.

"*I'm* a DuBose, Mom," I snap. "*Astrid* is a DuBose."

"And it kills me inside," she spits. Then she turns on her heels and storms out of the kitchen.

I hear the front door being slammed, and I'm left alone, reeling from her words. I've always known that she disliked the DuBoses, but Robert gave her husband a job. Sure, Dad died on one of his construction sites, but that was unavoidable.

Mom's deep-rooted hatred, though. That is something she always had.

Or had she? Now that the heavy tension in the room is fading, I'm starting to remember a time when she wasn't so cold with Fletcher. It wasn't for long. But once Dad died, she completely changed her attitude toward him *and* Robert. But there were a couple of years in the beginning when she was okay, wasn't there? Maybe, but she definitely started to hate Fletcher before the violence—that I do know.

I check my phone with a hand that won't stop shaking and see it is just after six. Outside, what little light there had been during the day has already started to fade. The idea of making dinner seems like a trek up the Alps, and I think I'll just order in when Astrid gets home.

A text from Reece bleeps as I'm holding the phone, and I swipe it away without reading it. I'm sure he is worried about me or thinking about me or something like that.

Without realizing I'm doing it, I scroll down through the names on my call list. When I get to the one saved as MICHAEL FOSTER, I click on it and delete it before entering a new one.

What is staring back at me is something I never thought I'd see again, and it is also something that I'm still not sure I fully believe. The name FLETCHER looks strange next to the call button, but there it is all the same.

Chapter 20

It's only as I'm turning into the long, gravel driveway and see the sprawling gardens with their hedge animals and sprinklers that I realize how long it's been since I've visited Robert DuBose's home. Actually, this is the first time I've been *invited* here since before Fletcher died.

As I edge the car along the drive, I hear the pebbles crunching beneath the tires. The window is open as it is hot today, but the breeze is doing little to cool me. The surprisingly nice weather is just another part of today that feels disjointed and out of place.

When Fletcher called me last night, I was still reeling from my argument with Mom. I accepted his invitation to lunch so quickly that it scared me, and I could already feel traces of the gooey-eyed teenager who fell head-over-heels in love with him returning. She is still only a whisper inside, but the fact that she is there at all is very worrying. She makes decisions with her heart instead of her head, and they are rarely good ones.

On my left, I see a tanned gardener as he waters a row of juniper bushes with a hose. He is wearing a red baseball cap, and when he looks up and waves, I do the same. The gardens on my right spread out so far that I can barely see the bright green bushes separating the DuBose property from some other millionaire's mansion.

Robert DuBose has always done things in an over-the-top manner that borders on being obnoxious. Even though he had been vehemently against me marrying his son, he still took charge when he knew he wasn't going to change Fletcher's mind. The wedding venue ended up looking like something from a gangster movie. Everything was bright white and grand, down to the ridiculously long flowing dress I was convinced to wear. All I had been able to think about at the time was how embarrassing it was to have two ladies I didn't know carrying the hem behind me as I walked down the aisle.

I quickly learned that what Robert DuBose wants, he gets. And he wanted his only son's wedding to be fancier and more expensive than everyone else's in his circle.

I never got to meet Harriot DuBose, but I know that she and Fletcher were extremely close. She died when he was thirteen, and I feel that he had trust issues from that day forward.

In all the time I've known Robert, I never once heard him talk about his wife.

The main driveway borders a circle of pristine grass about the size of a small swimming pool. The only car I see is a shiny black classic model that looks like a Bentley or something like that. I don't know exactly, as I'm not that knowledgeable on the subject, but it resembles something Al Capone would have been driven around in.

I don't know why, but I keep expecting to see a white Coupe parked somewhere. It's silly because Fletcher confirmed that it hadn't been him following me in the fog. In fact, nobody had been tailing me that night. It had all been my paranoia, which has pretty much refused to fade since. I'm still constantly jumping at shadows, and I'm uncertain of everything.

I park the car and just sit here. The wide steps leading up to the massive front door look intimidating. Why did I agree to meet Fletcher without thinking things through? I didn't even give him a chance to finish his sentence. By the time he had added that lunch was going to be at his father's house, it was too late. Would I have agreed even if I'd known? Probably, and that is the most worrying aspect. It means that the teenage me is having more of a say in things.

I take a deep breath and step out into the sun. The air even feels cleaner in this part of Boston, and I suppose the people that live here are farther away from all the traffic and fumes of the city. The house looks bigger than I remember, and the white brickwork shines in the afternoon sun. Flowers of the brightest colors sit in hanging baskets under all of the upstairs windows, and the marble pillars at the top of the steps look freshly polished. *Everything* looks freshly polished.

The front door slowly opens before I've moved from beside my car, and a man in an expensive cream suit steps out.

Robert DuBose still looks the same. His tan is almost milk chocolate brown, and his salt and pepper hair is slicked back. His piercing blue eyes are intense, even from fifteen feet away. He is stocky but not overweight. His shoulders are pulled back, yet it somehow doesn't look forced. When he smiles, I find myself swallowing nothing but warm air.

"Ah, Lilith," he chimes. "I'm so glad you accepted my invitation!"

Sure, I tell myself. *You invite me now that your son is back. Where was this friendly welcome when we were all grieving?*

"Hello, Robert," I call from the bottom of the steps. I'm trying to keep the disdain—and the fear—out of my voice. "Thanks for inviting me."

Robert creases his brow and looks at the car behind me. "No Astrid?"

"No, she is at a friend's today."

This is true, but Astrid didn't know where I was going, so she couldn't have come even if she'd wanted to. Actually, nobody knows about this lunch apart from Fletcher, Robert, and me. Mom would have insisted on coming, but that would have been a disaster. The tension between Robert and me that existed in the past was always multiplied whenever Mom was involved. Thankfully, their dislike of each other is mutual, so I don't have to worry about Robert having invited her.

"Oh, that's a shame," he tells me through that strange new smile. His teeth are as bright as the shining house. "I was looking forward to seeing the little scamp."

"She's seventeen, Robert."

"Of course she is."

We stand facing each other for a while like two poker players betting it all on an unturned card. Already I'm regretting this, and it was crazy to agree to meet Fletcher so soon after only one lunch together. Yes, the few hours I spent with him at Reginno's were nice, but I can't let him take control again. Besides, I'm still confused about who he is and if he's telling the truth.

The medical records, I tell myself. *The hospital confirmed them.*

Right, but is that enough to let him back into our lives? No, it's not. And it won't be my life that he becomes a part of, at least not in that way. I'm only doing this so Astrid can have a father again.

Are you, Lilith?

"Yes," I say under my breath.

"Excuse me?" Robert asks, still standing at the top of the steps. His attempts at sounding upper class and not a Roxbury native have gone up a whole new level over the years.

"Nothing. Sorry, I was just talking to myself," I say, laughing. It sounds ridiculous.

"I do it all the time!" That fake cheeriness again. It's so off-putting. "Well, come in. I'm sure Virginia will be here soon."

"Oh, I didn't invite her," I say as I walk up the steps. "I didn't know if I should."

"That's okay," Robert replies, nodding. "I invited her this morning."

Chapter 21

After Robert had led me through the huge, marbled foyer, we walked to the back of the house and out into the backyard. Well, "backyard" is a bit of an understatement. This is more like a country club. The grass is just as shockingly green as out front, and instead of the rows of bushes that run along the side, there are thick trees in the distance. Beyond, small rolling hills separate the DuBose property from the world, but they are so far away that I can only see their outline.

There is a long table on the patio with a huge lunch spread on the sparkling white cloth. I can see quiche, jugs of orange juice, an array of salads in glass bowls, and what looks like a whole side of salmon. Several platters of bread, rolls, and cold cuts are scattered throughout.

Robert leads me past it to a round glass table with four chairs around it. Next to that is one of those liquor stands that businessmen used to have in their offices from a time long ago. As he pours himself a drink from a crystal decanter, he asks if I'd like one.

"No, thank you," I say. It's the first words we've spoken since he told me he had invited Mom, and I'm still reeling a little.

Under normal circumstances, a father-in-law inviting his daughter-in-law's mother to a casual lunch at his home wouldn't be strange. But these aren't normal circumstances, and this is not a typical family. Robert DuBose doesn't make *any* decision—regardless of how insignificant it seems on the surface—unless he has an ulterior motive.

Come on, give him a chance. Maybe he has changed? Finding out that your only son is alive after twelve years would do that to anyone, right?

"It's early, I know," Robert declares, pointing his drink at me before taking a sip. He looks at the glass as he savors the brown liquid and sighs admirably. "But this is a special occasion, wouldn't you agree?"

"Maybe."

"Maybe?"

"I'm still unsure about all of this."

Robert looks at me like I'm a silly child who has spilled ice cream on his expensive suit. "Unsure of what, Lilith? You don't believe this man is my boy?"

"How can I?" I ask. I hadn't planned on this conversation happening so quickly, but I'm glad it is. "And where is he, anyway?"

"Fletcher? He is at work."

"Work? Why did he invite me if he's not coming?" I'm trying so hard not to show the anger that I'm feeling.

"Yes, he will go back to running one of my construction firms. Just baby steps at first, of course." Robert takes another sip and looks out over his vast land. "I don't want to put too much pressure on him. And he is on his way home as we speak."

"Okay," I say. I'm annoyed that Fletcher isn't here, but at least he will be soon.

"You don't believe it's him?" Robert repeats, shaking his head slowly. His tan looks electrified against his cream suit. "I must say, I'm a little surprised."

"Why?" I snap. Screw trying to keep the animosity out of my voice. This is a crazy situation, and here he is, trying to act like it's just a friendly little lunch. "You expect me just to accept it, no questions asked?"

"I'm sure you've asked questions."

"What's that supposed to mean?" I growl.

"Nothing at all, Lilith," he almost croons. "You're a thorough, professional young woman. I'm just saying that I'm sure you've made a few inquiries. Who wouldn't, in the same situation?"

I watch his face for a while for any signs of sarcasm and spot none. Up this close, I can see the wrinkles on his skin as they fight against the Botox. Years of tanning beds have taken their toll, but the finest skin creams seem to have held the natural aging process off somewhat. Robert DuBose would probably be considered devilishly handsome if his demeanor was different, but the coldness of his persona strips him of any charm.

"You're right," I say after a while. "I made some calls."

"And?"

"I'm sure you know a hell of a lot more than I do, Robert."

"How so?"

"Come on," I say, shaking my head. "With your connections? It should be me asking you what you've found out."

Robert nods approvingly. The only thing I've ever seen that remotely moves him is moxie. "I made a few calls. There are medical records at Hagerstown that confirm a man was found wandering and that it was later discovered that he had amnesia. The Michael Foster thing checks out, *and* the reasons why he was given a new identity. My lawyers are in the process of suing that shitty hospital for all its worth, which won't be much, I'm sure."

"Suing them?"

Any fake cheeriness that had been on his face vanishes, and that emotionless darkness that always sends a shiver down my spine takes over. His blue eyes look black.

"Of course, Lilith," he spits, his voice drenched in venom. When he gestures sharply with his hand, some of his drink sloshes over the side of the glass. "If those amateurs had dug a little deeper, they'd have found that a man had been reported missing at the Gauley River in the days prior to Fletcher being found. Even a monkey would have been able to put two and two together after that. Instead, I lost my only son for twelve years."

His words shock me, but only because they're true. It was so unprofessional of the hospital not to do more to find out who the man was that had ended up in their care, even if the rafting accident had happened around 150 miles away. How Fletcher came to be in Hagerstown a few days after the accident is another question, but that doesn't matter right now.

"I'm sorry, Robert, but I'm going to need more than that."

Robert swirls his drink and looks back out over his gardens. His calm exterior is back in full flow, and none of the seething rage I just saw remains. When he speaks to me, he does it over his shoulder.

"You need more than that?" he says, his voice like silk. "Why don't you just ask to see his tattoo, Lilith?"

Chapter 22

Fletcher got a tattoo on his chest when we first started dating. It was a three-inch lollipop with FOREVER written beneath it. That is all, just a simple tattoo. At the time, I wasn't even twenty, so the gesture seemed really romantic. In fact, even now, I still get a tingling in my stomach when I remember how I used to feel when I looked at it.

Asking to see it before now never crossed my mind, at least not until Robert mentioned it a couple of hours ago. Fletcher arrived at his father's house not long after that, and Mom pulled up a couple of minutes later. Since then, I haven't had a chance to ask Fletcher about it.

Okay, that's not the whole truth. I just haven't plucked up the courage.

For one thing, I'll have to ask to speak with him in private. Only Mom, Robert, Fletcher, and I are sitting out on the back patio sipping juice and eating quiche, but I still don't want anyone here to think Fletcher and I are getting back together. I especially don't want Fletcher to believe that.

But I will need to see it, and it will have to be soon. My head is a mess thinking about it.

"May I use the bathroom?" Mom says, standing up from her chair and dabbing at her mouth with a napkin. The denim dress she is wearing over a white tank top is slim-fitting, and I think I see Robert checking her out. It could just be my imagination, though, and the sun is in my eyes too.

"Of course, Ms. Townsend," Fletcher says.

Mom looks at him like he has just called her the nastiness name imaginable for a second and then turns to Robert. "Where is it?"

"Oh, I'm sorry," Robert replies. He points toward the back of the house, where both sliding doors are open. The perfectly white curtains billow in the light breeze. "Through the kitchen and take a left. Follow the hall until the end, and it's on your right."

Mom gives Fletcher one last hard stare and then sets off across the patio toward the back doors.

When she arrived here earlier, I have to admit that my heart was in my mouth. She refused Fletcher's hand when he offered it in the foyer and then did the same to Robert. Fletcher took it in his stride and even made a sweet joke about it. Robert remained calm on the outside, but I could see that he was boiling beneath the surface.

Hearing Fletcher refer to Mom as "Ms. Townsend" is beyond strange. Not once when we were dating did he call her that. In fact, I only ever heard him use her first name, and even that was said with a coldness in his tone.

My stomach grumbles, and I look at the nearly full plate on the table in front of me. I have absolutely no appetite, and my belly continues to do somersaults whenever someone speaks. The tension is palpable, but everyone apart from Mom seems to be trying to remain cordial.

"I'm sorry again for being late," Fletcher leans in and tells me for the fifth time since he got here.

"It's fine," I reply. I've been quite sharp with him for the last two hours, and I can't figure out why. I know we're not together anymore, but I keep getting these flushes of feeling like we are.

"Your mother is as charming as ever," Robert scoffs. He takes a sip of Scotch as he looks at me over the rim of the glass.

"This is a lot for her to deal with," Fletcher says before I can reply. "It's a lot for all of us."

Robert grunts and shakes his head. I feel like he wants to say more, but there seems to be something inside holding him back. Does he want Astrid, Mom, and me out of the picture? He never liked us in the first place, so I'm sure he just wants his returning son to start a new life without us.

The silence is as uncomfortable as I remember. On the rare occasions years ago when Robert actually made an effort to spend time with Fletcher and me, it was always awkward like this. The only time conversation would pick up was when Robert and Fletcher would start drunkenly debating politics or business. The rest of the time, it just became more and more evident that neither of them wanted to be there.

When I check my watch, I see that all three of us haven't spoken in over five minutes. It feels like sixty.

There is a sharp bleep, and Robert pulls his phone out of his suit pocket. I watch as he swipes open a message or an email, creases his brow, and says, "What the hell?"

"What is it, Dad?" Fletcher asks.

Robert stands up abruptly, still looking at the phone. He places his drink on the table and sniffs hard, like a bull getting ready to charge a lonely matador. "Wait here."

He stomps off across the patio, his spotlessly clean suit radiant in the afternoon sun. Fletcher watches him go with his mouth in a perfect O shape. He looks strangely young even though he is forty-five. In truth, he looks like the man I fell in love with all those years ago.

"Huh, that was odd!" he says, then utters a quick, nervous laugh.

"Probably business," I tell him.

"Yeah, probably."

When I sit forward in my chair and lean into Fletcher, it looks like he flinches a little. Is he genuinely nervous? If so, it's the first time I've ever seen him like that.

"Fletcher," I say. My voice trembles as the realization of what I'm about to ask kicks in. What if he shows me, and it's actually there? What then?

"Yeah, Loly?"

"I need to see the tattoo."

Chapter 23

"It was always confusing to me. All those years after Hagerstown, I would see it in the mirror and wonder what it meant," Fletcher tells me, pulling his white T-shirt back on. "I mean, a lollipop! How was I supposed to figure that one out?"

Now it's my mouth that is hanging open. I wonder if it is a perfect O like Fletcher's was a moment ago. The same tattoo. I mean, there is absolutely no denying it; it's identical.

What the hell do I do from here? Oh, God, do I have to tell Astrid now? What am I meant to say to her? Where do I start? How will this affect her? Oh, no. Oh, God, no, this is all too much.

"Loly?" Fletcher says. I hear him and see his lips moving, but I can't grasp his words. Even though it's just my name, I feel like it should mean more. "Loly? Are you okay?"

"I-I'm fine," I manage. But I'm not. I'm far from okay.

"You look like you've seen a ghost," he says.

I *have* seen one. That is basically what is happening here. A man died twelve years ago, and now he is sitting down beside me at the patio table, looking concerned.

"I know I've kept in shape," he says, playfully flexing his tight, sinewy bicep like a cartoon character. There is a huge, cheesy grin lighting up his face. "But I didn't think you'd feel faint if I took my shirt off!"

I snort a laugh, even though I really do feel dizzy and dazed. Seeing the tattoo has confirmed things that I still don't know if I wanted to be confirmed. The hospital records could have been explained away as sheer coincidence. The man who had been given the name Michael Foster was found a long way from where my husband smashed into the rocks along the Gauley River, so I could have maybe convinced myself over time that it wasn't Fletcher. But the tattoo *and* the medical records? Well, that's just too much to dismiss.

"Seriously, though, are you okay, Loly?"

"I'm okay," I say, and I mean it a little more this time. "Can I have a glass of water?"

"Of course," Fletcher replies, then slaps his forehead with the palm of his hand. "Jeez, what kind of a gentleman am I?"

You're not a gentleman, Fletcher, and you have never been one, I snap inwardly. Or has he really changed? *No, stay on your guard, Lilith. Don't you go falling for any tricks.*

Fletcher steps over to the long table with the food and beverages on it. The one that Robert clearly paid to set up before we got here. There is absolutely no way a man like Robert DuBose laid out that spread himself.

"Club soda okay?" Fletcher calls.

"Sure."

"You got it."

I see him pop the cap and pour it into a glass. As he walks back over to me, he smiles in a way I don't remember. There seems to be only kindness in it. Instead of comforting me, it puts me on edge even more.

The water is cold and fizzy, and it is wonderfully refreshing. I drink half of it in one go, then burp as I place the glass on the table.

"Excuse you!" Fletcher chimes, that smile still there.

The sound of footsteps makes me turn around in my chair, and I see Mom walking toward me. She is followed closely by Robert. Her face is bright red, and her mouth is screwed up so tightly that her lips have turned white. Robert looks flushed too, but his face is a little harder to read.

They've both been gone a while, and I hope they weren't arguing inside. I know how much Mom dislikes Robert, but surely she wouldn't go at him on a day like today?

"Everything okay, Ms. Townsend?" Fletcher asks.

"You can stop with that Ms. Townsend crap, *Michael*," she growls.

"Mom, please," I say. I feel like I've traveled back in time. The only thing worse than the times when it was Fletcher, Robert, and me locked in silence were the occasions when Mom was there doing her best to add to the tension.

She stands over me for a moment, looking down with her hands on her hips. I have to shade my eyes with my hand to see her properly. I think she is about to tell me we are leaving when she pulls her chair out and sits down sharply. Her back is dead straight, and she is looking past me at Fletcher.

Robert takes his seat again and picks up his drink. I can hear what's left of the ice clinking in the glass.

"Everything okay, Dad?" Fletcher asks. He sounds nervous.

"Not really, no," Robert snaps, then looks hard at Mom.

She turns her nose up and exhales sharply through flared nostrils. Again, I picture a bull getting ready to gore someone.

"Business?" Fletcher asks, clearly just trying to ease the tension now.

"You could say that, Fletcher." Robert is still glaring at Mom, who is pretending like she doesn't notice. When he finally peels his gaze away from her and settles it on mine, I feel my whole body run cold. Through a thin smile, he adds, "It all depends on how you look at it, I suppose."

Chapter 24

It is one of those days in winter when the air is cold, but it is so bright that everything seems reflective. The sky is so blue it looks freshly painted, and everyone we pass is wearing three layers. I like this weather—always have—and I feel good in the slim-fitting, black duffle coat and navy jeans I chose this morning. I've paired them with a black Gatsby hat and large-framed sunglasses.

Fletcher is wearing a dark brown wool coat that looks quite dapper and jeans that flare ever so slightly at the ankle. They are draped over sparkling white sneakers—something I never saw him wear back in the day—and his shaggy hair is tucked under a maroon cap. His stubble has grown out a bit, and I can see hints of gray on his chin whiskers.

The park is pretty full, considering how cold it is, but I suppose the brightness of the day has been so unexpected that people are taking advantage of it. Of course, we had sun a few days ago, but it has been so miserable since I think winter has finally kicked in for good.

The recent bad weather seems ominous, given how things have been with Mom since our lunch at Robert's house. She still won't tell me what happened between the two of them, and she actually denies that anything happened at all. I asked Fletcher the following day if Robert had mentioned anything, and he said he hadn't.

I guess I should have expected the lunch to end like that once I heard Mom was coming. She and Robert were constantly at each other's throats throughout my marriage, and nothing has changed. Each of them still thinks their kid could do better.

"Thanks for meeting me again," Fletcher says. His eyes seem a bit shifty today, and I feel like he wants to ask me something but can't quite do it.

"No problem," I reply. Walking so close to him still feels strange, especially with the beautiful, serene scenery around us. It's like we're in a rom-com. "My classes finished at one."

Fletcher smiles down at me, but it looks painted on. His smile has looked odd since he came back into my life nearly two weeks ago, but that's probably because it has been a sweet one. Today it's different, and not in a good way. He has been hinting at meeting Astrid lately, so maybe that's what is on his mind.

I'm still not sure if it's a good idea, but I know I can't keep spending time with him in secret.

We are on the north side of the park, near the duck pond. A few of them are waddling along the edge, seemingly reluctant to get in and look for their lunch below the surface. I can't blame them, as the water must be freezing.

There are a few couples slowly milling about around us. I wonder if any of them are as confused about life as we are right now. I seriously doubt it.

Fletcher takes his phone out again and checks it before stuffing it back into his coat pocket. The park is surrounded by red metal railings, and the street beyond is surprisingly quiet. When a nearby girl in a Boston University hoodie squeals as her boyfriend tickles her, Fletcher snaps his head around and scans the area.

"Is everything okay?" I ask.

He concentrates on the couple for a second and then looks down at me. "Hmm?"

"You seem on edge. Is something bothering you?"

"No, nothing."

We continue walking. To onlookers, we must seem like any other couple in their early forties. They would never understand the situation we are in as we stroll through the park together. How could they when I don't?

The last few days have been pleasant. Fletcher has been so sweet, but it has all just left me more confused about things. Mom has barely spoken a word to me since lunch at Robert's, and she's been spending a lot of her time away from the house. I've only seen her car in the driveway a handful of times, and on the rare occasions when I do speak to her, she replies with just vague, grunted answers.

"Did something happen with your father?"

Fletcher scrunches up his brow. "No. What? Come on, Lilith, just drop it."

"Drop what? I'm only asking if something is wrong."

"I'm fine," Fletcher snaps. It's not an overly aggressive reaction, but there is a sharp edge in his voice, nonetheless.

We've come to a small pathway at one of the other entrances. There is a parking lot beyond with only a few cars in it. Fletcher points to a bench to our left, and I nod. Wordlessly, we both walk over and slump down.

"I'm sorry," he tells me, shaking his head. "I've been a bit off today."

"That's okay."

"It's not okay, Loly." He drops his head and slowly shakes it. "You're such a sweet person. You don't deserve this."

"Deserve what?"

"This," he says and waves his hand at nothing. Then he clears his throat and smiles again. "I mean, this mood I'm in. You know?"

"Really, it's okay," I tell him, and I actually mean it. He has been through so much, and I need to remind myself of that more often. We all do. "This can't be easy for you. Remembering bits here and there. It's confusing."

Fletcher looks off in the direction of the parking lot and the buildings looming over it. I can only see the side of his face, but I can tell he is in pain. There is so much we need to talk about, and I know now that he is not ready to see Astrid. It would only add to his confusion.

"It is hard, but I need to make more of an effort." He looks off into the distance as he speaks. "What if we—"

Fletcher suddenly stops mid-sentence and sits up straight. His shoulders pull back, and I can almost feel the tension in his body. When he stands up and grabs my hand, his grip is tight.

"Come on," he says hoarsely. "Let's head back."

"Wait, hang on," I reply as he pulls me to my feet.

"It's nicer over here," Fletcher says as we start to move at a near jog. His voice is shaky, and he keeps looking back over his shoulder.

"Fletcher, slow down." I yank my hand out of his, but I don't slow my pace. "What's going on?"

"Nothing," he tells me, forcing that smile again. His eyes meet mine for only a second before he looks back over his shoulder again.

"Fletcher, wait!" I snap. When I stop walking, he does too. I can see his eyes trying to look back to where we came from, but he seems to be fighting the urge this time. "What is going on?"

"Nothing, Loly, really," he tells me. "I just prefer it over the other side of the park."

I watch his expression for a few seconds to see if I can interpret what's bothering him, but he just looks scared. I nod, and it seems to make him relax a little. As I start walking again, he exhales heavily. When I turn around to see if I can spot what rattled him, I don't know what I expect to find.

It's nothing. All that is there is the near-empty parking lot, the duck pond far away on the left, and two young teenage girls in school uniform sitting down at the bench we just left.

Chapter 25

The last hour has been awkward. Fletcher lasted five minutes at the south side of the park before he suggested leaving. When I asked him where he wanted to go, he just replied, "Anywhere." That ended up being a quirky little coffee shop on West Street with a chipped brickwork interior and mismatched tables that all have daily affirmations printed on their wooden surfaces.

I asked Fletcher a couple more times what the hell happened at the park, but he was evasive. Could he have seen something—something completely innocent—that triggered a painful memory for him that he couldn't process? I suppose that's as good a reason as any.

"How do memories come back to you?" I ask him. The latte I ordered came out in a jar, but it still tastes good despite the needlessly pretentious presentation.

"What do you mean?"

Fletcher removed his hat when we came in here, and his hair is slightly disheveled. Somehow it makes him even more attractive.

"Like, is it one long stream of images, or do the memories just slot back in like they were always there?" I ask.

He takes a sip of his coffee as he thinks about his answer. If I had brought him into a place like this twelve years ago, he would have taken one look at the decor and walked right back out again. Strangely now, he looks quite at home in his surroundings.

"A bit of both, really." His hand comes up to the huge scar on the side of his head. "I'll see an image of us together at Christmas or something, and then it will just become part of my memories."

"And the bad stuff?" I ask. It wasn't meant to come out so bluntly, but we need to discuss it at some point.

When I confronted him about this the night he first showed up, he claimed then that he couldn't remember. I'm not sure I want to know the answer because I've had this fear since he came back into my life: What if the first time he remembers one of the darker incidents is the moment when he snaps back into the old Fletcher? What then?

"Like the gambling?" Fletcher asks, dropping his gaze.

"Gambling?"

Of all the vices Fletcher DuBose enjoyed—and there were many—gambling strangely wasn't one of them. In fact, it was probably the only one he resisted.

"Yeah," he says, tilting his head slightly. He looks like a confused puppy. "Why, what else was there?"

"Come on, Fletcher," I reply. I look around to make sure nobody is sitting close enough to eavesdrop. I think we're safe, as the place has started to clear out now that it's three o'clock. "You have to remember some of it."

Why am I pushing this? What good can come from it?

Then it hits me. If Fletcher is getting a second chance at life, then how is it fair that he can do so, forgetting all of the horrible things he did? All of the tears I shed. Hell, all of the tears his little daughter cried as she hid in her room and covered her ears. He can't live the rest of his life without absorbing those moments; it would be like they never happened.

"I'm sorry, Loly," he says. "Only some of it came back when I hit my head."

The letter he handed Astrid to give me last week went into more detail about what had happened that time. He had been painting his apartment in Pittsburgh when he fell off a ladder and hit his head on the edge of the kitchen table. His neighbor found him and called 911, and a few days later, Michael Foster woke up and remembered that his real name was, in fact, Fletcher DuBose.

"That hospital in Pittsburgh," I say. "They'll have records of you being admitted there?"

"What?" Fletcher asks. He looks wounded, but I don't care. "You already called them."

"No, I called Hagerstown, not Pittsburgh."

"Okay. Isn't that enough? You've seemed okay with everything lately."

"No, it's not enough."

What just happened in the park has annoyed me more than I thought it had. He has been acting shady all day, and I know something is bothering him. Also, I have a right to know if his story about hitting his head is true or not. It's the least I deserve.

Maybe I could have timed this moment better, but it's too late now.

"Well, I'm sure they have a record of it," he tells me. He sounds like a pouting child.

Maybe meeting him so much has been a bad idea? What did I expect would happen? Even if this new, seemingly nicer version of Fletcher doesn't remember the awful things he did, I do. And more importantly, Astrid does. Even if they are faded memories for her, they are still imprinted in her psyche.

"I think we need to take a step back," I tell him.

His face washes over with something that looks like anger, and I instinctively retreat inside myself for protection. Then I see that what he is really showing is fear. Pure, unadulterated fear.

"Don't say that, Lilith," he pleads. When I go to stand up, he grabs my hand and looks up into my eyes. He is clearly terrified. "Please, please don't go."

"Why, Fletcher? You could just start again. If the memories aren't there, then what have you lost?"

"I need to see Astrid," he tells me.

"What? No, that's impossible."

His hand is still on mine, and it's shaking. I can feel the clamminess of it.

"You don't understand, Lilith," he almost whimpers. "I have to see her. I have to get to know her."

"Fletcher," I say. I'm still halfway between standing up and sitting down. "It's just not a good idea."

His grip tightens on my hand to the point where I wince. I can see myself in the whites of his eyes, and the green pupils looking back seem to scream at me. "You will not take her away from me, Lilith. I need to make sure she makes the right decisions."

"What are you talking about?" I snap. When I try to pull my hand away, he draws me closer. I can feel the gazes of the other patrons on us now. "Fletcher, let me go."

He leans into me so that our faces are only inches apart. "You have no idea what you're doing to me, Lilith. Either you tell Astrid about me, or I do."

Chapter 26

Two days have passed since I met with Fletcher in the park. Although he initially frightened me when he grabbed my hand, I later came to understand why he reacted like that. His anger was just fear—fear that he would never see his daughter again.

How would I feel if I was told I couldn't see Astrid again? I don't think I could bear it. Even if Fletcher's memories have only come back in fits and starts, the love he feels for his child must have remained deep inside.

"Can I sit here?" a man I only know to see asks. He is one of the teachers at Levinson High School, but I don't remember his name.

"Of course," I tell him, nodding at the chair on the other side of the table.

Only four of us are in the faculty lounge, and everyone else seems to have their minds on the weekend ahead. What plans they have, I don't know. But Levinson has the feel of a school where the teachers are as keen as the students to get out at the last bell on a Friday and spend as much time away from the place as possible.

I don't want to be here either, but for different reasons. I finished my last class at three o'clock, and I've been sitting in front of a cold cup of coffee, staring at my blank phone since.

When I unlock it for the one-millionth time, there is still no call from John Howerton. Of course, I would hear it ring when he does call, but I still feel like I will miss it if I blink.

Thankfully, the fellow teacher, whose name I don't know, doesn't want to make small talk. He has unfolded a copy of the *Boston Globe*, and as I watch him, he yawns into his fist as he reads.

I forgave Fletcher for his reaction in the coffee place the other day, but I haven't met him since. We've spoken on the phone a couple of times, and he's apologized profusely, but I'm still not sure if it's a good idea to meet face-to-face again.

So why can't I stop thinking about him?

The Fletcher that came back from Pittsburgh to see his family again has changed; that is a fact. How much? I'm still trying to figure that out. But when I see him smile—when it's not forced or expected—there is a softness in him that can't be faked. Also, I don't think I have much of a right to continue keeping his existence a secret from Astrid. She is seventeen and old enough to make her own decisions.

Mom insisted that I call John and get him to check out the Pittsburgh hospital that Fletcher said he was admitted to when he fell off the ladder. I did it this morning, and John said he would get back to me before four. I'm almost certain Fletcher's story will check out, but I'm also pretty sure Mom will find a way to dismiss the evidence once we have it.

Her presence recently has become intrusive more so than supportive. I'll never be able to thank her enough for all the times throughout the years she picked me up off the floor after an episode with the old Fletcher. But even then, she always seemed to do it with an I-told-you-so expression.

Maybe I'm being harsh on her. I know that if Astrid ends up with a guy like *that* Fletcher, I won't relent until she sees sense. But that man who has gone by Michael Foster for more than a decade is not the same person he used to be. I know that's crazy—and I'm not about to hand my heart over to him—but I can't just walk away from this either.

The teacher I don't know ruffles the pages of his newspaper again, and I let the sound shimmy down my spine. I've always loved the noise of a crisp newspaper, and it always brings me back to my childhood. Dad used to read the paper every Saturday morning as we sat down for breakfast, and I sometimes felt myself sinking into the sound.

I could start the drive home right now and answer John's call while I drive, but I just don't want to do it. Everything has been so hectic lately that sitting here and waiting feels like some slight grasp at a sliver of control. It's not much, but at least it's something.

I wonder where Fletcher is now? He told me on the phone that he would be starting with one of Robert's firms soon, and I was happy for him. Before the rafting accident, Fletcher only worked for his father out of loyalty that I never really believed he felt. As an only son, it was almost guaranteed that Robert's empire would have ended up in Fletcher's possession when the old man retired or passed away. Still, I don't think Fletcher ever actually wanted it all.

My phone blares into life on the table, and I pick it up. John's name flashes on the screen, and I stand up and walk out of the room with it held out before me. The corridor is empty, and I lean against the wall and take a deep breath before answering.

"Hey, John."

"Lilith," he replies. His tone is a little frosty, so I guess he is still pissed that I went against him the last time I was in his office. "The hospital got back to me."

"And?"

"There *was* a man named Michael Foster admitted there recently."

I nod, even though I'm alone. "I thought as much."

"It's not that simple."

"Oh?"

I can hear some papers being shuffled on the other end of the line. "When did he say he was there again?"

"Em, I'm not sure exactly," I reply, trying hard to remember. "I think he just said it was a few weeks ago. Why?"

"Because the Michael Foster that was at St. Olafson's Hospital was admitted over two months ago."

"Okay. What does that mean?" I ask. I can smell bleach and old wood. The corridors at Levinson desperately need to be renovated, but the cleaners clearly try their best to make it respectable.

"Not much, if he was simply confused when he said it," John tells me. "But the injuries listed here seem pretty severe for falling off a ladder."

"He hit his head on a table, John. That could do a lot of damage."

"Hmm, I suppose. But twenty-two stitches worth of damage?"

"Maybe," I say, shrugging. "Is that it, John? Too many stitches and a month out on the date?"

"He didn't have insurance."

"So?"

It's starting to feel like I'm talking to my mother. Why is everybody trying so hard to find problems where there aren't any?

"The bill was for two thousand dollars, Lilith," John scoffs. "Who pays a two thousand dollar bill with cash?"

Chapter 27

"Thanks for coming," Fletcher says. He is standing in the doorway of his father's mansion. The gray streaks in his shaggy black hair look more prominent today, and I like it. When he smiles, I sense some of that nervous energy he had in the park. "Come on in."

I had no intention of meeting up with him again so soon, but something about John's attitude on the phone made me want to come here. When I called, and Fletcher told me that Robert was away for the day on business, I accepted his invitation and drove straight here from the school.

Fletcher steps aside to let me pass. The day outside is cold but clear, but the house is toasty hot. He takes my jacket and hangs it up, then spreads his hands like a maître d' and gestures for me to go on through. I can smell dinner wafting to me from the kitchen, and Fletcher smiles again as he catches me admiring it.

"I'm just whipping something up," he tells me. "Would you like some?"

I haven't eaten since breakfast, but I still decline. My phone call with John an hour ago was strange, but only because of the last three words he said to me—"Be careful, Lilith."

It really does feel like everyone is trying to make this—whatever *this* is—fail. Yes, Fletcher was a horrible man during the last years of our marriage, but lots of people have pasts they wish they could change. This man walking beside me through the foyer has had twelve years to create a whole new him. Does the person he was before the accident have to remain part of the package? I don't think so.

Fletcher is wearing khaki pants and a white T-shirt. His skin is the faintest of light browns, and as I walk beside him, I can smell his cologne. He always went for a sharper, more old-school scent, and I always loved it. It's manly and strong, and it suits him perfectly.

"Are you sure you won't have some?" he asks as we step into the huge, modern kitchen. Everything in here is metal and sleek, and the glass table next to the wall shines under the lights.

The food smells so good that I keep expecting to see one of the maids appear. In all my years with Fletcher, I never once saw him cook anything more than a grilled cheese.

"What are you making?" I ask, looking at the two pots on the stove. Steam is billowing out from beneath the lid of one, and there is a smaller pot blipping next to it.

"Slow-braised pork and pea and mint sauce," Fletcher tells me.

"And you made it?"

He shuffles uneasily like a child, then looks up at me through his bangs. "Yeah. I learned how to cook in Pittsburgh."

"It smells amazing."

"I'm fixing you a plate, no arguments," he declares before walking over to the stove. He slips a towel from the rack and uses it to lift the lid off the big pot. After smelling the steam, he replaces it, flings the towel over his shoulder, and says, "Ten minutes."

When he points at one of the fancy chairs next to the table, I sit down. Fletcher takes the one facing me, then clicks his fingers and stands back up.

"Where are my manners? Would you like some wine?"

"I'm driving," I tell him, although I really think my nerves could do with having their sharp edges slightly dulled.

"I'll call you an Uber," Fletcher chimes, then starts pouring two glasses of red before I can protest. When he places one in front of me, I thank him and take a sip.

"Listen, Fletcher," I say. "I think you should know that I got a call back about the hospital in Pittsburgh today."

"Oh?" He looks slightly hurt but unsurprised.

"Yes. I had to check it out."

"And?"

"And they basically confirmed to us what you had said."

"Us?"

"Sorry, yeah," I reply. "My lawyer, John, called for me."

Fletcher flinches at the word "lawyer." "It's become that serious, has it?"

"No, no, not at all," I say. "It's nothing like that. I just wouldn't have been able to get the information myself."

Fletcher looks wounded, but when he nods, I don't see any anger in him. "Robert is the same way."

"You're calling him Robert now?"

"Hmm?" Fletcher replies, looking back up at me. "Sorry, I mean Dad. Wow, I'm still getting used to all of this. I've called him Robert a few times already. He doesn't like it. Can I be honest with you, Loly?"

"Of course."

Fletcher shifts in his seat and then leans in close. "Of the few memories that have come back to me so far, hardly any of them involve him."

"Your dad?" I ask. Fletcher nods, then drops his gaze again. When I reach out and place my hand on his shoulder, it's more toned than I remember. Then again, he has been doing manual labor for twelve years. "They'll come back, Fletcher. They all will."

"You think?"

"Yes, I do," I tell him.

Seeing him like this—vulnerable, alone, and trying so hard—it is nearly impossible to find any trace of the Fletcher who once begged me to tell a nurse that I had fallen down a flight of stairs. Whatever happened to him on the river seems to have unlocked the man I always believed he could be if he ever managed to beat his demons.

"I'm sorry," he says. I think I can hear choked tears in his voice. "For all of this. You have been dragged into my messy life."

I want to lift his chin with my hand and kiss his lips. I want to, but I know I can't. Not yet. Maybe not ever.

Instead of doing this, I ask, "What did you mean when you said that your father was the same?"

"What?" Fletcher looks up at me again. The whites of his eyes are tinted red. "Oh, right. I was just feeling sorry for myself."

"Come on, Fletcher. You can tell me."

Fletcher shrugs. "I just meant because he has been checking up on me, too, you know?"

I do know. Robert told me he had made some inquiries himself. "Sure. But you understand why we need to do it, right?"

"Yeah." Fletcher stands up and slips the towel off his shoulder. Then he walks over to the pots and speaks to me over his shoulder. "But a DNA test. I mean, that's a little bit much, don't you think?"

Chapter 28

"I've seen the results, Mom," I snap. "Fletcher showed them to me."

"DNA test?" Mom repeats, shaking her head slowly. "That's impossible."

We are standing in the tidy living room of her house. Through the window, I can see my own home. The light in Astrid's bedroom shines in the descending darkness, and I can't believe that I will be going up there after this to tell her that her father is still alive.

"My God," I say, shaking my head now too. "What is wrong with you?"

"Me?" Mom says, pointing at her chest.

"Yes, you. Why do you have to punch holes in everything?"

Mom stops poking her chest with her finger and points it right at me. "That man is *not* your husband, Lilith."

I throw my arms up in exasperation. "I saw the DNA test results, Mom. Fletcher showed them to me an hour ago. What more proof do you need?"

As I drove here from Robert's house, my emotions were as confused as they'd ever been. Breaking the news to Astrid is a terrifying prospect, but I found a weird excitement at the prospect of telling Mom. I thought *maybe* she would accept the truth, although I think I knew deep down that she would always continue to dismiss Fletcher's story. I don't know why I let myself even consider the former.

Mom barges past me into the kitchen, and I follow behind. For the first time in my life, her slim frame doesn't look sturdy—she seems weak and pathetic.

She opens the freezer and takes out a bottle of vodka that looks like it's been in there for a while. As she pours herself a glass without offering me one, I tap my foot impatiently. I'm waiting for whatever ridiculous answer she is considering, and I know it will be a mean one.

Mom takes a long, drawn-out slug of her drink and then levels her gaze at me. "I need more than that, Lilith."

"More than a damn DNA test?" I growl. "You really are impossible."

"It can't be him, Lilith," Mom repeats, taking another drink. "You have to trust me on that."

"Trust you? No, not anymore."

"Excuse me?"

"I know there is stuff you're not telling me, Mom," I growl. "Like lunch at Robert's. What took you so long to go to the bathroom, huh? And what were you two fighting about when you came back outside?"

Mom waves a hand at me. The gesture is so dismissive that I feel my blood boiling. "I told you that was nothing."

"Yeah, that's what you told me," I reply sarcastically. "You've always told me whatever works best for you."

"Now you're just talking nonsense, Lilith."

"Am I?"

"Yes."

Mom pours another drink as she looks out the kitchen window. I knew telling her about the DNA test and the hospital in Pittsburgh would play out like this, and I feel stupid for having ever thought otherwise. She has always been the most stubborn woman I know, and I wonder just how many opportunities and relationships I have missed out on throughout my life because of her outside interference.

"Look, Lilith," Mom says, turning back to face me. She seems to be making a real effort to sound caring. "Even if it were true, and it's not. But even if it were—why would you let that man back into your life? Don't you remember all the things he did?"

I nod and drop my gaze. She is right about the stuff that happened in the past, but that is exactly where it belongs—in the past. Everyone deserves a second chance, and apart from Fletcher's panicked moment in the coffeehouse when he grabbed my hand, there have been absolutely no signs of the anger that used to frighten me so much. And even then, he had believed he might not see his daughter again, so his reaction was only natural.

"Oh, I remember, Mom," I say. My voice is surprisingly even, given how angry I am. "And I also remember how you tried to turn me against him at every opportunity."

"Can you blame me?" Mom exclaims. She sounds like a kettle on a stove that is about to boil over. "After everything that happened, I would have thought you would see some sense."

"Sure, play it like that. You were turning me against him long before he raised a hand to me, Mom."

"That's ridiculous," she snaps. When she waves a dismissive hand this time, there is less conviction in it.

"Forget it. There is no point talking to you," I tell her. "Fletcher will be coming back into our lives, whether you like it or not. He is Astrid's father."

Mom takes a step forward and scowls at me. When she speaks, her voice drips with venom. "You would let that animal spend time with your only daughter?"

"She is *his* only daughter too."

"Great parenting," Mom scoffs.

"You can talk, Mom."

"You ungrateful cow," she sneers. "How dare you say that after all the sacrifices I made for you."

"Oh, get over yourself, Mom." I wave my hand over the kitchen. "You got a pretty little house out of your meddling, didn't you?"

"Lilith, that's not fair," Mom says, reeling a little.

"Fletcher is back to stay, Mom. Just accept it or—"

"Or what, Lilith?"

"Just accept it," I tell her again as I turn to leave.

"That is not the man you think he is," Mom barks behind me. "I forbid you to see him again."

That makes me stop in my tracks, and I spin back around to face her. She really looks pathetic standing there holding her drink. Has she always looked like this, and have I just painted her as a hero to suit the narrative? Seeing her as a protector has helped me to blindly accept the choices she has always insisted on making for me. But they haven't been choices so much as her need to control.

"You forbid *me*?" Any level tone I'd maintained in my voice is a thing of the past now. "You forbid me? Where the hell do you get off?"

"THAT IS NOT FLETCHER DUBOSE, YOU STUPID WOMAN!" Mom roars. The tendons on her neck stand out. When she throws the glass of vodka against the wall, it shatters in an explosion of shards and liquid. "FLETCHER IS DEAD. DEAD, DEAD, DEAD!"

I stay where I am, shocked but not afraid. Mom has shown her true colors, and the desperation in her actions only proves that her intentions have only ever been to meddle. She knows she has lost this one, and it is clearly too much for her to accept.

"I want you to leave, Mom," I tell her steadily. I can't believe these words are coming out of my mouth, but I think I've known for a long time that they needed to be said. "I want you to pack up your stuff and leave."

Part 2: Virginia

Chapter 29

He goes to La Piazza most days for lunch. I watch him making his way from his office in City Point each time, his driver cruising in the old Bentley just slow enough for everyone to see who is in the back seat. The routine varies sometimes, but usually it's the same. Of course, I'm not watching him every day—not even half the time—but it's definitely become more frequent.

Maybe that's because I've been living in town for the last two weeks. Ever since Lilith kicked me out, I've taken up residence in a small but cozy apartment not far from here. I was conscious of the location when I chose it, as being close to his office was a real bonus.

I know something is going on with him, and it has been for a long time. I just need to find proof.

Hearing about the DNA results was more than a shock; it was devastating. The man claiming to be Fletcher just can't be him. I know this for a fact, yet Lilith still won't listen. The real truth would destroy her, and I can't risk that happening. Even if it means her hating me forever.

The windows of the La Piazza restaurant are slightly tinted, so I can't see in from across the street. I could walk in and find out who he is meeting, but he would recognize me straight away, and that would not be good. Anyway, he usually eats alone, so it's not worth the risk.

I take my phone off the dash of my silver Ford Focus and check the time: 13:12. I could be here for another fifty minutes, so I may as well get comfortable.

I pull up Astrid's name and punch in a quick text: *Hope you're keeping well. Talk soon.* I hit send and toss the phone on the passenger seat. The coffee I got from the street vendor earlier is only lukewarm now, but it still tastes good. Outside, the rain is falling in irregular spits, and the sky is a gloomy gray. People in suits holding umbrellas over their heads pass my car with their eyes down. It is one of those Monday mornings when everyone out in the world seems dejected.

I wish Lilith would see sense, but she's been obsessed with that wife-beating scumbag from the moment she laid eyes on him. I thought she had finally learned her lesson twelve years ago, but it seems old wounds really do heal. Wally had warned me about Fletcher shortly before he died on one of Robert DuBose's sites. Well, that's what the police said, anyway. I've always suspected differently.

Following someone and tracking their movements is not something I expected to be part of my life, but a mother will do whatever it takes to protect her family. Lilith and Astrid are my only family, and I will die before I let any more harm come to them. Lilith will never know the sacrifices I've made to keep her safe, and that's just one of those things I have to deal with. I have many crosses to bear, and this one is no different.

Living away from them will be tough. Fortunately, I have some money squirreled away. Over the years, Wally's life insurance has paid me well. By living in the house next to my daughter,

I've hardly any expenses, and I don't have to pay rent to Lilith. I offered many times to help out with the bills, but Lilith always refused. Maybe she always knew that one day she would ask me to leave.

I worked a few part-time jobs in the decade after Fletcher's death, but Lilith needed me to watch Astrid while she went back to work. Weighing up her career as a fully qualified teacher versus me as a barmaid wasn't a hard one, so I decided that giving her the freedom to blossom was the most important thing.

Once Fletcher's life insurance kicked in and the new house was bought, Lilith got too used to having me around. When she had the smaller house built next to it for me, it was hard for me to say no. Deep down, I was glad. Even though Fletcher was dead, he wasn't the only threat to my family's safety. I needed to be close to protect them.

The rain on the car's windows has started to block my visibility, so I lower the driver's side window a crack and run the wipers for a bit. When I slide the windows back up, they squeak shrilly in my ears. The black Bentley is still parked across the street with the driver sitting inside, just like he is always made to wait.

I don't know what I've ever expected to find by doing this, but I know there are more secrets hidden out there somewhere. How I'll get to them and what they'll tell me, I don't know. I just hope that when my chance comes, I'll take it.

With my eyes locked on the front door of La Piazza, I reach across to the glove compartment and rummage for the pack of Pall Malls I keep in there. I rarely smoke, and never in front of Lilith or Astrid, but I always keep an emergency stash for when my nerves are acting up. My hand lands on the pack, and I slip a cigarette out and spark it up using the lighter in the side door.

The first couple of drags are horrible, but my lungs settle. The third puff is amazing. The car will stink tomorrow morning, but I don't care. It's not like anyone else will be getting into it any time soon. At least not if Lilith remains as stubborn as I know she can be.

As I smoke, I lower the windows again and sink farther into the seat. There is no way he'll spot me from here when he comes out, but it is always better to err on the side of caution. I could probably explain away my being here, but after what happened at lunch a few weeks ago, it will definitely look suspicious.

The door to La Piazza opens, and I sit up. It's only a man and a woman in business suits. The man opens his umbrella up as they walk down the street. He doesn't once look at the woman he's with to see if she wants to step under it with him. I watch her try to keep up beside him with her leather satchel held up over her head.

"What a gentleman," I say to nobody, slowly shaking my head.

What happened to men? Even my own Wally had his demons. He liked to bet on the horses far too much, but he would still hold a door open for me and insist on walking on the outside of the sidewalk whenever we were together. Nowadays, it seems like it's a competition to see who can be the most chauvinistic.

I bring my gaze back to the restaurant just in time to see him stepping out into the drizzle. He waits by the door until his driver hops out with an umbrella. Once he's under it, he walks toward the back of his car with his shoulders pulled back so far that it looks like they might meet at his spine.

I toss the butt out the window and start my Ford just as the engine across the street roars to life. Again, I'm not sure what I'll achieve by doing this, but I know it needs to be done. Robert DuBose is the man behind my husband's death, and I'll prove it one day.

Chapter 30

"I'm still in shock," Reece tells me, running a shaking hand through his strawberry blond hair. "Did she mention anything to you?"

"As I said, Reece," I reply, trying not to sigh, "I haven't spoken to her in two weeks."

When Reece called me out of the blue last night and asked to meet for breakfast at a diner in town, I thought it might be a good idea. I thought that maybe he might have some news on how she's doing or why she is being so irrational. I can already tell this will be a waste of time.

Even though Reece has been dating my daughter for over a year, I've only met him a handful of times. Lilith rarely had him over to the house, and I only ever spent time with him when he invited us all out to his place or to a restaurant for dinner.

Reece looked fidgety before we sat down in the booth five minutes ago, but he is a nervous wreck now. I was not at all surprised to hear that Lilith ended things with him. My only fear now is that she is picking up where she left off with the man calling himself Fletcher. That could be devastating in more ways than one.

Reece shakes his head, and a clump of his bangs come loose and dangle just above his eyes. I look at his receding hairline with no surprise. A man that carries himself in the manner that Reece McElroy does can't expect to have flowing locks or even live past fifty-five. For people like him, even the most insignificant event in their lives brings insurmountable stress. Unfortunately for them, every iota of that stress is simply down to them being them.

"But why? Why would she do this?" he asks.

He isn't looking at me as he speaks, so I don't answer. What am I meant to say? *Hey, Reece, my daughter was never going to stay with you, regardless of what has happened with this imposter. You are too weak a man for her and always will be. In fact, you're far too weak for most women.*

No, that would do no good. Also, I have no intention of hurting him further. Despite him being a clingy and annoying man, he is essentially harmless.

"She didn't say anything else to you?" I ask. This is why I'm here. As guilty as it makes me feel, I only wanted to meet Reece to see if he had any information on Lilith and Astrid. Neither of them has replied to me since I left.

"Hmm?" he asks, lifting his puppy dog eyes up to meet mine.

"Lilith," I say. Again, I have to fight to keep the sigh out of my response. "Did she say anything else besides it being over between you two?"

"Just that she didn't think it was fair to drag me into it," Reece whines. "What does that even mean?"

Good. If she didn't tell him about Fletcher, it probably means that they aren't an item. If they were, she would have informed Reece. I know my daughter, and she is usually as honest as they come.

"I'm not sure," I tell him, shrugging.

Reece shakes his head again, and this time he actually physically groans. I have to cringe at the sound. Really, what has happened to men?

My tailing of Robert yesterday led to nothing. After his lunch at La Piazza, his driver drove him to a cafe on the other side of town. Robert got out, said something through the driver's window, and the Bentley pulled away and left him on the sidewalk. After that, he walked into the cafe alone and didn't come out for another half hour.

When he did come back out, he waited on the sidewalk for about a minute before he was picked up by a—

A waitress appears beside us, snapping me back from my thoughts. She has a pad in her hand and taps it with a pen as she speaks. "Ready to order yet?"

"Oh, I can't even *think* about eating!" Reece declares, his face scrunched up.

When she looks at me, I say, "Scrambled eggs, a side of bacon, sausage, and three slices of bread."

The waitress smiles at me before waddling off behind the counter.

"Look, Reece," I say, turning back to him. "Lilith is going through some stuff. If I were you, I'd just accept it and move on."

"But I need to know what I did wrong!" he whines.

I should never have come here.

"You didn't do anything wrong." This time I'm unable to keep the exasperation out of my tone. Reece doesn't notice. He's too busy shaking his head again. "Sometimes things just end."

I could be finishing my unpacking instead of being here. I have plenty of empathy for this man, but my patience is wearing thin. Also, there are many more serious things going on right now than his pain. Reece will get over it and move on. My daughter and my granddaughter could be in real danger. Comparing the two scenarios isn't even in the same ballpark.

I'm starting to realize this whole meeting might be a bust, so I take one last try at salvaging even a shred of it.

"Lilith didn't say anything else at all? Nothing? Maybe Astrid spoke to you?"

Reece's head moves from side to side once more before he buries it in his hands. As he mopes, I sip my coffee and try to figure out where I go from here. Only one thing matters, and that's getting to the bottom of this Robert situation.

Digging up the truth about what happened to Wally has always felt like an impossible task, but I feel like everything is connected. The DuBoses are not to be trusted. This man who showed up a few weeks ago certainly isn't Fletcher, but he clearly intends to see out this act. That can only mean trouble, as there would be no nice reason for him to do it.

The waitress returns with my food and plunks a stacked plate down in front of me. Reece still has his head in his hands as I eat. Under any other circumstances, I would console him. Right now, I don't have the mental space to deal with his issues. There are too many questions that need to be answered.

What happens if Lilith really does take this Fletcher back? Why won't Astrid get back to my calls and texts? And who was driving the white Coupe that picked Robert up from the cafe yesterday?

Chapter 31

My apartment on Dorchester Street kind of looks like the first place me and Wally shared all those years ago. We lived there before and after Lilith was born, and things always seemed so much simpler. Lilith was a great kid, and life was wonderful for a long time. Everything only started to change for the worse when Wally got a job with DuBose Construction. That was when it all began to turn sour.

With the back windows open, I can hear the traffic down below as it grumbles past. There is a strong breeze outside that keeps ruffling the drawn curtains. The salad I made for dinner still sits on the breakfast bar half-eaten, and the glass of wine I poured myself tastes bitter.

I'm wearing blue jeans and a gray hoodie this evening as I sit on the couch staring at a blank TV screen. Even though I showered this morning, somehow my hair feels like it needs a good wash. I can smell cigarette smoke and curse myself for having gone through half a pack in one day. Watching Robert more intensely has taken its toll.

The worst part is that nothing he has done has stood out. He still shows up at his office and hangs around inside for a few hours. He goes for lunch every day—at La Piazza more often than not—and he goes home in the evening. He has been picked up in the white Coupe a couple more times, but that's about as off-routine as he goes.

My breakfast with Reece last week was pointless. I've felt bad ever since for how dismissive I was of him, and I even sent him a text apologizing the following day. He replied with some epilogue about how confused he was at Lilith's breaking up with him, and I found myself rolling my eyes once more. Thankfully he wasn't there to see it this time.

I pick my phone up off the coffee table and call Astrid. As always, it rings for a while and then goes to voicemail. I leave a message asking her to get back to me, then hang up.

Across the room, the curtains lift in the breeze again, and I catch a glimpse of the night sky and a spattering of stars. I used to love looking up at the darkness when I lived on Beacon Hill, but it helped that I had my daughter and grandchild in the next house. There is something magical about the vastness of space that always brought me a strange sort of comfort.

If I believed in God a little more, then maybe I would think that Wally was looking back down at me. But Wally is gone, and he's never coming back. Robert DuBose saw to that.

The big question has always been, why? Wally was a hard worker and was employed at DuBose Construction for years before his so-called accident. Sure, his moods darkened near the end, but I can't imagine what he could have done to get on Robert's bad side. So far as I know, he rarely had any contact with him.

He often told me about Robert's famous temper and the shady dealings he'd always suspected, but his death still came out of the blue. Of course, *any* death is a surprise, but Wally had always kept his hands clean throughout his life. And therein lies one of the biggest issues: What if Wally had been involved in the darker side of Robert's dealings, and I never knew?

It seems unlikely, as we were very in love and extremely close. I feel like Wally told me most of what went on in his life, but how can anyone be 100 percent sure of how much they know their partner? We were really struggling financially early on in Wally's time with Robert, so maybe he got into debt somewhere along the line? Our money troubles then seemed to vanish overnight, but I was just so glad we were out of it to ask too many questions. Lilith had been starting high school then, so not having to worry about making rent each month had been a huge relief.

Wally had been acting strange in the months before he died. I remember one particular evening when he'd had a few too many beers and seemed like he wanted to tell me something big. I pushed him at the time, but his mood had darkened, and he asked me to drop it. I had, but there is not a day that goes by when I don't regret that decision.

My phone vibrates on the table, and I pick it up again. The text is from John Howerton: *Any more info?*

I type: *No, nothing*, and hit send before placing the phone on the armrest of the couch.

I know I should concentrate on this Fletcher imposter situation more so than on Robert, but I feel the two are linked. A man like Robert DuBose doesn't let some stranger waltz into his life and claim to be his dead son so easily. Watching the two of them interacting at that lunch at Robert's a few weeks ago had been enough to raise my suspicions even further. Robert's behavior had been so nonchalant, and he is a man who is nonchalant about nothing.

I pick the wine glass up and try another sip. It is even worse than the last one, and I grimace as I swallow it. I put it back and take a cigarette from the half-empty pack. Even as I light it, I know I'm going to regret smoking it in the morning. I haven't gone through this many cigarettes in a day since I was in high school.

The problem with tailing Fletcher is that I know he is spending a lot more time with Lilith and Astrid. That is two extra pairs of eyes that could spot me, and the last thing I need is my family thinking I'm some obsessive nut that has to keep watching them from afar. I know I'll have to do it soon regardless, but I need to bide my time. Hopefully, Lilith can see sense before I have to do anything drastic.

Although, could I ever do anything more drastic for her than I've done in the past?

The answer is probably no, but who knows what the future will bring? This is not an ordinary situation, so it may call for out-of-the-ordinary solutions. If Robert or this Michael Foster character thinks I won't go to any lengths to protect my family, they are gravely mistaken. They might not know what I've done to fix things before, but they will soon find out if they hurt my girls.

My phone vibrates sharply next to me again, and I gasp. Every muscle in my body is tense, and I need to calm down. I take a couple of hard drags on my cigarette before picking up my phone.

The message is from Astrid, and I instantly feel tears stinging the corners of my eyes at the sight of her name. Her text reads: *Sorry I haven't been able to reply. Are you free tomorrow? I really need to see you.*

Chapter 32

"Thanks again for meeting me, Nana," Astrid says. Her long black hair is tied up today, and she is wearing denim overalls with one of the straps unclipped. Her green eyes look troubled, yet there is defiance in them too. "I don't like going behind Mom's back, but I really needed to see you."

"You don't have to feel bad for wanting to see your grandmother," I reassure her.

We're sitting in my car in a parking lot not far from Astrid's school. The rain is falling steadily outside, and visibility beyond the windows is almost nothing. It isn't yet eight-thirty, and the day is dull and gloomy. We are both holding paper coffee cups, and Astrid sips from hers as I watch her.

"Thanks for the coffee," she tells me, lifting the cup and taking another sip.

"You're welcome."

We both drink and listen to the sound of the rain pounding the Ford's shell. It's so great to see Astrid after so long. When I picked her up down the street from her house twenty minutes ago, I gave her such a long hug that I think I worried her a little. I'm so mad at Lilith for pushing me away from her.

"Now," I say, slotting my coffee into the cupholder. "What is it you wanted to talk about?"

"Fletcher," Astrid says without hesitation.

She's not calling him Dad yet, which is a good sign. At least, I hope it is. I nod at her. "Okay. What about him?"

Astrid drops her eyes. It is such a strange gesture for her. She is always so full of confidence. "I don't really know. That's the problem, Nana."

"Don't really know what?"

Tread carefully, Ginny. You need to tread carefully.

"What to make of all this," Astrid tells me, shrugging. "What to make of Ma."

"Your mother? What do you mean?"

Astrid shrugs again. "I don't know. This whole thing. It's just changed her, that's all."

"In what way, sweetie?"

"She's been... different."

I reach across and touch Astrid's face. She leans into it and brings her hand up to meet mine. Her eyes are closed as I speak, and I'm glad because I'm struggling to keep my expression neutral. "Has she let that man move into your home?"

"No, no," Astrid replies. "Not yet, anyway."

"Has she mentioned it?"

Astrid lifts her head back up and smiles. She is still holding my hand. "No. But he is over more and more often."

"Okay," I say, nodding.

"Yeah. At first, he was over every third or fourth day, but he was there for dinner nearly every night last week."

"Is he staying over?" I ask, then regret it instantly. I'm not sure I could handle one of the two possible answers. I promised myself on the way over that I wouldn't put too much pressure on Astrid by bombarding her with endless questions.

"Not that I know of," Astrid replies. "I'm so sorry I didn't reply to all of your texts or answer your calls, Nana."

"Hey! Look at me," I snap. Astrid brings her eyes to meet my gaze. "I told you when I picked you up that all this stuff between your mom and me has nothing to do with you. I said some mean things during our argument, and she has every right to be mad at me."

"She shouldn't have told me not to contact you, though," Astrid spits.

I completely agree with my granddaughter on this one, but I don't say it. The silence between us is enough of an answer for her, I'm sure. Also, I'm glad that Lilith told her straight up that it was her decision that we don't communicate. A lesser woman would have made it sound like I was the one not wanting to see her family.

I pick my coffee up and drink some more. Astrid does the same. She will need to get off to school soon if she doesn't want to be late, but I have so many more questions.

"Is he being nice to you?" I ask.

"Who? Fletcher?"

I hate hearing her calling him by that name—I'll never believe, even for a second, that he is Fletcher DuBose—but it's better than her referring to him as her father.

"Yes. Is he being kind?"

"Sort of," Astrid tells me.

I can feel my blood starting to heat up. If that asshole has even looked at her wrong, so help me. "What do you mean, sort of?"

For the third time since we've been parked here, Astrid shrugs. "That's the thing, Nana. He's always concerned about where I've

161

been or who I've been talking to, but he hasn't even tried to hug me once. He barely looks me in the eye."

This gives me more relief than I could have ever imagined. If he's not bothered about Astrid, it means he is after Lilith's money. But what payment there was following Fletcher's death has been mostly used up, so far as I know. Even if it hadn't been, there was never enough to go to the amount of trouble this imposter has. So why do it at all?

"Anyway," Astrid says, reaching down by her feet and grabbing her bag. "I need to go, or I'll be late for school."

My hand snaps out and grabs her wrist before I can stop it. "Please don't leave it so long next time, Astrid."

My granddaughter smiles, and I can see so much of Wally in it that my heart aches. "I won't. We can meet up again soon."

"When?" I ask, hearing the panic in my voice. I knew I had been missing her, but seeing her now has really brought it home.

"Well, I can't tomorrow," Astrid says. She taps her chin with her forefinger as she thinks. "How about Thursday night? You can take me to McDonald's. It will be like when I was a kid!"

"Sure. Sounds great," I say. "What's tomorrow?"

Astrid has already opened the door. It's still raining, but it's died down considerably. Thankfully, the school is only a two-minute walk away. She looks back over her shoulder to face me.

"Tomorrow?" Astrid says. "Oh, right. Robert is coming over for dinner. He says he has some big announcement."

Chapter 33

I called Lilith right after leaving Astrid, but as always, she didn't pick up. I know she is still mad at me since our argument, but that was three weeks ago. She needs to swallow her pride and admit that we both said some nasty things. Even though mine were true, I have to try to see it from her side too.

After checking the parking lot and finding Lilith's car, I waited outside the school for an hour for no other reason than to collect my thoughts. After driving into town and grabbing another coffee and a bagel, I returned and parked a little way down the street. I can still see the lot's entrance, so I'll know when she leaves. Following my daughter and cornering her when she gets out of her car isn't exactly a nice way to go about things, but I need to speak with her. If even a few of my words get through, there might still be a chance.

The worst part is that I'm not even sure what the worst outcome of all of this could be. If I knew Robert's and Fletcher's—

I hate calling him that.

—motives, I would have a better argument. Right now, all I can say is that I don't trust them, which is something Lilith has always known. If anything, it was always one of the biggest issues between us in the early years of her relationship with Fletcher.

I light a Pall Mall and lower the window a crack. Lately, it feels like I've spent more time hunched down in the driver's seat of my Ford than anything else. It makes me feel like I'm the one in the wrong. I know what really happened to Fletcher twelve years ago, though. I just need my daughter to accept it again.

This new guy is impressive; I'll give him that. There were times in the days after his return when I could almost *see* Fletcher in him. The features were a bit off, but as Lilith said several times—we all look different from how we did twelve years ago. But the over-the-top niceness; that's what convinced me. That and the fact that I know Fletcher is dead.

The Fletcher of old was able to turn on the charm when needed, but it was always hollow. To anyone who had lived a bit, his act could be seen as just that—an act. Even then, he rarely brought out the puppy dog eyes. He only made an effort to be nice when he needed Lilith to lie to a doctor or stay in for a few days until it all died down.

The clock on the dash tells me that it is 12:57. I've been here for a couple of hours now. If Lilith worked full time, I'd have more of an idea of when she might finish up for the day. Since she is a substitute, her classes can end at any time.

I've spent all morning sitting in the car smoking and drinking coffee, and I still have no idea what I'll say when I confront her.

When the silver SUV comes slowly rolling out of the school gates, I almost miss it. Thankfully, I'm already slightly hunched down as it passes. I see Lilith, but she doesn't see me. I hope she didn't see me, anyhow.

I start my car and make a U-turn, falling into line about fifty feet from Lilith. The rain from earlier has completely died off, but the roads are still slick, and I watch as she drives the car with caution. The SUV was probably the only real splurge Lilith made with Fletcher's insurance money, which didn't surprise me. My daughter has always been smart with her finances, and that has never changed.

Lilith takes a left up ahead, and I slow down and do the same. I'm still a long way back, so the chances of her spotting me are slim. Still, I wish another car would pull out and come between us. Fortunately, there are a lot of Ford Focuses on the roads in Massachusetts, so she would have no reason to be suspicious of one behind her.

What are you going to say to her, Ginny? What if she dismisses you again? Do you even know what you're worried about?

"The DuBoses," I tell the empty car. "That's what I'm worried about."

It's always been them, and that point of view will never leave me. Robert is secretly known in some circles as a gangster. His construction company has several legitimate firms working under it, and it's very successful, but not multi-millionaire successful. I had my suspicions from day one, and the stories of racketeering, loan sharking, and gambling have only grown in the years since Wally's death.

Lilith always plugged her ears at the mention of the DuBoses' shady dealings—even more so after Fletcher died, as she wanted to protect his memory for Astrid's sake—and I suspect she has buried her head even deeper now. Of course, whenever Robert or his companies would come to the attention of the authorities or the press, someone important would suddenly be seen with a new car or on vacation in the Bahamas, and the problem would miraculously go away.

Wally used to say I was overdramatizing the whole thing and looking for problems that weren't there. Lilith mentioned the same thing on a few occasions too.

A sign for a 7-Eleven on our right comes into view, and Lilith's blinkers come on. I flick mine too, and my heart starts to beat through my chest. The same question keeps racing through my mind: What the hell am I going to say to her?

I know what happens when I walk into serious situations with no plan in place. My temper has caused some terrible things to happen, yet here I am, steaming in headfirst once more. Whether the outcomes of my actions have been for better or for worse will always be up for debate.

Lilith is already at the pumps as I get out and walk toward her. She sees me coming and replaces the nozzle before using it. Even though it is gray and dull out, she is wearing sunglasses with huge lenses.

My mind instantly goes to all those moments in the past when she tried to cover Fletcher's handiwork, and all hope of a rational conversation leaves me in a millisecond.

"What has he done to you?" I hiss. I'm only a couple of feet away from her now.

"What?" Lilith snaps. "What are you talking about? What are you doing here?"

"Don't change the subject, Lilith. I'm not going through all of that again."

"All of what?" Lilith exclaims, the brow above her sunglasses creased. "Are you crazy?"

Before I can think about what I'm doing, I whip my hand out and try to snatch the glasses off her face. I only make the slightest contact with them, but they fly off and hit the ground beside us. Lilith cringes, and I realize she thought I was going to strike her. I haven't raised a hand to her throughout her whole life, and the notion that she believes I could stings me hard.

"W-what the hell are you doing?" Lilith asks as she brings her face back around to me. "Did you just try to hit me?"

I want to answer, but all the fight has left me. My daughter has her hands on her hips now, and she is looking at me like I'm some crazed lunatic. I suppose I might be because I've just tailed her and then swiped at her for no good reason.

There are no marks on her face, no black eyes. She is wearing the sunglasses because she likes them or because they look good. In fact, I've seen her wearing those particular frames a thousand times.

What has got into me?

I watch with my mouth open as Lilith picks up her glasses and hooks them onto the lapel of her black blazer. Then she shakes her head in disgust, climbs back into her car, and drives away.

Chapter 34

"What happened the other day?" Astrid asks as she takes a seat across from me. It's just after five, and McDonald's is packed with people. Then again, McDonald's is always packed with people. "Mom was on me the second I got home from school. She told me to stay away from you."

I'd expected that. Truth be told, I would have done the same thing if some crazy old woman had followed me to a gas station and then attempted to strike me. Of course, I was only trying to remove Lilith's sunglasses, but I still did it in an aggressive manner. Seeing her wearing them like she had done so many times in the past set something off in me, and I lost control.

"What happened was something that looked a whole lot worse than it really was, honey," I say, shaking my head.

Astrid is wearing a long, slim black buttoned-down jacket that matches her shiny hair. The latter is down today and frames her petite, cutesy features perfectly. The flared blue jeans she has on are tight around the thighs, showing me just how grown up my grandchild has become. She looks like a woman in her early twenties, not one still in her teens.

"Well, she was livid," Astrid tells me. When she laughs into her hand, I look at her with surprise. Through her fingers, she says, "I'm sorry. She was just comical in her own silly way."

"I'm confused," I say, feeling myself smiling, even though nothing is funny about the situation. Astrid's moods—whether good or bad—have always been infectious. "I thought you said she was livid."

Astrid clears her throat and makes a visible effort to look serious. "She was. I shouldn't laugh, but I've never seen her like that. I guess that's why I'm laughing. It scared me a little."

"And she didn't tell you why?"

"Uh-uh," Astrid tells me, shaking her head. "She was grunting under her breath, and I heard something about a gas station."

"That makes sense."

"So, what happened?"

I sigh loudly and look around the crowded restaurant. We haven't ordered our food yet, which is a big no-no in a place with a turnover like McDonald's. They want their customers in and out without delay. I've been sitting here fifteen minutes already, and two families could have been fed and rushed out the door in that time.

"Let's order first," I say, standing up. "Then I'll tell you all about it."

When Astrid goes to stand up, I stop her with my hand. "Keep our table." I lean in closer in an over-the-top conspiratorial way, then nod at some of the people walking around with full trays. "The vultures are circling."

Astrid giggles and hunches her shoulders, and she has transformed right back into my young grandchild again. My need to protect her and my daughter spikes, and I instinctively pull my shoulders back as I walk to the counter.

I order two Big Mac Meals—both with Fanta—and bring the tray back to our table. Astrid is scrolling through her phone as I approach, but she slots it back into her jeans pocket when she sees me. She has taken off her jacket since I left, and her T-shirt hangs loosely off one smooth, milky shoulder. The little girl who giggled at my silly joke vanished once more.

"Dig in," I say as I sit down and plunk the tray in front of us.

"I haven't had McDonald's in ages," Astrid exclaims, reaching for her straw.

"Same here," I reply. "How was school today?"

"Fine." Astrid smiles over her Fanta as she gulps some down. Lowering her cup, she says, "Stop procrastinating."

I smile, then fill Astrid in on what happened at the 7-Eleven as we eat our burgers and fries. She nods as I speak and, at one point, reaches over and touches my hand. I leave out the severity of how Fletcher used to treat her mother and only say that there had been times when he'd been aggressive. Thankfully, Astrid was made aware of *some* of Fletcher's outbursts a couple of years ago after one particularly boozy New Year's Eve when Lilith had drunk a little too much and the alcohol loosened her lips for a few minutes.

Astrid had never known just how bad it had been near the end, and she was too young when he died to really remember anything at all about him. In a way, I've always been grateful for that small blessing. It also kills me that the bastard left such a trail of destruction and pain, yet he is remembered as someone who "was taken from us too soon."

When I finish telling her what happened with Lilith, Astrid sits back and dabs at the corners of her mouth with a napkin. She looks around as I did earlier to make sure nobody is in earshot. When she seems satisfied, she smiles and says, "You were tailing her?"

I throw up my hands in mock exasperation. "You make it sound so sinister."

"Ah, I'm sorry," she says sarcastically, nodding. "You were doing that old friendly, I'm-just-*kind*-of-stalking-you sort of thing?"

I lean my head back and laugh. It feels so good that I'm shocked when it almost instantly turns to tears. I catch them just in time and blink the feeling away. I haven't realized the full extent of how much being away from my family has hurt me, and this sudden feeling of unadulterated joy brought it all home.

"You okay, Nana?" Astrid asks, still giggling.

"I'm fine," I reply. "I'm more than fine, sweetie. I've just missed you."

Astrid's face sinks into sadness. "I know. Me too. This whole thing is so messed up."

"I know. Anyway, let's not ruin our time together by being depressed."

"Right!" Astrid says, perking up a little too much.

I lean across the table, making sure not to plant my elbows in a big pool of ketchup. "Now, tell me what Robert's big announcement the other day was."

Chapter 35

Michael Foster turns his Porsche 911 onto Herald Street, the top down, even though the sun is barely visible through the thick, gray clouds. There are a couple of cars between us, which is good. Although I don't think he would have the awareness to be conscious of anyone but himself, never mind an unassuming Ford Focus several vehicles back.

He drove out the massive gates of Robert's house at 8:32, and I've been behind him for about fifteen minutes since. He seems to be heading toward City Point, so I presume he's going to the DuBose Construction offices. If that's the case, then I've probably wasted my time. Still, I want to keep this scumbag as close to me as I can for the foreseeable future.

Dinner with Astrid yesterday was lovely. Seeing her woke something inside me that I thought I had buried twelve years ago. Ever since I was kicked out of my home, I've spent the whole time keeping a close eye on Robert. Inside, I've been dealing with a lot of anger, and I've tried to repress it. Not anymore.

Three cars ahead, Michael Foster brings the Porsche to rest at an intersection. I slow my Ford and come to a stop thirty feet behind. As we wait for the lights to turn green, I light up a Pall

Mall and inhale deeply. I have a sudden urge to get out of the car, walk up to the Porsche, and drag him out of it by the hair.

I manage to repress the compulsion. Getting aggressive with Michael is precisely the sort of thing he would use to manipulate my daughter even more. He used to do it in the past, and on more than one occasion, Lilith and I fell out over some game he had decided to play. Like all narcissists, he is very clever when it comes to tearing people apart for his own amusement.

I thought this wasn't Fletcher, I tell myself.

"Shit," I hiss. "Now I'm thinking as if it's the same person."

I know it's not Fletcher, more than Lilith will ever understand. Whoever he is, he has done his homework. Even when he is alone, I can see some of Fletcher's mannerisms in his demeanor. The constant running of a hand through his hair, the perfectly vertical back, and the knowing smirk. They were all classic Fletcher moves.

The light switches to green, and the traffic takes off again. I smoke as I drive, my mind still like Swiss cheese. It has been since Astrid told me what happened.

Hearing that Robert's "big announcement" ended up being nothing more than some self-congratulatory nonsense about a new merger didn't surprise me one bit. I can't even begin to figure out why he decided to do it at Lilith's house. Probably just to show off. With Robert DuBose, it is often something as simple as that.

No, it wasn't the news about Mr. DuBose's merger that slapped me in the face. It was what Astrid told me a few minutes later that has me tailing his pretend son.

Someone behind me blares their horn, and I look up to see a large space between me and the car in front of me. For a second,

I think that Michael has turned off somewhere without me spotting him. Then I catch a glimpse of him edging the Porsche into the right-hand lane, and I move in the same direction.

When I look in the rearview mirror, the male driver of the car behind flicks his hand at his chin a couple of times. I give him the tried and tested middle finger, to which he returns the gesture in kind.

Lucy—that's what Astrid said her name was. I knew this imposter was hiding more than he was telling us, and I'll use this name as my first piece of evidence to bring him down. It will hurt Lilith to discover his secrets, and she'll probably hate me for a while. But she needs to know the truth. I'm just going to have to follow Michael Foster for as long as it takes for him to lead me to this Lucy person.

Still, it could mean my daughter will lose her husband twice in her lifetime. That will be a wound that will take some time to heal. I just hope she hasn't developed deep feelings for him a second time.

According to Astrid, it might already be too late for that. Lilith and Michael have been spending a lot of time together. He is still being indifferent toward Astrid, which I suppose is a good thing. I just can't figure out what his end game is or why he is playing it at all.

Robert is undoubtedly involved. Or is he? How would I feel if someone claiming to be my dead daughter—my only child at that—showed up after twelve years? I'm sure that a massive part of me would need to convince myself that it was her. When the heart has a hole that size left in it, the human spirit will do whatever it takes to fill it, especially when such a scenario had seemed completely impossible beforehand. Maybe that is what's happening with Robert.

Robert DuBose is not a nice man; I know that more than anyone. But he always loved his son. Even if he was involved in this whole thing, what could possibly make such a fiasco worthwhile? Just to hurt Lilith? He never liked her, but something so elaborate would be too much, even for him.

Every time I think I've made a step forward, a new thought hits me, and I'm knocked eight steps back.

Ahead of me, Michael turns onto East Broadway and 4th. I don't follow him any further, as he is clearly going to the office. I'll come back later and hope I see him leaving. I need to tail him in his free time; only then will I catch him up to no good.

I crush out my burned-down cigarette and light another one up right after. The sun has come out a little more now, and I drop the visor to keep it out of my face. I can still picture Astrid as she sat across from me at McDonald's, her eyes downcast as she filled me in on what she had overheard a couple of days ago.

"Fletcher was on the phone," she told me over the tray of empty burger wrappers. "I didn't mean to eavesdrop, but he was standing just outside my bedroom. I think he thought I wasn't home."

"What happened, sweetie?" I asked.

"He was half-whispering 'cause Mom was downstairs. But when he ended the call, he said, 'Okay, bye. I love you, Lucy.'"

Chapter 36

Although I'll never fully grasp what Lilith saw in Reece, I can understand why she liked him. Underneath all the neediness and suffocating affection is a good man. Not the type of man I'd ever find attractive, but a kind one, nonetheless.

When he called again asking to meet, I nearly said no. I'm dealing with the blowback of hearing that Michael Foster is seeing another woman while he strings my daughter along by pretending to be her once-deceased husband. Add to that the fact that I can't seem to find a single bit of dirt on Robert, and my patience is hardly in the kind of state needed to deal with Reece McElroy.

"I like your apartment," Reece tells me as he sits on the couch.

"Thanks, Reece." Most of the furniture came with the place, and I only added a few touches here and there. I don't bother telling him this, though.

Outside, night has started to fall, and there is a slight chill in the air. Thankfully, this building has a great heating system, and my apartment is nice and warm. I had planned on staying in tonight and trying to come up with a new angle to come at this whole situation, but the agony in Reece's voice when he called got to me, despite myself.

When Astrid left yesterday, I told her to be extra careful around Michael Foster. She agreed, and I'm certain she had already been thinking the same thing. It seems that my granddaughter has a better asshole radar than her mother.

"Would you like something to drink?" I ask, sitting down at the kitchen table. The living room, kitchen, and dining room are one large space in my apartment. I have to say that I quite like it that way. I never thought I would. "I have iced tea, Diet Coke, or water."

"A water would be great, Virginia."

I nod and stand up. As I walk to the fridge, I hear Reece groan to himself as he thinks of some pain or other that he is dealing with internally. The sound makes me cringe inside, and I have to physically stop my head from shaking in disgust. I have to remind myself that he is a good man and a kind one too. Just because he is hard work, it doesn't make him not worthwhile.

Wally was a good man too. But there was also a mysterious—and even a little dangerous—side to him. He wasn't a troublemaker, but there was always an undercurrent of a chance that he would react if another man was rude to me or something like that. There was a hint of brooding aloofness to who he was, but only the slightest hint. It was so buried that I would sometimes think it wasn't there at all.

I bring two bottles of water back and hand one to Reece before taking my seat at the table once more. He struggles with the cap for a few seconds, finally gripping it between the hem of his T-shirt and his hand and straining until it pops. I twist mine off and take a sip.

"So, I finally got an answer from Lilith," he tells me, his tone petulant and his perfectly round face screwed up.

"And?"

"I think her mind has slipped."

I know where this is going, but I nod for him to go on anyway. I need to see all of this from as many angles as possible. That way, I can be sure I'm reacting in the right way.

"She told me that Fletcher is back!" Reece tells me, his voice suddenly far too high-pitched. "Can you believe that?"

"Yeah, I know," I say. "But he does look a lot like him, Reece."

"You knew about this?"

"Yes, but it was up to her to tell you," I say. Then I shrug. "Frankly, I was hoping she would see sense before then."

"So you don't believe it?" he asks. His voice is still high, but there is something like hope in it.

"No, I don't."

"It's just"—he rubs his chin for a few seconds as he tries to come up with the appropriate term—"crazy. Is it still acceptable to use the word crazy?"

"Who knows, Reece? What else did she say?"

"That was it, really. Just that Fletcher was back, and she had to give it another chance for her daughter's sake."

For her daughter's sake. Yeah, right.

According to Astrid, this so-called Fletcher has been indifferent to her since he returned. It sounds like Lilith is seeing what she wants to see again, which has only ever led to trouble. When she buries her head in the sand like this, more often than not, it comes back up with a black eye or a bloody nose.

"Okay, Reece," I say, nodding. "Well, thanks for telling me."

"You already knew," he replies sadly.

"Right, but you didn't know that. You're a good man."

"Fat lot of good that has ever done me."

"I'm sorry?" I ask.

"Being a good man," Reece says, shaking his head. "Just look at Lilith. She's gone back to *him*, and she told me some of the stuff he used to do to her. And here I am, apparently,"—he brings his hands up and makes air quotes with his fingers—"a 'good man,' and she's left me for him."

It makes no sense, and I feel for Reece on this one. Unfortunately, there have been women going back to their abusers since the beginning of time. Whether it's because they have some internal issues that insist they deserve to always be unhappy or they have something ingrained in their DNA, I fear that it will always be an issue for a select few.

Reece groans to himself again, and I don't react inwardly or physically. He's got a point: He offered Lilith everything she always claimed she wanted, and she threw it back in his face. Did the package come wrapped in neediness instead of paper and clinginess instead of a bow? Sure, but whatever Reece's issues, he is still twice the man Fletcher was.

When my phone vibrates on the glass coffee table, Reece jumps in his seat. Again, I fight back a head shake and force a smile instead. I pick the phone up and see JOHN HOWERTON on the screen. I check the time and see it is nearly eight. Why is John calling so late?

"I have to take this," I tell Reece, then turn my back to him. "Hey, John. What's up?"

"Virginia," John croaks. He sounds out of breath. "You have to come to the office first thing in the morning."

"Okay," I say. "Is something wrong?"

"I can't discuss it over the phone," he says, his voice barely a whisper now. "But I've got something on Robert that will expose his criminal activity."

Chapter 37

After Reece left, I couldn't sit still. I texted John a couple of times during the night, but he never got back to me. After that, I called, but it was the same result—no reply. I wish he had just told me what he had on Robert because I couldn't sleep thinking about it. If it were something about Wally, then John surely would have met me last night. He is the only person in the world who knows about my suspicions regarding my husband's death.

The traffic is painfully slow this morning, and it feels like everyone is out to annoy me. It's always the same when you're rushing, but it never brings any comfort to know that it's just your impatience making everything seem worse.

I called John again this morning, and he didn't answer. He told me before he ended our call last night to be at his office by 8:30. Even with the traffic, I'll be there early. I just hope he is too. Something in his voice last night was different. I've seen him get excited in the way that only a lawyer can before, and this wasn't it. Usually, having a piece of evidence that could bring someone like Robert down would have John electrified with excitement.

Lilith has never known it, but in the years following Fletcher's passing, myself and John Howerton became quite close. On a couple of occasions, it nearly passed over from a client-lawyer relationship to something more. Both times, one of us stopped it before it could. John is a bit too metrosexual for my tastes, but he is a man who takes charge of situations, and I like that aspect of his persona.

Of course, I'm twelve years older than him, so that might have become an issue at some stage.

Our friendship—if you could call it that—started one day years ago when I asked him some questions regarding private detectives. He asked why I wanted one, and I ended up telling him a little about my suspicions regarding Robert DuBose and Wally's death. As it turned out, John had represented a man a few years before. This guy had been an employee at DuBose Construction who had seen some things he didn't quite like. John had filled me in on the details on a need-to-know basis, but what little he told me confirmed a lot of my earlier suspicions.

Soon after taking on the case, John began receiving threatening phone calls. His ex-wife—wife at the time—also claimed that she was being followed. John refused to be intimidated, but a few weeks later, his client showed up in a cast and told him that he no longer wanted to pursue the case.

John never forgot the harassment he and his wife were subjected to and has held a vendetta against Robert DuBose ever since.

A gap opens up in the line of traffic, and I edge the Ford forward. I hang a left and swing onto Essex Street. A glint of sunshine reflects off the fender of the car in front, and I squint. My sunglasses are on the dash, so I slip them on. They make me think of Lilith at the gas station and how scared she seemed when I swiped at her. The image makes me cringe.

When the traffic slows once more, I grab my pack of Pall Malls and light one up. The smoke calms my nerves a little, but not nearly enough. If John has something that can blow the lid off Robert's criminal activities, then everything changes. The scary part is that I don't know what sort of chain reaction I might set off. What if this explodes in my face? Even worse, what if the aftershock hurts the two most important people in the world to me?

A line of cars has come to a stop behind me. When I look in the rearview mirror, I see a white Coupe directly behind me. The sun on the windshield makes it impossible to see the driver. The car makes me think of Robert, but so does everything these days. Ever since Michael Foster walked into our lives, my desire to hurt Robert DuBose instantly became an obsession.

Soon I fall into the habitual routine of navigating early morning traffic. The stop-start-wait-and-start-again of it has never sat well with me. I'm a foot down sort of gal, but I need to keep my cool. I'm not far from John's office, and I have a feeling that something big is about to happen. I just pray it's for the better.

The coroner and the police said that Wally's death was an accident. They claimed that he had been unblocking the industrial compactor from the inside when someone had mistakenly pressed the button to run it. Those machines are meant to have a safety sensor that stops this from happening, but the police claimed that Wally had disabled it to allow himself to climb inside. Apparently, it happens more often than people think, they said.

We couldn't even give Wally an open casket.

I feel a tickle on my cheek and realize that I'm crying. Wally had his faults, but he was a great husband and an even better father. It was his need to give us the best of everything when he didn't have the means to do so that sometimes got him mixed with the wrong crowd. But a few high-stakes poker games throughout his life didn't make him a bad person. A gullible one, maybe, but not bad.

John Howerton's office building comes into view, and I see a free parking spot right along the street. If I believed in omens, then surely this bit of serendipity would be a good one.

I'm parked and out of the car in seconds. I crush my cigarette under my shoe and dry my eyes before replacing my sunglasses and walking toward the main doors. John shares his building with a couple of other lawyers and some new-aged therapist who uses burning sage like it is the missing piece of the puzzle to unlock the meaning of life. Along with sharing the building, each office uses the same receptionist, a lovely young girl named Molly.

"Hey, Mol," I say as I approach.

Molly is in her early twenties and stunning. I don't know much about her personal life, but I always get the feeling that she will succeed in whatever she does. There is just an air of confidence about her that never even comes close to wandering over to arrogance.

She smiles through shiny red lipstick and tucks a lock of her wavy black hair behind her ear. Her dark skin looks like a doll's, and her big brown eyes must make every man she meets feel like he would never find his way out if he fell into them.

"Hey, Ginny," Molly chimes. "How are you?"

"I'm good," I reply. The clock on the wall behind her says it is still ten minutes before 8:30. "Is John in yet?"

"He didn't call you?"

"Last night, yes."

"I mean, this morning," Molly asks, confusion on her pretty face.

"No."

"He left a message for me last night to say he was going to be a little late. He had to meet a contact in town this morning."

I nod and say, "No problem."

Molly tells me to wait in John's office, and I thank her and make my way upstairs. As I walk, I call John's number again. It's not like him to be late, even with prior arrangements. If he is meeting a contact, then maybe it has something to do with Robert.

This time, his phone doesn't ring out. Instead, it goes straight to voicemail.

Chapter 38

John Howerton's office is just an extension of the man himself. The faux-leather chairs and heavily varnished desk are too much, and the choking air freshener and years of drenching himself in cologne before court appearances are overwhelming. Everything about the room is very John, with his crowning cliché being the tray of crystal decanters and brandy glasses on the counter on the far wall.

How many times I've paced this office today, I don't know. But neither Molly nor I have heard from John all morning. It's now quarter after ten, and I know something is wrong. It's not like him to be even a few minutes late, never mind a couple of hours.

I force myself to sit in the chair facing the desk, but my legs keep twitching. I pull out my phone and check it again, almost like I believe I might have somehow missed a call or a text from him. Molly has popped up a couple of times and is concerned, but not as much as I am. All she knows is that he had to meet a contact. She has no idea it might be something to do with Robert DuBose.

Even if she did, would she be more worried? Robert is rumored to have his hands in some sleazy, illegal pies, but it's hardly public knowledge. It is more so a whisper among criminals and the rare few who have investigated him, like John and me.

Maybe John's meeting has nothing to do with Robert. Could that be a possibility? Of course, but I know deep down that it's connected.

I think of the white Coupe I've spotted a couple of times and shiver. Has Robert had me followed? No, that's ridiculous. What reason could he have to react in such a way? Sure, I've been tailing *him*, but I'm confident he doesn't know that. Even if he did, I've kept some form of tabs on him for years. Okay, so I've stepped it up a lot since Lilith kicked me out, but still.

If Michael Foster had never come into our lives, everything would be fine. Well, not fine, but at least we'd be where we were in our lives. Things had gone stagnant for Lilith and me. I know that, but we were safe. Now I feel like danger is looming over my daughter, and there is nothing I can do to help her.

I realize I've stood up, and I'm pacing again, so I force myself to stop. It's doing nothing to ease my mind. All those years of suspecting Robert and sneaking around, it always felt less dangerous. Now, I can't help thinking we're all in real trouble.

When he caught me snooping around his house during his impromptu lunch, I could have kicked myself. What made it worse was that his office door had been left wide open, and his computer unlocked. If I hadn't heard him coming down the corridor, I'm certain he would have found me doing a lot more than stepping out of his office.

He'd known, though. His smirk had said it all. I made some excuse about getting lost looking for the bathroom, but we had both known it was bull. My reaction and the way I demanded

Lilith leave with me had been embarrassing, and all it had done was confirm what I had been up to before Robert had found me.

And then there is Michael Foster. Lilith says he showed her the DNA results, and John confirmed his hospital stay in Hagerstown. Also, the scar on his face: That is exactly where such a mark would be following what happened in the river, and I sometimes find myself believing that it just might be him. Not often, of course. But it does happen.

I know it's not him, though. It can't be. It just can't.

Without thinking, I walk over to the decanters of brandy and scotch. I pour myself a glass—I don't know the difference between them—and choke it down. The liquid is like fire, and I gag a couple of times before it settles. Despite the horrible taste, it helps me relax.

When I know I won't throw up, I sit back down and pull Lilith's name up on my phone. She won't answer if I call, but she will probably read a text if I send one.

I type: *John is missing. I think this could be related to our situation. Please call me. Let me explain things, at least.*

I hit send. The clock on my phone says that it is 10:35. If John was going to be here, he would have arrived by now. Waiting here is a waste of time. I could call or text Astrid, but she would be in school. I don't want to worry her unnecessarily. She has enough going on, and I won't drag her into it until it's unavoidable.

My black parka is on the back of my chair, and I slip it off and fold it over my arm. As I leave the office, I consider checking John's desk for any notes concerning meetings or any information at all, but I change my mind. It is spotlessly clean, and anything of importance would be locked away. Even if it wasn't, he would never have kept a record of his meeting with a contact if it was anything to do with Robert.

After taking the stairs, I stop and talk to Molly at the reception desk for a moment. She still hasn't heard from John, and I see a little more concern on her face now. I tell her to call me the second she hears anything, and she asks me to do the same. Then I step out on the bright, cold day and walk over to my car. As I do, I slip my sunglasses on and scan the area for any strange cars or people. There is nothing of note.

I sit in the Ford, toss my jacket on the passenger seat, and lock the doors. Once my cigarette is lit, I inhale deeply and start the car.

I've only just pulled out into traffic when my phone rings. It makes me jump, and I have to slam on the brakes when I nearly rear-end the car in front. With my heart beating far too hard, I struggle to get the phone out of my pocket and check the screen. It's a number I don't recognize, but I hit answer anyway.

At first, there is only silence. Then a familiar voice crackles through the line, and all the taste leaves my mouth in an instant.

"Hi," Robert DuBose says. "How are you, Virginia?"

Chapter 39

Someone behind me blares their horn, and I nearly drop my phone. I can hear Robert breathing on the other end. Even though I can't see him, I know he is grinning.

With the phone tucked between my ear and shoulder, I edge the car back into a space on the side of the street and shut it off. The man who had honked at me drives past, giving me two fingers in the process, which I ignore.

"Are you there?" Robert asks, his voice like sour honey.

"I'm here. What do you want, Robert?"

"Why so frosty, Virginia?" he asks.

"What do you want, Robert?" I repeat.

"I just thought I'd check in and see how my favorite in-law is doing."

When I swallow, I can hear it clicking in the back of my throat. I don't know what game he is playing, but it can't be a coincidence that he is calling me right now. In fact, I don't recall us ever talking on the phone, even when Fletcher was around.

"Look, I don't know what game you're playing, Robert," I say, hoping my tone sounds braver than I feel. I crush the end of my cigarette out in the overflowing ashtray. "But I'm not in the mood—"

"Tut, tut, tut," he interrupts. "Why does it have to be a game? Our only children are reconciling, and you still have to hold grudges?"

"Lilith will see through this. It's only a matter of time."

"See through what?" Robert asks. He sounds like a DJ on AM radio. "Why have you always been so paranoid?"

"You know why," I tell him through clenched teeth.

"Oh dear. I think you've spent the last twenty years chasing a hunch. Maybe you should have used the time more productively."

"How do you know what I've been chasing?" I snap. "Huh?"

"I have my connections too, Virginia."

The line goes silent, and all I can hear is his steady breathing. I have a feeling that mine isn't close to being as even as his is, and that pisses me off. I hate showing weakness, especially to someone like Robert DuBose.

Beside me, the slow traffic continues to edge past my car. The window to John's office looms above, the red velvet curtains still closed against the bright morning sun. With shaking hands, I take my cigarettes off the dash and light another one up. I need something to calm my nerves, and the first couple of drags seem to do the trick.

For a third time, I ask, "What do you want, Robert?"

"Okay, okay," he says. "Let's cut to the chase, hmm?"

"If you would."

"I think we should try to find a way to bury the hatchet, so to speak."

"With you?" I scoff.

"For the kids' sake."

"No."

"I expected nothing less," he tells me. This time, there is absolutely no doubting the grin in his tone. "But don't say I didn't offer."

He is playing with me, and I can't figure out why. Does he know what I've been doing, following him and Fletcher? Why is he calling me the moment John Howerton has gone missing? Did he have something to do with it?

"You know," he continues, "Lilith and Fletcher really do seem so happy."

"That's not Fletcher," I growl.

"Oh, but it is, Virginia. I've seen the DNA results."

"I don't care. That's not him."

"And how can you be so sure?"

"Because," I say, carefully choosing my words. "Just... because, Robert."

"Stellar argument," Robert replies, chuckling. "Have you ever thought about being a lawyer?"

"Cut the crap," I snap.

"Oh, that's right!" Robert chimes. "You already have a lawyer, right?"

I bolt upright, my cigarette clenched between my fingers. "What's that supposed to mean? Have you done something to John?"

"There is that paranoia again, Virginia. You really should work on that. It's a very unsavory trait," he tells me. I want to tear into him, but I feel like he is holding all the cards. When I don't respond, he says, "Can't you just be happy for your daughter? Her husband is back and—"

"*That's not her husband*," I hiss. "No DNA tests will convince me otherwise."

"Maybe," he says. "But their marriage was only dissolved through a technicality. *I* have a fancy lawyer too, Virginia. And he tells me that said technicality can be fixed like that." I hear him snap his fingers on the other end of the line. "So maybe you should swallow that poisonous pride of yours and accept things."

"Never," I tell him. I feel like my phone is going to break in half if I grip it any harder.

"So be it," Robert tells me. Then I hear him actually yawn. "I've offered an olive branch."

"Well, you know what you can do with that olive branch?" I snap. "You can take it and shove it up your—"

The line clicks as Robert ends the call. I keep the phone pressed against my ear for another while, my chest heavily rising and falling as I breathe in the stale smoke of my smoldering cigarette. It's like I've just been punched in the gut, and I don't think I've ever felt so alone.

When I believe I won't crash if I drive, I crush the burned-down butt in the ashtray and start the car. As I pull out into the morning traffic, I suddenly have no idea where I should go. My family has been snatched away from me, and the only other person who knows of my suspicions is missing.

How did it come to this? And what the hell can I do to stop it when I don't even know what's happening?

Chapter 40

Every car I see looks suspicious, and all the people I pass on the street seem to watch me. It's been over an hour since Robert called me, and my nerves are still shot. It wasn't a coincidence, and it certainly wasn't to offer an olive branch, as he put it.

Since he hung up on me, I've driven aimlessly through the city. My mind won't stop racing, and I feel like danger is waiting around every turn. Maybe it is? Perhaps my meddling has led to this, and all I've done is drag Lilith and Astrid into real danger.

When I look in the rearview mirror, the same brown eyes I've always known stare back at me, but they look defeated. My hair seems to have more gray than I remembered, and my skin feels wrinkled to the touch. I've always considered myself a strong woman, but not right now.

You were strong before, my mind tries to tell me. *Oh, you were very strong all those years ago, weren't you?*

That was in the past, and I was acting on maternal instincts.

I pass a sea of buildings, their edges sharp in the afternoon sun. The trees peppered along the sidewalk are bare. They look like black, poisoned veins against the concrete that surrounds them. A white car falls into place behind me, and I jump in my seat. Then I see it is an old Corvette and not a Coupe, and curse myself for being so weak.

You already have a lawyer, right? That's what Robert said to me, his voice so mocking in its tone.

Could he be so bold as to do something to John Howerton and then call me so I would know it was his doing? John said he had something on Robert—something *big*. If Robert DuBose knew about whatever it was, I'm sure he would have reacted. But to what extent?

The cars in front of me stop, and I bring the Ford to rest. As I wait, I check my phone to see if Lilith has responded to my text. I can see that she has opened and read it at some point, which is something, at least.

I think about calling Molly, then decide against it. I'm close to John's office building, so I might as well just go there in person. I don't know what I expect to find, though. The longer it goes without hearing from John, the more I'm sure something terrible has happened to him.

Soon I'm on John's block again, and I'm edging the Ford into the same space I vacated earlier. My hands feel numb as I park, and I know I'll have to sharpen up if I'm to be of use to anyone. I can't go up against a man like Robert if I shake with fear whenever he calls me.

Why now? Why has his voice suddenly become so intimidating?

Because you know for certain now that he is dangerous, Ginny.

Yes, that's it. Before now, a tiny part of me had clung to some shred of belief that Wally's death really had been an accident. It was this part of me that had caused me to ease off on my suspicions and my investigations over the years. Sure, Fletcher's death and the needs of my daughter and grandchild had also interrupted things somewhat. But still, I think I had been trying to forget about it and move on before then.

I get out of the car and slip my jacket and sunglasses on. The air is still quite chilled, but the sky is a perfect blue. I watch the people that pass me on the sidewalk for a moment, wondering if any of them are as shaken as I am. I suppose they've all got their own issues and fears to deal with, but they probably don't involve a dangerous man like Robert DuBose.

"I'm procrastinating," I grunt to myself, making a young man in a suit who is passing me look up. I smile, and he smiles back, his ten-thousand-dollar dental work glinting in the sun.

As I walk toward the building's entrance, I realize that my aimless driving through town following Robert's call wasn't so aimless after all. I must have subconsciously planned to come back to John's office the whole time; I'd just needed to gather myself before I did. What I'm about to do is illegal, but I have no other choice. I need something to go to Lilith with, and I think that maybe it's time I told her what I think happened to her father.

I step into the small reception area to see Molly looking very worried. It is nearly noon, which means John hasn't checked in with anyone for over three hours. Molly knows as well as I do that this is unheard of, and I'm sure she is starting to feel some of the fear I have been experiencing.

"Any word?" she hopefully asks as I approach. When I shake my head, she says, "Oh, no. This isn't like him at all."

"I know," I say, nodding now. "But maybe he just got held up with his contact."

"Maybe," Molly replies, but her voice has no conviction.

I would love to stay here and keep her company—I know she is scared—but if I'm going to do this, it has to be now. If someone connected to Robert has threatened John, then maybe he will want nothing to do with me when he finally resurfaces.

And that's if he actually *does* resurface.

"I'm going to wait in his office again," I tell Molly, moving toward the stairwell before she can ask questions.

Thankfully, she is far too preoccupied.

I start up the steps toward John's office with my head down and my mind focused. Going through his client files is wrong on so many levels, but I might never get another chance. If I find what I'm looking for, then who knows where it might lead me.

Chapter 41

The problem I have is that I have no name for the man I'm looking for, which means I don't even know where to begin. Also, how do I even know if John still has a hard copy of the file? It was over two decades ago, so he could have easily had all of his records computerized by now. Although, I don't think he would have.

John Howerton is a man whose vision of himself portrays a man in a different era. You only have to look at his office to know that, so I'm pretty confident he will still have files kept in the two filing cabinets on either side of the wall behind his desk.

I've never seen him open them before, though. Until now, I've always assumed they were decorative, and they probably are. And there is a very expensive computer on his desk with plenty of memory for storing client records, I'm sure. I tried the latter as soon as I came in, but it was password locked, as I had expected.

I step over to the first filing cabinet and try the top drawer. It has a keyhole on it and doesn't budge. I bang it with my fist and curse. The smell of air freshener and cologne is somehow worse now, and I walk over to the window and open it. The red velvet curtains I opened when I first walked in billow in the soft breeze.

There are three drawers on the side of John's desk, and I try them all. The top two are locked, but the bottom one opens. There is nothing in it but a Filofax and a silver hip flask that is so dusty I wonder if it's ever been used for anything more than show. Cursing, I step back from the desk and examine it again. Standing on this side, I realize that the far wall is barely decorated. John has clearly placed everything he thinks looks impressive on his side of the desk so that the people facing him see it all.

Shaking my head and smiling despite the situation, I try the rest of the drawers on each of the filing cabinets. Of course they are all locked. I'm starting to think this was a waste of time. Even if they were unlocked, the odds of me finding the one client file I'm looking for are extremely slim, especially without a name.

I slump down in John's oversized faux-leather chair, getting an extra pungent waft of cologne as I do. As I sit, I try to remember the year I told John about my suspicions regarding Wally's death.

I know it was before Fletcher passed away, but how long? John was my lawyer before he was Lilith's, and I hired him not long after Wally died. He had been great with the life insurance and stuff, but there had been a long period after that when I didn't see him. It was only when Lilith got engaged—

"That's it!" I exclaim to nobody but myself. "That was when I wanted to hire a private detective."

Nineteen years ago, that was when Lilith got engaged. I remember being terrified that she was going to be married into a family that I suspected of killing her father. If I had told her then, could all of this have been avoided? No, she was and still is too headstrong. Lilith would have gone ahead with the wedding whether she'd had my blessing or not. That was why I never told her. It would have only caused heartache.

You could have told her about the other thing, Ginny. You could have told her when you got back the next morning.

I shake my head hard enough to see red dots. The decisions I made in the past can't be undone now. No, all I have is the present. Now that I know how long ago I discussed Wally's death with John, I can figure out a year in which the other guy came to see him.

"Three years ago," John had told me as we sat in this very office nearly two decades before now. His young face had been lit up with excitement as he spoke. "Three years ago, a guy came to me and mentioned Robert DuBose."

"What was his name?"

"The guy?"

"Yes."

John laughed, his features still smooth enough that they didn't need to be touched up with concealer. "I can't tell you that, Ginny."

"Okay."

Then John had sat forward in his chair, adjusting his silver cufflinks as he spoke. I'd listened intently, my belief that Robert DuBose had killed my husband growing with each word. John's tone had grown in pitch as he fell into the role of Hollywood lawyer, and I don't think he ever really understood just how poisonous the nettle was that he was trying to grasp.

To him, it was a juicy case, and he was the suave young lawyer who would make his name off it. In truth, he had always been more suited to low-key divorce settlements and DUIs. He hadn't been able to tell me much that day, but I always remembered that one of his clients had decided to go up against Robert and the shady dealings that go on at DuBose Construction.

That, and the way the guy had suddenly decided that maybe he had made a mistake.

I clap my hands once and stand up, more determined than ever to find something on Robert. All these years, I've only ever scratched at the surface. Images of John's wife being followed or his client showing up with his arm in a cast always tried to hold me back. The thought of putting my family in danger had finished the job.

Now, my family seems to be in peril regardless, so there isn't anything that can stop me.

"Think like John," I mumble to myself as I stand behind his desk, tapping my foot. "Think like him."

John has always seen himself as a 1920s throwback. The crystal decanters, silk ties, velvet curtains, and filing cabinets speak volumes to his character and his mindset.

I kneel behind the desk and open the bottom drawer again. The hip flask wobbles on the wood as I do, and I hear a light sound. I remove the flask and the Filofax and place them on the plush carpet.

It takes me nearly a minute, but after pressing and pushing the base of the drawer several times, I hear a pop. The bottom comes out easily enough, and I peer into the secret compartment. Looking back at me is a set of keys.

Chapter 42

Amazingly, it seems like John has kept physical records of every client he's ever had. What is even more surprising is that he's sorted them in chronological order. In the ten minutes I've spent examining the contents of the filing cabinets, I've found that he has them filed by year and then alphabetized within each year.

My hands are shaking as I flip through the files, some of them yellowing and dog-eared. I've narrowed it down to a two-year period just to be safe, but it will take me ages as I don't have a name. I have to open each file individually and skim through it hoping I catch Robert's name or his company's or something that links to him.

Through the open window, I can hear the traffic below as it slowly rumbles past. I removed my jacket a while ago, but I'm still sweating. Several of the files I've already checked are piled up on the desk, and I have more out on top of the filing cabinet as I stand next to it, frantically leafing through pages.

Nothing is standing out. Nothing. And what if I have the year wrong? What if I have the memory wrong? Did John say three years or a few years? The latter could relate to any timeframe, really. People regularly say "a few" when they mean five or ten or whatever number.

No, I need to concentrate and stick to my instincts. Molly could walk in here at any moment and catch me rifling through her boss's personal files. What then? How would that look with John missing? Not good; that's how it would look.

"C'mon, c'mon, c'mon," I whisper, closing yet another file and putting it on my makeshift out pile.

Most of the records involve divorces and insurance claims, as I knew they would. They are pretty easy to dismiss after a couple of lines, which is some sort of a positive. Still, I have so many left to go, and I have no idea how long I have to check them before someone catches me. Even if I find what I'm looking for, what then?

"I go see him," I tell myself, nodding. "I go see whoever it was that came to John and ask some questions."

I toss another file on the desk and pull the next one out. The first line reads *Jennifer Fonseca. Parking fine: Stillwater*, and I groan. I know I should move on to the next one, but John represents these clients in more than one case. He is their lawyer, so there could always be more on the later pages. A quick skim proves fruitless, and I throw the file on the stack.

The unmistakable sound of a police radio echoes up from the street outside. I drop the file I'm holding and walk to the opened window. I can see two state troopers standing next to a police cruiser. One of them is sitting in the driver's seat with the door open and a receiver to his mouth. The other is standing on the sidewalk directly below me. I'm only on the second floor, but I can't make out what is being said through the general noises from the street. It's just muffled sounds.

As I watch, the one on the radio looks up at the window, and I instinctively duck back. When I edge myself forward again, I see the tops of their hats as they walk into the main door right underneath me.

"Oh my God," I hiss.

Did Molly call the cops? Is there a camera in here that I've never noticed before? It doesn't matter now, as I'm done if they walk in. There are files all over the desk, and both of the cabinets have drawers open.

My heart is in my mouth as I frantically stuff the files back into the drawers. My mouth tastes like old pennies, and I drop one of the manila folders when I try to slot it in. Several pages fan out and land on the floor. I quickly stuff them back in and ram the file into the drawer.

Somewhere downstairs, the police are asking Molly which office it is they need to check. How long will it take them to walk up here? One, maybe two minutes?

I grab as much of the stack on the desk as I can carry and hold it in the crook of my arm as I load folders into the cabinets. As I stuff them in, I try to think of an excuse—any excuse—that I can use to explain myself. There is nothing that will pass as plausible. Nothing.

I step across and pick up the rest of the pile, moving over to the second cabinet and dumping some in. They don't fit properly, and I have to push them down with force. Even if I somehow get them all in before the cops walk in, it will be obvious to anyone who opens the cabinets that someone has been searching through them.

Deal with that later, Ginny. You can deal with that later. Just get the hell out of here.

I can hear footsteps out in the corridor as I force the last of the files in. The cabinet drawer won't close, and I can hear the two cops talking now. Molly's voice is mixed in with theirs, and I can tell that she is upset.

"You *should* be upset for calling them on me," I hiss. "You bitc—"

The drawer clicks shut just as the handle of the office door rattles. In one movement, I slip around to the other side of the desk and land in the chair.

A trooper steps in through the door. He is in his mid-thirties with sharp features that make him look like a rodent. Behind him, his partner—mid-forties, strangely handsome—seems to take the entire scene in through intensely alert eyes.

Molly steps in beside them and dabs at her eyes with a tissue.

"Are you Ms. Townsend?" the younger trooper asks.

"Yes," I reply, trying to act casual, even though my heart feels like it might explode.

The trooper nods once and says, "We're going to have to ask you a few questions."

Chapter 43

"He did what?" I ask, still in shock at what I've just been told. Molly whimpers next to the state trooper, who introduced himself as Officer Liam Whitely, and I suddenly feel awful for having thought she had called the cops on me.

"We are in no doubt," Officer Whitely repeats. "Molly told us you were meant to meet him here this morning, Ms. Townsend?"

The three people who walked into the office a millisecond after I closed the last drawer on the filing cabinet are standing over me. I'm still sitting in the chair in front of John's desk, and I think my mouth is hanging wide open. It's hard to tell because I'm so numb.

"Y-yes," I say, nodding. Everything around me seems to be coated in air that is twice as thick as it should be. "He said to be here first thing, but he never showed up."

The other officer—the older one—pulls up the spare chair and sits facing me. When he removes his hat and places it on his lap, the light from outside shines on his blond crew cut. His blue eyes seem caring, and I feel like collapsing into his arms and weeping.

I don't, though. I have to stay strong. Robert had done something. I just never believed it would be this.

"I'm Officer Tony Demarco," the older cop tells me. "I know this is all hard to process, but we will need to ask you some questions now, okay?"

As I hear Molly groan, I nod. She is still standing next to Officer Whitely.

"Good," Demarco says, nodding. "Now, when was the last time you spoke to Mr. Howerton?"

"Last night," I reply.

"Okay, and did he sound depressed or anxious?"

"He was excited," I tell him, and I mean it.

John had been champing at the bit to bring down Robert. I should probably tell the officers this part, but I don't know how deep I'm entangled in it all. I have to choose my words carefully until I know more about what is going on. If Robert could have John killed and make it look like suicide, he would have no hesitation in doing so to me. Or even worse, to Astrid or Lilith.

"Excited?" Officer Demarco says, his brow creased. Then it clears, and he nods. "Um-hmm. Sometimes that is the way with suicide. When someone has made up their mind to go through with it, a sort of calm washes over them."

I want to scream, to yell at him and tell him that John was murdered, but I can't. Would they believe me even if I did? They walked in here a few minutes ago and told me he had been found in his car in an underpass not far from his office with a belly full of Xanax and a quart of vodka. Not exactly a smoking gun scenario.

Demarco turns to his younger partner and says, "Officer Whitely, can you get Ms. Townsend some water, please?"

Whitely stands where he is for a moment, then grunts a reply and walks out of the room.

"Maybe you should go too, Ms. James?" Demarco says to Molly, that warm smile lighting up his face again. "We will need to ask you more questions later. Go get some water and sit down. You've been through a lot."

I watch as Molly tries to force a smile for me, and I feel that sting of guilt again at having suspected her. The cops had arrived at the office building without her ever having picked up the phone. Once a 911 call had come in regarding the motionless man in the fancy Mercury parked below the underpass, it was only a matter of time before the police showed up at John's place of business to ask some questions.

With the two of us alone, Officer Demarco sits back in his chair and looks deep into my eyes. His smile has faded by the time he speaks.

"Is there something you're not telling me, Ms. Townsend?"

"What do you mean?" I ask. There *are* parts I'm not telling him—significant parts—but I can't bring myself to open up. Not yet. I need to understand the situation better before I put anyone else in danger.

"You say you were meant to meet John here this morning, right?"

"Right."

"At what time?" Demarco asks.

"Eight-thirty."

"And it's now... " he says and looks at his watch, "twelve thirty-eight. Seems like a long time to wait around to see your lawyer."

"I was worried," I tell him, instantly regretting it when his eyebrows shoot up.

"Worried? Why?" Demarco asks.

"He's never late," I tell him, trying to sound sure of myself. It's quite easy because this part about John is completely true. "Not even by a minute."

"Hmm, I see," Demarco says. He looks at me for another few seconds, and then his smile returns. "Okay, well, I'm sorry for laying these questions on you. You're still in shock. I can see that."

"I'm sorry I can't be of any more help, Officer."

Demarco stands up and cracks his back. "You've been plenty of help. But I will still need you to come down to the station and give a statement, okay?"

"Sure," I reply, my eyes involuntarily flicking to the filing cabinets behind him. Thankfully, he doesn't seem to notice. I smile at him. "Could I just have a few minutes to collect myself?"

"Of course," Demarco says, nodding. "I'll just be downstairs. Take all the time you need."

With that, the state trooper walks out of the office and closes the door. Before I can second-guess myself and lose my nerve, I'm up and opening the filing cabinets again.

I need to find that client file, and I'll probably never get another chance to look.

Chapter 44

Enrico Suarez—that was the name on the file. It actually only took me another four or five minutes to find it yesterday after Officer Demarco had left me to "gather myself." I spent the next while making sure everything was put back the way it had been before I started looking. Well, everything except the set of keys. I kept them along with the manila folder with the Suarez address.

West Concord is way out of town, and it has taken me a while to get here. I punched the address that was in Enrico Suarez's file into my GPS, but I have no idea if he still lives there. There had been a phone number in the records, but it was out of service. Suarez was in his forties when he came to see John, and it was twenty-three years ago at that.

I hope Suarez is still alive and well. And if he is, at the same address too.

I turned off the Concord Turnpike a while ago, but the GPS now has me confused. It just keeps leading me down country roads and around sharp bends. Brown trees that only have a hint of green in them stand tall on either side of me as I slowly edge the Ford along. Beyond them, endless fields stretch back until they hit the horizon. I've never liked the countryside, and oddly enough, it's the wide spaces that actually make me feel claustrophobic.

I think I'm still a little shaky from yesterday. Coming so close to getting caught snooping in John's office rattled me. Hearing that he had committed suicide was much worse.

I gave my statement at the police station. It was mostly just a repeat of everything I had already told Officers Whitely and Demarco earlier that day. Throughout the entire experience, my mind kept drifting to the manila folder in my car. I had stuffed Enrico Suarez's client file into my jacket and carried it straight by the waiting cops in the reception area. As I passed, I told them I was grabbing my cigarettes. Thankfully, they simply nodded and waited for me to return.

The police seem completely satisfied that John killed himself. They are going on the fact that a couple empty bottles of Xanax and vodka had been found on the floor of his car. My own suspicions are entirely different, but I kept my mouth shut on that part.

Will my withholding of what I suspect come back to haunt me? Maybe, but I don't think it would have done me any good to speak up, either. Robert DuBose doesn't do things halfway, and if he had paid someone to make John's death look like a suicide, then no mistakes would have been made. That means that there will be no traces of foul play, and I would look like a crazy paranoid person for even suggesting it.

Maybe I am those things? It certainly feels like my mind is slipping.

The GPS tells me to take a left again, but I can already see that it has brought me in circles. I'm definitely in West Concord—I've seen signs—but finding the actual house is proving to be a nightmare. Pressing the screen so hard that my fingerprint lingers on the surface for a moment, I shut the GPS off. I'll have to find this house the old-fashioned way.

Enrico Suarez's file was very thin. From what notes John had taken, the man came to him one day twenty-three years ago and said that he suspected his boss of money laundering, racketeering, and running an illegal gambling ring. John's chicken-scratch handwriting had noted a few things: that Enrico claimed he was a staunch Catholic and couldn't stand by and let these crimes happen and that he worried about the aftereffects of going to court and seemed terrified. The notes also said that John believed Suarez would have a strong case, but only if he continued to work for DuBose Construction and gathered some form of solid evidence.

Apart from two short pages of handwritten notes, the only other useful information was Suarez's phone number and address. The former was out of action, and I'm hoping the latter gives me something. Anything at all.

It has started to drizzle a little, and I turn on the wipers. As I come over a small hill, I see a man walking his dog. The large German Shepherd is bounding along beside its owner, its bushy tail high as it surveys the fields around it. I slow as I come up beside them, and the man leans into the open window of the passenger side the second I come to a stop.

"Lost, little lady?" he asks. He looks to be in his mid-fifties, with massive shoulders underneath a thick, woolen sweater. His eyes are the same color as the grass behind him, and he drums his mucky fingers on the doorframe as he smiles in at me.

I know a lot of modern women would be offended by being referred to as "little lady," but I have a soft spot for old-school men such as this.

"I think so," I reply, leaning forward a little and turning sideways so I can look him in the eye. "I'm looking for a place called Pine House. I think it is close to here."

"Close 'nuf," he tells me, grinning. "But you'll need to turn this car 'round and head back the way you came. It's about five minutes south,"—he points behind me—"and it will come up on yer left. You probably passed it already, sweetie."

"Thanks," I say, nodding.

"No problem," he replies, giving me a cheeky wink.

I can't help but smile, and I wave to him as I bring the window back up. He steps almost into the ditch to let me turn the car around, his dog obediently sitting by his feet. After a moment of edging the Ford around, I honk the horn and head back the way I came. I can see him waving a meaty hand in the rearview mirror as he slowly disappears behind the hill.

Enrico Suarez's short film ended abruptly, with John simply writing: *Client no longer wishes to pursue the case.*

If John hadn't told me all those years ago that his client had shown up with his arm in a cast and fear in his eyes, I would have known no different. He made no note of that part, which makes me think John was feeling some of the trepidation Enrico was at the time.

The friendly man walking his dog hadn't been wrong. I've driven past this house twice already this morning. My heart sinks when I realize why, and I suddenly know for sure that I've wasted my time. All that's left now is to drive back into town and tell the police what I suspect. It will probably lead to nothing, but at least I'll have tried.

The house I'm looking at is almost certainly abandoned, and for many years by the look of it. Overgrown shrubs cover several of the windows, and the front garden is nothing but a huge tangle of reeds and vines. There are no other houses for half a mile on either side, so I know this is the Suarez place. Or was, at least.

A sign partially covered by ivy with the faded words PINE HOUSE on it confirms my fears.

"Shit," I snap, banging the wheel with both of my palms. "Shit, shit, shit."

Chapter 45

I nearly start the car up again and head for home, but change my mind and get out at the last second. I've driven all this way, so I might as well have a look around. My coat is on the back seat, and I slip it on against the drizzle. The driveway up to the house—or is it a cottage?—has weeds protruding from the surface all the way along. When my feet crunch on the filthy pebbles, a flock of birds takes flight from a nearby bush, making me jump.

Like all abandoned houses—especially ones in the countryside—this place looks eerie. With the dark, gray morning skyline behind it, the crumbling roof looks like a gaping mouth. I feel silly for letting my emotions get the better of me, but it's hard to fight them. On top of the creepy look of the place, my last shot at finding something new on Robert has just been obliterated.

There is no way someone lives here. My only hope had been to find this Enrico Suarez and ask him some questions. Maybe he had found some evidence before Robert and his heavies went to work on his arm? And perhaps that was *why* they went to work on his arm.

Wally is dead, and he's never coming back. I had been too scared and in shock at the time to really look into his so-called accident on the construction site. When I finally was aware enough to make a few tentative inquiries, too much time had passed. Even if I'd acted right away, I'm sure Robert had covered all the angles. He wouldn't have had my husband killed without putting precautions in place.

Why did it have to be a murder, Ginny? Maybe it really was just an accident? Wally was an honest guy. Robert would have no reason to get rid of him.

"No," I say aloud, the sound getting lost in the clean, country air. I realize that I've only made a couple of strides up the driveway and stopped still. I make no effort to push on.

I've been through so many scenarios over the years, and I think I've spent a lot of the time actually trying to convince myself it was an accident. I wanted it to be so because my daughter was married to Fletcher DuBose. She had been through enough already herself. When the black eyes and dropped gazes started happening, my attention switched from Robert to his son. Robert and his involvement in Wally's death became a thing of the past, at least consciously. In the back of my mind, I guess I was always hoping something would come up that would expose him.

I force myself to take another few steps, knowing that when I knock on the door and nobody answers, everything ends. After that, all I can do is try and get my family back. If that means swallowing my pride and accepting the choices Lilith has made, then so be it. I've done it before, so I can do it again.

The front door looks to be in better condition than the rest of the house, and I suppose it might have been reinforced to keep squatters out or something like that. The porch steps creak so loudly when I step on them I wonder how I haven't gone right through the soft wood. Some weeds and ivy have grown up through them, and one vein of the latter has wrapped itself around the handrail like some macabre barber's pole in nineteenth-century London.

A mouse stops at the top step, his beady black eyes seeming to scan me for danger before he wrinkles his nose and scampers off into a darkened corner. I suck in more fresh air, closing my eyes as it tries its best to soothe my nerves. I can't figure out why I'm so on edge, as it is clear there is nobody living here.

When I'm at the door, I bring my hand up to knock and just hold it there. I can't stop thinking that this is the end somehow and that all avenues have been exhausted.

Would it be so bad to just accept this new Fletcher as my daughter's estranged husband? He did seem a whole lot nicer than the old one, so there is that, at least.

Maybe he survived, Ginny? that evermore intrusive part of me sneers. *You saw the scar on the side of his face, right? That could easily have happened at the Gauley River.*

"He can't be alive," I say to myself, but it sounds less convincing than usual. "He just can't be."

Then what is left? John is dead, and I have no doubt it's because I involved him in this whole Robert DuBose situation again. Lilith is with a man claiming to be her husband, and it's getting harder for me to deny the similarities. This man seems to have little interest in his daughter, at least when it comes to showing her affection. Astrid says that he is still constantly asking where she has been and what she's been up to but appears to be otherwise unconcerned.

Wally has been gone a long time, and no amount of retribution will bring him back. Maybe it's time I just let it all go and get on—

"Can I help you?" a gruff voice calls behind me, making me gasp. I turn around to see a Hispanic man in his mid-to-late sixties. He is wearing a bucket hat and holding a rod. Dark green fishing waders that come up to his chest glisten in what sunlight there is, and his grizzled face looks suspicious.

"I'm sorry," I say, looking down the steps at him. "I thought nobody was home."

"Can I help you?" he repeats, this time with a little impatience in his tone.

"Yes. I'm looking for Enrico Suarez."

The old man in the fishing gear squints his eyes and looks me up and down. Then he spits on the ground and says, "I'm Enrico Suarez. Who's askin'?"

Chapter 46

The inside of the house isn't at all like the dilapidated shell. In fact, the two rooms I've seen—the living room and kitchen—are actually quite charming. We are sitting in the kitchen now, a tidy little stove burning in the corner. The table looks handmade, and the wooden floors are worn and scuffed yet clean.

Several potted herbs run along the windowsill that looks out over a shabby backyard, and the yin and yang effect between in here and out there is amazing. I can smell the sweet odor of the red maple logs Enrico has just thrown on the flames. When he closes the small metal stove door and turns to face me, I see worry as well as curiosity in his expression.

"How's your tea?" he asks me, nodding at the cup in my hand.

"Delicious." It really is lovely.

"Look, I'm sorry you've come all the way out here," he tells me. "But I left that part of my life behind long ago."

The first ten minutes of our meeting were spent with Enrico sizing me up, his questions sharp and to the point. I had mentioned why I was there off the bat, and I had seen the way his demeanor had shifted from wary to outright defensive. After he decided I was not here on *behalf* of Robert DuBose, and I had actually mentioned his old boss because I wanted to bring him down, he'd invited me in and made some tea.

After changing out of his fishing gear, he joined me in the kitchen. Now that the fire is lit and we have our cups in front of us, I can sense his defenses going up once more.

"I know you want to leave all that in the past," I tell the old man, nodding. "But my daughter and grandchild could be in danger."

"If they got on the wrong side of Robert DuBose," Enrico growls, "then they are most definitely in danger."

I tell him it's me who is on the wrong side of Robert, and Enrico simply nods for me to go on. As I fill him in on Wally and the returning Fletcher, he listens with his mouth ajar. I finish with the news I got yesterday that John Howerton died of a suspected overdose—but that I believe it was murder—and Enrico sits back in his wooden chair and clicks his tongue.

"It seems like the work of Robert DuBose, all right," he says, his voice as rough as sandpaper. Then he rubs his upper arm with his hand. "He didn't stop at just ruffin' me up. Oh, no. Ol' Robert didn't leave it at that."

"What happened?" I ask.

"Destroyed my whole life," Enrico tells me, shaking his head sadly. "Ruined any job I ever got afterward and terrorized my family until my wife packed the kids up and left me. I don't blame her, either. Robert made sure she knew the dangers of stayin' around."

"How long?" I ask. The pain in this man's voice is only matched by the anger and fear that seem to bubble up with every word he speaks. "I mean, how long did he terrorize you all?"

"The wife and kids? Around a year. Liza stuck it out for that long, but when the dog was poisoned, she had enough." Enrico snorts hard, then takes a sip of his tea. "There was lots of other stuff before then, like cars bein' followed and the kids sayin' some strange van drove beside them as they walked to or from school, stuff like that."

"I'm so sorry," I tell him, very aware that Wally was working with DuBose Construction while all of this was happening. Hell, I had probably chatted with Robert at one of the staff parties while his hired heavies were out harassing Enrico and his family. "I really am."

"Look," Enrico says, sitting forward and opening the stove door again. He tosses a few sticks into it and snaps it shut. "Ain't nothin' to be sorry for. It's all in the past. At least, I thought it was till you showed up."

Enrico's expression tightens, and I see all the color leave his grizzled cheeks. "You didn't tell no one you were comin' here, did you?"

"No, no," I answer quickly. His voice is a little high and panicked, so I try to counter it with calmness. "No, nobody knows. I only decided last night after I got your file and saw the address."

"Good," he says, looking around like there might be other people in the kitchen with us, watching from the shadows. "Good. That's good."

We sip our tea for a while, and I can almost see the cogs going in his head. He doesn't know me at all, and I have just shown up at his door, mentioning the name of a man who ruined his life over two decades ago. I can see in Enrico's demeanor that he has never fully recovered from that experience. How could he when he lost his whole family because of it, and all he'd try to do was the right thing?

Suddenly, he sits upright and brings his hand up to his chin.

"What did you say your husband's name was again?" he asks.

"Wally. Wally Townsend."

Enrico sucks in air through his teeth. "I think you might be right to believe your husband was killed."

"Why?" I ask, my heart pounding. "Why? Why would you say that?"

"Your husband worked for Robert, all right," Enrico says, nodding slowly. He seems to talk to nobody in particular as he drags up memories long buried. "But not just on the construction sites."

Chapter 47

The drive back from Enrico's place was mostly a blur. I really thought I had known my husband, but it turns out there was a lot more to Wally than met the eye. For one thing, Enrico told me that Wally was one of the men who ran the books for Robert DuBose's gambling ring. Enrico hadn't seen all that much—just enough to raise his suspicions—but he'd been almost positive that had been the case.

My questions following this information had been rapid and a little aggressive, I have to admit. I'm still in shock now as I sit in the living room of my apartment, looking out at the pitch-black night sky.

Could Enrico have been lying? No, I don't think he had any reason to do that. Also, he seemed almost embarrassed to tell me.

I'd always known Wally liked a bet but presumed it had never been anything more than a once-in-a-while thing. Gambling isn't that taboo these days, but for the type of bets Robert was accommodating, the police would certainly have been sniffing around. According to Enrico, there had been men who were a lot deeper into the running of the books than Wally, but he had undoubtedly been a part of it.

I crush out yet another cigarette, with barely any memory of having smoked it. There were times when I felt there was more to Wally's life with DuBose Construction than he let on, but I tried to tell myself it was nothing more than a few late-night poker games or a trip to the track with the fellas. Could my husband's running the books have led to his death? Maybe he was skimming a bit off the top for us.

These are all new questions that open up so many unforeseen doors. No matter how many of them appear, they all still lead to the same thing: Robert had Wally killed.

In fact, this new information only strengthens my belief that Robert had something to do with my husband's death. Before now, the only thing holding me back from fully accepting that particular outcome had been the reasoning behind it. Why would Robert have risked killing a man who simply laid bricks for one of his construction firms? What would be the point?

Clearly, Wally had been in too deep and couldn't find a way out. Whatever the reason, it had angered Robert enough to deal with him in the most horrific way imaginable.

I pick up my phone and stare at Lilith's name for a while. I know if I call her, she won't answer, and the number of text messages she hasn't replied to up until now is getting silly. I need to talk to her face-to-face. If she won't listen, I'll have to make her. She needs to know how deep this thing runs.

"Damn it!" I snap, replacing the phone on the windowsill and pulling out another cigarette. "How did I let it get to this?"

Anything I tell Lilith now will look like desperation on my part. She already thinks I'm crazy. If I start filling her in on my suspicions about her father's death and the strange old man in the countryside who confirmed them, I'll look even more insane.

As I smoke, I pull Officer Demarco's card out of my jeans pocket. He told me to call him if I remembered anything else about John Howerton. I know I should have relayed my fears about Robert when we spoke yesterday, but I was too lost in my own confusion to know what was best. If I call him now, I could start fresh. The only problem is that I'd have to tell him about Enrico Suarez, and he told me without any hesitation that he would deny everything he said if the police or anyone else got involved.

I grab my phone yet again and pull up my chat with Astrid. I write: *Hey, how are you? Miss you and love you*, and hit send. It's not much, but I've tried to have some form of contact with her every day since I was asked to leave my home. She responds most of the time. For those times when she doesn't, at least she knows I've been thinking about her.

The worst part is that all roads lead back to one thing and that opening Lilith up to that truth will probably drive her away for good. Can I ever be completely honest with her while that hangs over my head? Probably not, but I can't do it yet; I'm just not ready.

Sighing, I stand up and walk into the kitchen. The cigarette between my fingers leaves a trail of smoke behind me as I walk. Tomorrow, things are going to change, whether I go to the cops or to my daughter. There really is no place to hide anymore. John Howerton's death—I know it was really murder—has changed everything.

I make myself a sandwich and then just look at it for a while. After deciding I'm not hungry, I wrap it up and put it in the refrigerator. I wander back into the living room and take my seat on the sill again. The smell of the overflowing ashtray is awful, but I can't be bothered to empty it.

My reflection in the window is faded, but I can see how haggard I look. All of this started when Michael Foster decided to play his game. I'm fully confident now that he is in cahoots with Robert, as there is just no other explanation. If I can figure out the *why* then maybe I can start working on the *what*. *What* do they want, and *what* can I do to stop them?

Taking a deep breath that feels like it will never end, I pick up my phone and the business card. As I dial, a massive part of me tries everything it can to turn the phone off again. Somehow I stop it, but it takes a monumental effort.

The line rings for what seems like forever, and I'm starting to think the late time of the call has saved me from making a stupid mistake. Then Officer Demarco's already-familiar voice answers. I can picture him sitting at home—probably with his wife as they watch *SportCenter* or *Jimmy Kimmel*—his blue eyes curious and his strangely handsome face alert.

"Hello?" Tony Demarco says.

"Hi, Officer Demarco," I manage. My voice seems distant, and my thoughts are cloudy. "This is Virginia Townsend. I think we need to talk."

Chapter 48

"These are very serious accusations, Ms. Townsend," Officer Whitely tells me, his rat-like features even more prominent under the fluorescent bulbs of the Boston Police Department's interview room. "Robert DuBose is a highly respected member of the community."

Like hell he is, I think but don't say.

I could have sworn Officer Demarco's face twitched when his partner mentioned Robert being respected, but it could just be my imagination. All of my senses seem heightened and dulled at the same time.

Coming here suddenly feels like a mistake. Even as I ended my call with Demarco last night with the plan to come to the station the following morning, I felt like he was only humoring me. Why wouldn't I have said anything two days ago when John Howerton's body was found, and I gave a statement in this very room? Why wait until now?

The two officers have already asked these questions, like I knew they would. My only answer was that fear and confusion had played a part, which is basically the truth. I needed to know how I felt about the whole situation, and now I'm sure I'm in too deep and need their help. But not being able to tell them about my conversation with Enrico Suarez is killing me.

His confirmation of Robert's nasty character feels like it makes everything I'm saying so much more concrete.

"I *know* these are serious accusations," I say, wishing it was just Demarco interviewing me. Whitely seems to be not only rattish in appearance but in personality too. "And I'm only telling you about my suspicions."

"You have to understand, Ms. Townsend," Demarco cuts in. "We can't really start investigating someone on a gut feeling—we need some form of evidence to get the ball rolling. You would be surprised how often the police have to deal with false accusations made by a disgruntled ex-boyfriend or an angry wife."

"I'm neither of those things," I snap, then reel my neck in a little. Officer Demarco is only trying to help me understand the situation. "I'm sorry."

Whitely smirks and gives his head the smallest of shakes. Demarco smiles and says, "It's okay. I get it."

I sip the horrible coffee they gave me in a polystyrene cup and wait for them to talk. I've told them everything I can, and I need to know what my next step should be. One that I will undoubtedly take will be approaching Lilith and telling her everything I've said here. But apart from that, I'm in the dark.

Someone knocks on the door, and Demarco tells them to come in. A large man in a short-sleeved blue shirt that looks ready to explode against his gut leans his sweating head in and mumbles something about an important call.

"I'll handle it," Whitely tells his partner, patting his shoulder as he stands up.

When he is gone, Officer Demarco leans across the table and says, "I know he is a little rough around the edges, but he means well."

"It's fine," I tell him. And it is. I've always respected law enforcement officers and the work they do, especially considering the terrible salary they get for such stressful work. Obviously some of them are going to be bitter and angry at times. "Honestly."

Demarco gives me that wonderfully calming smile of his, and I feel instantly better. Not great, but secure.

"Why don't you run me through it one more time?" he says, picking up his pen and leaning over a yellow legal pad.

I start at the beginning, telling him that Wally worked for DuBose Construction for many years and always seemed happy enough. I already told them that I suspected my husband might have been involved in some illegal gambling with Robert, and I say it again. I don't mention that a man named Enrico Suarez gave me this information only yesterday. I fill him in once more on the stranger that is claiming to be my dead son-in-law and everything else that has happened, and I end on the feeler that something terrible will happen to my daughter and grandchild if I let this game continue.

Demarco nods and scribbles notes throughout, and when I'm finished, he says, "We have someone inquiring about those hospital records right now."

"I'm sure they'll check out," I tell him. I didn't sleep much last night, and I'm tired. The clock on the wall says it is just past ten in the morning, and the thought of the day ahead makes me want to slink down onto the table and close my eyes against the world and everyone in it.

"Oh?" Demarco replies, his blond eyebrows raised. "Why's that?"

I shrug. "Robert doesn't do things halfway."

"I still don't see what he would have to gain by pulling such an elaborate stunt, Ms. Townsend. I mean, finding someone who looks like his dead son just to mess with your family. It seems a bit much."

Unlike his partner, there seems to be no accusation in Demarco's tone, just curiosity. When the imposter situation is laid out like this by an external person, it always makes me feel like I'm the crazy one. Hiring a man to play the part of a deceased son just for shits and giggles is insane. And for all of Robert's faults, he's shown no signs of being evil for the sake of it.

For business and power, yes. But for something like this?

The door opens again, and Whitely walks in, holding a manila folder. As he sits down, he flops it on the table and grins at me. Then he leans into his partner's ear, cups it with his hand, and whispers something indecipherable. When he's done, he sits back and opens the file.

"Ms. Townsend," Whitely says. "Our team has made some calls, and it seems like the hospital records—on both the second accident and the Michael Foster incident in Hagerstown—check out."

"I thought they might," I say.

"Right. The DNA results too. That is pretty powerful evidence, hmm? It would suggest that this Michael Foster really is Fletcher DuBose, right?"

"Look, I came to you about *Robert* DuBose," I say, losing my cool a bit. This rat-faced asshole knows how to push my buttons. I'll give him that. "This Fletcher nonsense just happens to be an unwelcome part of the situation."

"Yeah, well. About Robert DuBose," Whitely says, his grin growing. "It seems his lawyer—working on behalf of Mr. Du-

Bose—put in a restraining order on you a couple of days ago. It's only reached us now."

"A restraining order? On me!" I exclaim, genuinely shocked.

"Seems you've been following Mr. DuBose and his son."

"That's crazy," I say. I know I have been, but there is no way to prove it.

"Mr. DuBose's lawyer just sent these pictures to us, and I printed them out before I came back in. Some of them date back quite far, Ms. Townsend. You've been quite busy," Whitely says, his ever-growing grin seeming to touch both ears now.

He opens the manila folder he just carried in and takes out several large A4 photographs. I can already see myself in some of them—sitting in my car or on a bench across from Robert's office.

Demarco drops his gaze, his face turning red. I look back at Whitely, who nods once and says, "Maybe you would like to take a look?"

Part 3: Lilith & Virginia

Chapter 49: Lilith

"More wine?" Fletcher asks, smiling. His shaggy black hair has been slightly trimmed, and it frames his strong features nicely. The green eyes looking at me across the kitchen table show only friendliness.

I nod, and Fletcher tops my glass up. Drinking at one in the afternoon isn't something I usually do, but today it just feels right. Things between us have been going well these last few weeks, and today's lunch seems like a natural addition to that.

Since Mom left a month ago, Fletcher has tried his best to fill the hole left by her undeniable presence. He has been more concerned about it than I would have expected—he never liked my mother before—but he hasn't exactly been pushing me to reconcile. His thoughtfulness on the matter feels more like a duty than actual worry. If I'm being honest, getting to know him again has been a lot easier without Mom's interfering. I think deep down Fletcher feels the same way.

"So," he says, tipping his glass to mine. The salad he prepared is divine, and I continue to be shocked by his culinary skills, among other things. "What have we got planned for Astrid's eighteenth birthday? It's only a few weeks away."

"I've rented a room at Liuxin," I reply, sipping some wine. "It's her favorite restaurant."

"I don't know it," Fletcher says, then shrugs.

"Really? You used to love it there."

Fletcher blushes, and I feel bad. There is still so much he doesn't remember. All of the major events in our lives together—our wedding, vacations, job promotions—seem to have returned. But little things like this remain lost.

Or is it just the stuff concerning Astrid? I ask myself, then push the negative thought to the back of my mind where it belongs.

"Did I?" Fletcher asks, giving me a half-smile. "I'm sure I still will, then."

"Did you have something else in mind?"

Fletcher places his glass down on the table and links his hands under his chin. It's another of the gestures that he seems to have picked up in the twelve years when his name was Michael Foster.

"Rober... I mean, Dad," Fletcher comically slaps his forehead with the palm of his hand and chuckles. "*Dad* was thinking we could do it at his house."

"Really? Seems like a bit much."

"It's Astrid's eighteenth birthday, Lilith," Fletcher says, his voice a little sharp.

The old Fletcher hasn't shown himself fully since his return, but there have been a few occasions when the hint of a temper seems to bubble under the surface. Then again, every human being needs to get angry at times. I need to cut him some slack. He has been through so much, yet he often seems to be the one being strong for me.

"I know," I say, smiling. "I just mean that your father never showed that sort of interest before."

Fletcher sighs. He looks exhausted suddenly. "Listen, Loly. You say that sort of thing to me a lot, but Dad is trying, just like I am. People change, and with everything that happened that day on the river and the years that followed, of course we are going to feel differently about things."

"I get it," I say. When I reach my hand across the table and place it on his, he smiles. "I should be more considerate."

"So we can do it at Dad's place?"

"Whoa, whoa!" I exclaim, lifting my hands up in mock defense. "Slow down, cowboy. I'll think about it. How's that?"

Fletcher squints his eyes for a second, then he grins. "Sure. Maybe you should just leave it up to Astrid?"

"Maybe," I say, shrugging.

If Astrid had her way, there would be no money spent on her birthday at all. The idea of a show being made for her is already making her cringe, and that's when the plan was to have it in a down-to-earth restaurant like Liuxin. If she knew we were thinking about letting Robert throw his enormous checkbook at the event, then she would probably die of embarrassment.

I know I should consider it, though. Fletcher is back now and has been for a while. Things aren't perfect, but we're intimate again and spending a lot of time together. He seems a little off with Astrid at times, but she has been the same with him. Still, after his panic in the cafe at the beginning, when I said he couldn't see her, I'd expected him to be a bit more involved.

It's only been a month, I tell myself. *Give it some time.*

Fletcher starts talking about work, and I half-listen. His job with DuBose Construction appears to be going well, but he seems to have a lot of time off. There are also days when he leaves for work and I feel like he isn't actually going. Not many—maybe one a week—but that could also just be my old paranoia acting up. Fletcher was never the most trustworthy of men before his accident, and I think some of the old fears I had back then are still affecting me.

When my phone vibrates on the table next to me, Fletcher stops talking. I pull it closer to me and see that Mom is calling. It hurts me to do it, but I swipe the red icon to cut her off.

"Who was it?" Fletcher asks.

"Nobody," I say, nodding for him to go on with the retelling of his workday. "It was nobody."

Chapter 50: Virginia

The phone only rings twice, and then it's cut off. I curse to myself and stuff it back into my jeans pocket. I'm standing on the steps outside the police station on West Broadway and Fifth, and I feel like I've been kicked in the stomach. The words of Officer Whitely are still ringing in my ears. I can't believe what he just told me.

Robert DuBose has a restraining order on *me*! The arrogance of the man, after everything he's done over the years. And that's the thing, isn't it? He had been gathering photos of me following him long before this Michael Foster person showed up. Why would he have been doing such a thing? How come he has waited until now to kick up a stink about me watching him?

I pull my battered pack of Pall Malls from my handbag and light one up. The early afternoon sky is a pale blue that is almost gray. I can hear seagulls as they drift around above, looking for scraps, apparently not full from the slim pickings in Boston Harbor. I put my sunglasses on despite the lack of brightness, and the relative anonymity they bring comes as a surprising relief.

I hadn't expected Lilith to answer the phone—she never does anymore—but I'd hoped she would. She needs to know what is happening, and I have to tell her what Robert has just done.

"Oh, God," I say, my hand gripping my stomach as I feel it lurch. "That sneaky bastard."

Lilith probably already knows. I can picture Robert showing up at her door, cap in hand, as he bows his head and tells her how he tried everything he could to settle things with me amicably, but there was just no hope. He was simply left with no other option than to get a restraining order.

She just wouldn't leave me alone, he'll tell her, his voice as smooth as silk. *Look at these, Lilith. I had my private detective take these photos. Some of them date back as far as seventeen or eighteen years ago, Lilith. Virginia has never trusted me. She was stalking me even before Fletcher's accident.*

I feel like I might throw up right here on the steps of the police station. A man walks past, holding an unopened umbrella, and creases his brow. It looks for a moment like he might stop and ask me if I'm okay, then he quickens his pace and pushes on through the spattering of people on the sidewalk.

So, *I* was being followed while I followed *him*. Is that how it was? Surely it couldn't have been that serious? There had only been a handful of pictures, and they were spread out over a long period of time. Maybe Robert always has someone watching his back, making sure nobody is planning to do the big man any harm, and I just happened to stumble my way into the surveillance. If that's the case, then Robert DuBose wields a hell of a lot more power than I initially thought he did. And if this is true, then he is far more dangerous than I ever could have imagined.

Somehow I get myself moving, my cigarette burning away as I walk down the street toward my car. I stub it out under my boot and take another out of the pack, lighting it and sucking hard before blowing a thick plume of smoke into the crisp air. The people who pass me are faceless, as unimportant as the seagulls that continue to squawk above. They have their own problems, I'm sure, but could any of them be as in shock as I am at this very moment?

A thought suddenly makes my heart jump: What if there is someone across the street taking pictures of me right now? My whole body shudders, and I feel violated in a way I'd never known possible.

So it was okay when you did it, Ginny?

"I never took photos," I grumble out the side of my mouth like the world's angriest ventriloquist.

Ah, that makes it okay then, my mind mocks.

I know this part of me is right. What I did was just as bad, but I tailed Robert because I knew he did bad things. He had me followed because he wanted to make me look bad. And why? I must have been getting close to something; that's why.

Once I'm in my car with the door closed and the windows up, I feel a little better. Cars slowly drift past on my right, and people wander by on foot to my left. Any one of them could be Robert's guy, and the thought makes me shiver again.

If he had only been having me watched since Michael Foster came back into the picture, then I'd feel somewhat better about things. But he has been keeping an eye on me for a lot longer than that. Did it start when Wally was killed? Or was it before even then? I can't imagine it being the latter, as it makes no sense.

Before I know what I'm doing, I pull up Lilith's name again and hit call. Once more, it gets cut off before the third ring. I could try Astrid, but she'll still be in school. As much as I've wanted to keep her out of the messier side of what's happening, I know I can't do that anymore. She is probably in as much danger as her mother and me. I need to sit her down and explain the bits that I can. Not everything, but enough so that she keeps her head on a swivel.

As I idly scroll down through my call list, I see the strange number Robert called me from yesterday when John was missing. I'm sure it was a phone that was used once and then dumped, but maybe it wasn't? The restraining order declared that I had to stay at least two hundred yards away from him at all times, but it also stated that phone calls came under the same category. Am I falling into his trap already if I hit dial? Probably, but the temptation is hard to resist.

Strangely enough, it's not fear holding me back. I'm still terrified of everything he can do to my family, but something has shifted now that he is playing out in the open. This restraining order has shown me that he is taking real action, and it is all part of a larger game. He has a much greater advantage over me, and I'm sure Lilith will be leaning toward the my-mother-is-crazy angle Robert is playing. Regardless, I need to fight back. Calling him now will do nothing for me, and it will just give him more ammunition.

I've never had his actual number; I never needed it. When I think of Lilith having the name JERK pop up on her screen whenever Robert decides to call, I smile. Instead of making me feel better, the action of smiling saddens me. All it does is remind me how bad everything has become.

I crush my cigarette out and toss the phone on the dash. Calling anyone right now—even Lilith—will be counterproductive. I need to regroup and strategize. If Robert is going to play dirty, then I need to step things up and come at him from a different perspective.

The engine of the Ford purrs to life, and I swing it out into the afternoon traffic. Amazingly, I suddenly feel a little better now that I've made some solid decisions. There is a long way to go, but Robert DuBose better know that he has messed with the wrong woman.

Chapter 51: Lilith

"Hello, Gemma," I say after answering the phone. Gemma Travers is the Levinson High principal and one of the only other faculty members at the school who seems to care as much as I do about the students' education. I like her a lot, but her calling me at home—especially at night—is strange. "Is everything okay?"

Through the living room window, I can see that the dark sky is cloudy. A full moon has lit up the trees in our front yard, and they look silver as they shine against the darkness. I can hear the faint sound of music from upstairs as Astrid listens to some band or other. Fletcher went back to his apartment an hour ago, and I have to admit I was glad when he did. My growing feelings for him are getting harder to deny, but they can weigh heavy on me too.

Having him back has been nice, but it's also been the most confusing time in my life. I have to keep reminding myself that my strongest emotion when I heard he had died on the Gauley River twelve years ago was relief. If he had simply left me back then and returned after so long, would I have been expected to welcome him back with open arms? No, I wouldn't. But this Fletcher is so different from the man who made my life a living hell so often in the past.

Of course he is the same man underneath it all, but maybe that is where the problem lies. Perhaps I need him to take responsibility for the things he did before I can forgive him fully for them and we can move on together. It still feels like he has dodged accountability.

"Did you hear what I said?" Gemma Travers asks.

"I'm sorry, Gemma. What was that?"

"I said I'm sorry for calling so late. Is everything okay, Lilith? You sound a bit off?"

"I'm fine," I tell her, smiling to myself. Then I clear my throat. "My mind just drifted, that's all. What can I do for you, Gemma?"

"As I said, I'm sorry for calling so late, but something has come up," Gemma says, her voice suddenly all business. "Mr. Hankwell has had another incident."

Gemma drags out the last word, and I can almost hear her making air quotes. Gerry Hankwell is one of two full-time English Lit teachers at Levinson. He has been on and off the wagon for years, apparently. I've smelled booze off his breath a couple of times in the faculty lounge and had it out with him once. I pity anyone suffering from addiction, but when it could cause harm to young students, I don't believe in dancing around the subject.

When Gemma says "incident," she surely means that he has either been kicked out of his home again or checked himself into Cherryview Rehab Center for the umpteenth time.

"Is he okay?" I ask, genuinely concerned. As annoyed as I was the time he came in to work tipsy, I know he has an illness.

"Not this time," she says. "He quit."

"Drink or work?"

"Both, I think. He called me in floods of tears. He's admitted he has a problem and that he needs to get himself well before he can ever even consider teaching again," Gemma says. To her credit, she sounds sympathetic toward the man.

"That's admirable," I say and mean it.

"Sure, but I don't think he'll make it back to a classroom. He's only a few years away from retirement as it is."

"I guess."

I'm wondering why Gemma is calling me about this at eight-forty-five in the evening. Although, she did say that Gerry had just called her, so maybe she is only off the phone with him and wanted someone to talk to about it. Still, we've never even chatted outside of the school gates. Does she have nobody else to talk to?

I can understand that. Ever since Mom moved out, I've realized how few friends I really have. Maybe if I'd had people close to me, I could have discussed everything that has been happening to me and I wouldn't be so confused all the time. It's been tough to figure it all out on my own. Astrid tries to help, but I don't like dumping all of it on her when she is in her final year of high school. She has enough to worry about with exams and everything else. Also, I don't think she is very fond of her father. At least not this version of him.

"Anyway," Gemma says after a moment's pause. "I'm calling because I wanted to offer you the full-time position he has vacated. I know this is sudden and quite unprofessional of me to call you about it at this time of night, but I thought I'd get a head start."

"Oh, wow. That *is* a surprise."

"You don't have to answer this second, of course. But if you could have a think about it tonight, perhaps?"

"Sure," I say, nodding. "I'll think about it, Gemma."

"Okay, well, I'll leave you to it," she says. Is there disappointment in her tone? Did she actually expect me to give her an answer right away? I hear a ruffling sound as she presumably switches the phone to her other ear. "Oh, and Lilith."

"Yes?"

"It goes without saying that what I told you about Gerry stays between us, yes?"

"Of course, Gemma," I tell her.

We say our goodbyes, and I hang up. I can still hear music coming from Astrid's room, but it seems even lower now. As I move out into the hall, I already find myself leaning toward taking the position at Levinson. Some of the students there have shown real promise, and Astrid will be off to college next year. With Mom living in town, I'll have plenty of free time.

What about your husband?

Right, of course. Anyway, our marriage was annulled when he was declared dead, so technically, he is just, what? My boyfriend? Ex-husband?

As I ascend the stairs, I switch my thoughts back to the job offer. I know for certain that Astrid will tell me to go for it. She understands how much I love teaching and how badly I've missed doing it full time. Still, it would be nice to discuss it with her.

Her bedroom door is open a crack, and as I approach, I hear the faintest sound of Robert Smith warbling about a giant spiderman that comes to him in the evening time. I loved The

Cure when I was Astrid's age, and I smile at yet another similarity the two of us share.

The music is down low, so when Astrid speaks on the other side of the opened door, it comes through pretty clearly.

"Okay, I will," she says. There is a pause as whoever is presumably on the other end of the phone speaks. "I won't say anything. I promise, Nana."

Chapter 52: Virginia

"Just keep an eye on things," I tell Astrid. I can hear light music in the background on the other end of the line. It sounds like The Cure.

"Okay, I will."

I smile at my granddaughter's maturity. She is all of Lilith and my best qualities rolled into one. I hadn't wanted to fill her in on my fears that Robert is up to something, but I've called Lilith a few times today, and she won't pick up. On top of that, she isn't even reading the texts I'm sending.

"You'll have to keep this to yourself until I've spoken with your mother, okay?" I say, the guilt eating me alive as I speak. I hate going behind my daughter's back, but things have become far too serious for pussyfooting around. "I'll call on her tomorrow, and we can talk it out face-to-face. Until then, this is just between you and me."

"I won't say anything. I promise, Nana," Astrid says. I can tell she is smiling through the phone.

There is a ruffling sound as Astrid presumably presses the mouthpiece against her sweater or something. I can hear muffled words that I can't make out, then the phone moves again, and it's clearer.

"... not to talk to her, Astrid," a voice I know is Lilith's says.

"Ma, she is my grandmother," Astrid counters. "You can't stop me from talking to her."

"Hang up the phone," Lilith commands.

"Why are you being like this?"

"Just hang up the—"

The line goes dead, and I sit at the kitchen table with my mouth hanging open. Leaving it until tomorrow to talk to Lilith isn't an option. For all I know, she will be straight on the phone to Fletcher after having it out with Astrid, and I know how that conversation will go. He will play the innocent card right out of the gates. Then he will tell her that he doesn't want to come between her and her mother and say, "but if you want my opinion, Loly..."

Fletcher was always able to turn Lilith's head.

"That's not Fletcher," I growl, shaking my head as I stand up and make my way into the bedroom.

I change out of my faded sweats, replacing them with a white zip-up hoodie and baggy beige pants. That done, I run a brush through my hair and quickly tie it up. My jacket is hanging on a hook by the front door, and I throw it on as I grab my car keys. My foot is halfway out of the apartment when my mind goes to all of the unlocked windows and back door.

It's probably my paranoia talking, but if Robert is willing to have someone snap photos of me over such a long period of time, then he would have no qualms with hiring someone to come into my home. They wouldn't find much here, but who knows what they could plant.

"Yep. Definitely paranoia," I mutter as I rush around the apartment regardless, double-checking windows and doors. When I'm satisfied, I clap my hands together and say, "Let's do this."

The street outside my building is eerily quiet. Only one man shuffles along the sidewalk across the way. His dog stops and sniffs the air for a second, then points its tail up and continues on its way. Several cars are parked on both sides of the street, and I instinctively check if one of them is a white Coupe. None are, but the glare of the streetlights makes it impossible for me to see if anyone is sitting inside the vehicles I do see.

It doesn't matter. If Robert is having me followed, then so be it. There is nothing I can really do about it. All that matters now is getting to Lilith's house and trying to get through to her. Astrid seemed to be in the process of doing the same thing when she hung up, so maybe Lilith will see sense if it is coming from the two of us.

When I get to my car, I take one last look around the empty street. Nothing stirs, and I climb in and start her up. As I edge the Ford out, I start to go through everything that I'm going to say to Lilith—*if* she will hear me out. Or, more to the point, everything I can say to her without having to mention a couple of very serious points.

Will I have to tell her about her father? I don't want to, but maybe it will be the only way. If she knows he was into running the books for Robert's illegal gambling ring, then she will at least know that the DuBoses aren't above board. I'm sure she knows this already, but Lilith has always had a way of burying her head in the sand when it comes to that sort of thing.

The clock on the dash tells me that it's 20:13. Lilith's house is just over ten minutes away. If I hurry, I'll be there in five.

Putting my foot down, I ignore that twinge inside me that says I'm driving much too fast. If Lilith gets in contact with

Fletcher—or worse, Robert—they will have convinced her I'm crazy before I've even pulled into her driveway.

What if they told her about the restraining order already? How bad will that make me look?

The cautionary part of me niggles at my insides as my foot pushes down on the gas again. I ignore it as the lights outside my windows whiz by at alarming speed. I need to get to my daughter as soon as I can. She needs to know the truth. Maybe not the whole truth, but enough to bring her back around to something bordering on reasonable.

"I'm coming, baby," I say through clenched teeth as the car rattles under the strain of the speed it's being forced to endure. "Mom's coming."

Chapter 53: Lilith

"Come on, Ma," Astrid snaps. Her wholesome, pretty face is screwed up. I don't think I've seen her like this since she was a little girl and I wouldn't let her walk to school on her own. She puts one hand on her hip as she looks at me and tosses her phone onto the bed. The low hum of The Cure has been replaced by the intricate guitars of Led Zeppelin. "This is getting ridiculous."

"What is?" I ask, knowing the answer. I never thought I'd be the type of mother who stops their kid from seeing someone simply because *I* have an issue with them. Yet here I am.

"It's unfair of you to tell me not to see Nana. If you have a problem with her, then that's exactly what it is—*your* problem."

"Nana isn't thinking straight lately," I say. "She is paranoid and aggressive."

"Aggressive!" Astrid exclaims, screwing her face up even more. "She tried to take your glasses off. She wanted to see if Fletcher had—"

"How do you know about that?" I snap.

"How do you think, Ma? Did you really think I wouldn't see her just because you told me not to?"

"I thought you might take my side, yes," I tell her, hating the petulance in my voice.

"Taking sides? Unbelievable." Astrid shakes her head. "This isn't a game, Ma. This is a man who has been missing for twelve years waltzing back into our lives. This is a man that used to hit you."

"That was the old Fletcher," I say. "He's changed."

"They could stick that phrase on a flyer for abused women who keep going back to their husbands," Astrid growls.

"That hurts, Astrid."

"Yeah, well. I'm sorry if it does." She looks me up and down, then shakes her head. "Did you ever think to ask me about all of this?"

"I did ask you."

"Right," Astrid scoffs. "When you had already been seeing him for a couple of weeks. Did you think I'd object when you came to me all doe-eyed and asked if I'd be okay if he spent some time around here? You had already made up your mind, Ma."

"He's my *husband*, Astrid," I plead. "He's your father."

"Is he?" she snaps.

"What?"

"Is he really my father? I don't feel it. And he certainly doesn't. To me, he is just some guy who looks a little like the man who left us twelve years ago."

This is crazy. Where is this coming from? Has Astrid really felt this way the whole time?

Would you have noticed if she did, Lilith? She isn't wrong when she says you came to her with love in your eyes, talking about your husband and second chances at life. Didn't you even use the word "miracle"? Yep, you did. What kind of a person would shoot down their mother's hopes and dreams after they used a word like that?

"He needs time," I tell her. "We all do. This isn't a normal situation."

"Where does he go, Ma?" Astrid says. Her tone has softened, but she sounds like she is explaining something simple to a child who just can't grasp it. "You must see those times when he gets a text or a call, and then he suddenly has to go out for a few hours. Where does he go?"

"He has to work, Astrid," I tell her. Or am I telling myself?

"Even on a Sunday?" Astrid scoffs.

"What are you getting at?"

"What do you think?"

"I think you're trying to stir up trouble where there isn't any," I growl, my indignation at her secret calls to Mom coming back to me. What else have they discussed? Do they just sit around laughing about what an idiot I am, snickering at the sucker who took back her abusive husband?

I point my finger at Astrid, and I'm surprised when it is steady. "If you and your grandmother were in the same situation, I would be supportive."

"Really?" Astrid exclaims, shaking her head. "You would want me to go back to a wife-beating husband?"

All my strength and anger disappear in an instant. For a moment, I feel like I might faint. Astrid's words hit me like a steam train. The sheer disgust in her voice hurts like nothing I've ever experienced. I can see the pure disappointment on her face. Not only is she mortified by my apparent acceptance of marital abuse, but I've also unwittingly admitted that I would encourage her to go back to a violent man if she was in that situation.

Is that really what I've just said? In a way, I suppose I have. That's the example I'm setting. By tolerating it back then and forgiving Fletcher now, I'm telling the world that what happened is okay.

But doesn't everyone deserve a second chance? Hasn't Fletcher been a different person since he came back?

Maybe he is a different person altogether?

I shake my head. No, not again. I've worked all this out already. There was DNA evidence, for God's sake.

Oh, that's right. You physically went to the hospital and confirmed it, right?

"Look, Ma," Astrid says, sighing. "I'm sorry you walked in on me talking to Nana. I should have told you before, and that's on me. But I'm going to keep doing it because I love her, and this is *your* argument. Also, I think you really need to hear her out."

"No."

Astrid throws up her arms in exasperation. "Okay, well, there seems to be no way to get through to you." She walks over to the speakers and turns them off. Then she sits at her desk and looks up at me. "Ma. Ask Fletcher who Kelley is. If he explains his way out of that, then we'll talk."

"Kelley?" I ask. My head is spinning. So much has been thrown at me in the last five minutes. "Who is Kelle—"

The loud shriek of the doorbell interrupts me, and Astrid jumps up and makes her way down the stairs before I can finish.

Chapter 54: Virginia

Astrid has already invited me in, and I'm standing in the hallway when Lilith appears at the top of the stairs. As she marches down them toward us, she looks several years older than the last time I saw her. Whether she'll admit it or not, everything that has happened is grinding her down too.

"Please, Mom," Lilith says to me as she reaches the bottom step. "You need to leave. This isn't a good time."

"There has never been a better time," Astrid cuts in. She is standing next to me as we both face Lilith, who is only five feet away. "We're all in this together."

"No," Lilith snaps. She is staring at me as she speaks. "We're not."

I take a step forward, and my heart sinks when Lilith takes one back. Is she still shaken up about what happened at the gas station? Surely she has realized it was a misunderstanding.

"Listen, Lilith," I say, stopping where I am before she backs up more. "We all really need to sit down and talk."

"You two have done enough talking," she snaps, and I see Astrid roll her eyes.

"We have just been keeping in touch," I tell her. "Nothing more."

"Sure, and gossiping about me. Isn't that right?"

"Ma, seriously," Astrid says. "You need to see sense."

"You've caused enough trouble," Lilith snaps, looking at Astrid for the first time.

I turn to my granddaughter. "Did I miss something?"

Astrid shrugs. "I told her about Kelley."

"Oh."

"Yes, " Lilith growls. "*Oh.*"

I spin back around to face Lilith, who is shaking with either anger or fear. Anger in her eyes that she is being teamed up on and fear that her husband is having an affair. At least, that is what it feels like to me. I realize now that I don't even know what they discussed about the Kelley matter.

"Has Micha—"

"Still can't say his real name, I see," Lilith interrupts.

"—Fletcher, then. Has Fletcher explained who this Kelley is?"

"Have you not done a bit of digging?" Lilith scoffs, and I know that Fletcher or Robert has told her about the restraining order. Then she says, "I can't imagine you heard something like that and let it be."

Maybe she hasn't heard yet, then. Keeping it in the holster, Robert, huh?

"I didn't check anything," I tell her, which is the truth.

"Neither did I," Astrid adds.

Lilith sighs loudly and drops her head. Under any other circumstances, I would already be hugging her so tightly that her eyes would pop out. But these aren't ordinary circumstances, and I know I need to tread carefully with her.

"Who is she?" Lilith asks.

"We don't know," Astrid says, putting a hand on my arm as she steps forward.

"How much do you know?" I ask. Then I turn to Astrid. "What exactly did you tell her?"

"Just the name," Astrid says. "Then you came to the door."

"To be honest, Lilith," I say. "That's all we have anyway. Astrid heard Michael... sorry, Fletcher—talking on the phone. When he was saying his goodbyes, he said, 'I love you, Kelley.'"

Lilith lets out a low groan, and this time I do step forward and hug her. She allows me to hold her for a moment, then steps back sharply. She shakes her head, and I can see her eyes have become red. Behind her, family photos adorn the walls of the hallway, images of the three of us at different stages of our life playing out against the flawless cream paint.

Astrid steps by me and takes over the hug that had been cut short. This time, Lilith doesn't fight back.

"Does the name mean anything to you, Ma?" Lilith asks. Astrid is the same height as her mother, and I'm hit with that familiar feeling of time having passed too quickly. Lilith shakes her head in her daughter's embrace, and Astrid says, "Okay. You believe me when I say I heard him say it, though, don't you?"

Lilith nods, then steps away, wiping her eyes. When she looks at me, her expression changes to one of stone-cold aggression. "This must make you happy?"

"What?"

"You never liked Fletcher, and now you have another stick to beat him with," Lilith spits.

"It's Robert that I never trusted, Lilith, and you know this," I snap. Then I shrug. "But if you want the truth, I never liked Fletcher either. I was glad when he died."

Lilith shakes her head. Her voice is filled with venom as she spits her words at me. "You bitter old woman."

Again, I shrug. I know it's a passive-aggressive gesture, but I can't help myself. Lilith is behaving like a spoiled child, and it is starting to get to me.

"Ma," Astrid says. "Will you just hear her out?"

"There is nothing to hear," Lilith snaps, turning to her daughter. "Your grandmother has always interfered with my relationship. And this is no diff—"

"OH, OPEN YOUR EYES, LILITH!" I shout, making both of them jump. It takes everything I have to lower my voice, but it's still quite loud when I continue. "The DuBoses are criminals—always have been."

"How can you be so sure?" Lilith barks. "You've always acted like you know more than anyone else on the subject. What could they have possibly done to make you hate them so much?"

I take a deep breath and let it out slowly. I look at Astrid and mouth the words, "I'm sorry." Then I step up next to my daughter and say, "Because I'm certain that Robert killed your father, sweetie."

Chapter 55: Lilith

I'm still in shock, even though Mom left over two hours ago, and I've had all this time to think about things. After her bombshell, the three of us somehow ended up sitting at the kitchen table for nearly three hours, talking about her suspicions regarding Robert. Some of it made sense, but a lot of it seems very far-fetched.

If this Enrico Suarez she kept mentioning is telling the truth, then my father was into a lot of illegal stuff with Robert. I can believe it simply because there would be no reason for him or my mother to make that part up. There would be other ways for her to convince me Robert is a dangerous man without tarnishing the memory of my father and her loving husband in the process.

The temptation to call Fletcher has been strong, but I've fought it away so far. Anyhow, it's after two in the morning now, so he would surely be asleep. I want to find out who this Lucy person is, but I don't want to at the same time. Saying "I love you" can only mean one thing, and Astrid seemed so positive that is what he had said on the phone. Why would she lie? To back up my mother? No, not Astrid. She is honesty personified.

So, what does it all mean, then? Is Fletcher cheating already? Was he in a relationship when he was Michael Foster and just hasn't broken it off yet? Is he even who he says he is?

At least Mom didn't push that side of things this time. Her need to insist that Michael Foster is an imposter seems to have faded. She seemed to genuinely be more interested in Robert. When she told me she had suspected his involvement in my father's death throughout my whole courtship with Fletcher, I nearly broke down in tears for a second time.

How did she carry that with her all that time and still support me as if nothing had happened? It must have taken a monumental effort. I know my mother, and she loves to speak her mind. Keeping something like that to herself while we had family functions and outings with Fletcher must have killed her, yet she did. Why? So I wouldn't have to carry the burden, simple as that. She wanted to have solid proof before she made waves.

I've been tossing and turning since I came up to bed over an hour ago, and I'm no closer to sleep. I kick the covers off and stand up, stubbing my toe on the nightstand as I do. Hissing through my teeth, I half-hop to the bathroom and look at myself in the mirror. The woman staring back looks beyond tired, which makes the lack of sleepiness I'm feeling all the more frustrating.

With the pain in my toe spreading up through my foot, I limp out of the bedroom and down the hall. Astrid's door is partially open, and I pop my head in and check on her. She is sound asleep, and the preciousness of my little girl makes me smile despite how shitty I feel.

I step quietly back from the bedroom—wincing as the pain in my toe flares up—and make my way down the stairs. Maybe some warm milk and a book will help me drift off, but I doubt it. I don't think I've ever been so confused, scared, worried, and hurt in my life. Powerful emotions, all. And none of them are good, even on their own.

Sending Mom back to her apartment tonight felt wrong, but I'm not ready to open up my home to her again just yet. She explained what she was doing when she knocked my sunglasses off at the gas station, and it made sense. If I'm being honest, I had come to that conclusion by the time I had driven home that day. Still, the manner in which she went about it had been very aggressive.

Wouldn't I do the same to Astrid if I thought she was concealing a black eye?

Really. You would want me to go back to a wife-beater? Astrid's words come back to me, and I shiver. She was right to be so blunt. At the end of the day, I was basically defending domestic abuse. Of course, it's easy for those on the outside looking in to make snap judgments. It's not their marriage they're trying to salvage, after all. But Astrid is a modern woman, and she sees such things for what they really are—unacceptable.

I've always considered myself a modern woman too. At least until the first time I lied for Fletcher, that is. That moment had come a couple of years into our dating, on one of Mom's visits to our old apartment.

"She won't understand the things I have to deal with, Loly," Fletcher had crooned as he tenderly wrapped a bandage around the dark blueish-pink bruise that ran all the way up my bicep. "She'll think I did this on purpose."

And I had worn the long-sleeve sweater he'd picked out of the closet, even though it was a painfully hot day. I'd covered the bandage and smiled as Mom looked at me quizzically, clearly knowing something wasn't right. The same woman who I kicked out of her home because she questioned a very questionable situation.

I pour some milk into a saucepan and put it on the stove. As it slowly heats up, I sit at the kitchen table. Through the window, I can see only stars. No moon tonight.

My thoughts won't seem to settle on one issue, but that's probably because there are so many problems in my life right now. Mom seems to think that we can get through it if we all stick together, but I'm not so sure. How can I be when I don't even know what I want? I still love Fletcher. And he is Astrid's father, even if he is struggling to find the feelings for her that he used to have.

We need to give him time, that's all.

I love you, Lucy; that's what Astrid told me she heard him say. Why? Why would he be seeing someone else? Why would he come back if he loved another woman? Maybe Astrid misheard? They haven't seen how much Fletcher has changed.

They could stick that phrase on a flyer for abused women who keep going back to their husbands.

"How has it gotten to this?" I ask the empty kitchen.

A sharp hiss snaps me out of my thoughts, followed by the pungent smell of burning milk. I jump up and grab the pot, scalding myself on the milk that's bubbling over the side. The pain in my hand instantly combines with the throbbing in my toe, and I realize that I'm crying again.

I need answers to the endless questions running through my head, and the only person who can give them to me is Fletcher.

Chapter 56: Virginia

It went better with Lilith than I had expected, but she is very clearly in love with Michael Foster. I had started to look at our situation as if we were forever falling out or were never close, but the opposite of that is true. I'm as close to my daughter as any mother could be, and vice versa. We've always had a strong bond, and one silly argument over a month ago isn't going to change that.

Still, I know time is of the essence, and I need her to come around faster. What Robert has planned, I don't know, but I feel it is something nasty. He wouldn't have gone to this much trouble otherwise.

The buzzer in the hallway goes off, and I stand up and walk over to the receiver on the wall. When I pick it up, Astrid says, "I'm here."

"Come on up," I reply, pressing the button to release the main door downstairs.

My apartment is spotlessly tidy, but I find myself giving one last frantic look around to be sure as Astrid comes up the stairs. I'm generally not superficial like that, but this is the first time she has been here. Besides Reece, it's the first time *anyone* else has been here. I want her to feel like I'm doing okay, or she'll worry.

I know that sort of thing should be beneath me, but I've built my whole persona around being a brave woman—the protector. I didn't have a choice. Wally was taken away when Lilith was only a teenager, and that coincided with my daughter getting involved with Fletcher DuBose. When Astrid was born, my role as head of the family was cemented. It wasn't a position I chose, but one that was given to me by circumstance.

Astrid steps through the front door. I can see her from the kitchen/living room area at the end of the short hall. She smiles as she walks toward me, and I see Lilith in her. After a long embrace, we sit at the kitchen table.

"Yesterday was something, huh?" Astrid says, giving me that smile again.

"Sure was," I agree, nodding.

We decided through text after I left last night to meet at my place at noon the following day, and here we are. Outside, the day is muggy, and it seems to fit with how claustrophobic and penned-in I feel. Even with the windows open, dead heat hangs above the kitchen table.

I watch as Astrid places her bag on her lap and starts digging through it. She pulls out a small notepad, a pen, and her glasses. She pops the last of them on, picks up the pen, and says, "Let's look at the facts, Nana."

I chuckle softly, and Astrid creases her brow. Through snorts of amusement, I say, "I'm sorry. You're just amazing."

"Quit it!" Astrid scoffs, but she is smiling again.

"Okay," I say, nodding at the pad. "Let's get down to business."

"What do we know as fact?" Astrid asks.

I feel my mood dampening. This has been the big issue for me all along. Almost everything that I suspect is nothing more than a gut feeling, even Wally's and John's deaths. Okay, I'm certain that they were killed, but that means nothing until there is proof. I know for sure that the man claiming to be Fletcher is lying, but I can't prove that, either. I can tell them *why* I know this, but they will either think I'm insane or lying.

Why would someone lie about such a thing, Ginny?

I shake my head and point at the pad. "What do you think, Astrid?"

"I think you're telling the truth, Nana."

"About which parts?"

"All of it."

The urge to break down in tears is overwhelming, but I manage to keep my composure. I'd had no idea how much the thought of nobody—especially my family—believing me had been weighing me down.

"Thanks," I say after taking a moment to gather myself. "Really."

"You're welcome, Nana." Astrid reaches her hand across the table and squeezes mine once. It is reassuring, and I can see in that instant what an incredible person she is and will be. "Now, let's start with granddad."

"Robert? There is so much, but my biggest fear is that the worst of it is unknown to us."

Astrid nods. "Okay. What about this Enrico guy? You said he was adamant he would deny everything he said?"

"Yep. Even if he were willing to come forward, it would all be dismissed as hearsay or just bitterness because he lost his job."

"His wife?" Astrid asks. "What about her? He said she had been harassed."

"I thought about that, but she was terrified by the whole experience. And I wouldn't drag her back into it," I say. "We probably wouldn't be able to find her, anyhow."

"Sure, I understand, Nana." Astrid jots something down on her pad, then places the pen down and looks back up at me. "I don't think we're going to get anything from the past that will prove what Robert did."

"I know," I reply, shaking my head. I think I've always known, but the instant dismissal of it by an external person seems to have hammered it home. And not softly, either.

Astrid sits back in her chair and drapes her arms over the sides like she is some stereotypical misogynist businessman in the 1920s who just patted his secretary's ass as she passed by.

"What?" I ask, mildly amused at her change in demeanor.

She grins at me. "We gotta double up on the surveillance."

Chapter 57: Lilith

"She said what?" Fletcher snaps, and I feel my whole body tensing up. Instinctively, I find myself scanning the living room for the quickest way to escape without getting too close to him. "Why would Astrid make that up?"

"What?" I ask. His reaction has surprised me as much as it has frightened me. I thought he might get defensive when I asked him about Kelley, but I didn't think he'd claim my daughter made it up.

Fletcher nods slowly. "It makes sense, I suppose. She's confused, and she never wanted me back. Things must have been easier when she had her mommy all to herself."

"That's ridiculous. She's not a ten-year-old," I snap, then cringe back into my seat when he glares at me.

I hate myself for feeling this way. I swore I would never retreat back into the person I used to be, but one stern look from Fletcher and my mind instantly started to look for things to say that would placate him. It's weak and pathetic, and it makes me feel useless.

"I know what age she is, Lilith," Fletcher says. Amazingly, it sounds like some calmness has come into his voice. I don't think I've ever seen him fight his anger away so quickly. At least not in the years before his accident. He tries to smile at me, and my heart melts. "I'm just confused. Why would she say such a thing?"

His piercing green eyes seem to look right into my soul, and his crooked smile somehow manages to take control of my stomach and make it flutter.

Maybe Astrid did mishear? Or perhaps she made it up as Fletcher said? It's not that far-fetched to think that a teenage girl would get jealous of her mother spending time with someone, is it? It happens all the time, and Astrid *is* only seventeen. Sometimes because of her maturity, I see her as older.

No, I won't go down that road. Astrid would never do something like that. How the hell am I thinking such things?

Fletcher gives me another half-smile, and I get my answer.

"She wouldn't make it up," I say, sitting up straighter in my chair.

"I should never have done this," Fletcher says, shaking his head. His freshly trimmed hair ruffles in the afternoon light spilling through the large front window.

"What?"

He continues to move his head slowly from side to side. "It was never going to work. Why did I listen?"

"Listen to who?" I ask. "Fletcher? Listen to who?"

"Hmm?" he replies. He looks like a boxer who just got sucker-punched in the jaw, and he's trying to remember where he is. "Oh. Why did I listen to myself? I should have ignored the memories when they tried to come back."

"Don't say that, Fletcher."

"It's true," he continues. "There is too much risk involved. I should have listened to my instinct and made a run for it when I could."

I go to plead with him and stop myself. This is another classic Fletcher tactic from back in the day. Usually, this happened when he wanted me to cover up his actions from the previous night or when he came home in the early hours smelling of perfume. He played this game—the passive-aggressive guilt game.

"We're not talking about that right now, Fletcher," I say. "I'm asking you who Kelley is."

"There *is* no Kelley," he tells me without making eye contact. "Astrid misheard."

"Which part?"

"What?"

"The name or the 'I love you' bit?"

"Both."

A heavy silence falls on us, and it's not the muggy air coming through the slightly opened window. I love my husband, but I need to figure out exactly what type of love it is that I'm feeling. Is it the surge of adrenaline I got when I was sixteen and his beautiful good looks won me over the second he winked at me? Is it the everlasting type that I used to convince myself we had in the mornings following one of his more aggressive outbursts? Or is it a hopeful one—the kind we all cling to when we know the relationship has nothing else to keep it afloat?

It could be any of those and more. One thing is for sure, though: There is some kind of love there. And it is different from any of the feelings I felt or thought I felt twelve years ago. Why? Because the guy sitting on the armchair across from me is a more loving man than he ever was. I feel it in him every time we're together.

"Please, Fletcher," I say. "You need to be honest with me if we're going to make this work. Do you want this to work?"

"It can't," he almost whines.

"Why not?"

"There are too many complications. This isn't the love you think it is, Lilith."

"That doesn't make sense."

"Maybe none of it makes sense," Fletcher says, shrugging. "Maybe it's not supposed to."

"Do you love me, Fletcher?" I ask, suddenly terrified at what the answer might be.

He stands up and walks over to me, then leans down and kisses me on both cheeks.

"Of course I do," Fletcher says. His eyes look like emeralds in the light. "More than I ever thought possible."

Chapter 58: Virginia

Getting Astrid involved too deeply in this is not an option, but she is strong-willed and stubborn. After much deliberation, we agreed that for her to keep an eye on Fletcher, all she had to do was continue her life as she had been. He is spending more and more time at Lilith's house, and Astrid already lives there. She just needs to be more vigilant around him and stay alert.

I insist that she pull in the reins the second it seems like he might be getting suspicious. Astrid agreed, but I'm sure my words went in one ear and out the other. Still, I'm hoping she will be able to sense any danger before it gets too serious.

All of this means that I'll be keeping a close eye on Robert again. It's going to be hard, as I know he is having me watched. Also, he has that restraining order on me. Astrid had been shocked to hear about that, but luckily I'd already told her about following him before then. She agrees it is best not to tell Lilith just yet, as it looks bad. I hate keeping it from her, and I'm actually surprised Fletcher or Robert haven't said it to her yet.

Yesterday with Astrid was one of the most amazing days of my life. I know that sounds crazy, given the things we are dealing with, but our already rock-solid relationship has become so much stronger. I could feel it the whole way through our discussion in the kitchen. I suppose that such bizarre—and yes, dangerous—situations create these impenetrable bonds. It must be the same for soldiers going into battle.

One of the biggest issues we discussed regarding tailing Robert was how I could do it without getting close enough for him to have me arrested. I still can't believe the cops bought the whole restraining order nonsense, but those pictures of me did look very incriminating.

I realize that my thoughts are drifting, and I bring them back to the present. All around me, people are dressed in black. A woman across the room, introduced earlier as John Howerton's sister, groans and collapses into floods of tears again. A younger man—presumably her adult son—passes her a tissue and stands back, looking awkward. A man holding a tray hands me a glass of whiskey, and I nod my thanks to him. He smiles wanly at me and moves off through the crowd of mourners.

John Howerton's home is much like I expected, and it feels like an extension of his office and the man himself. Everything looks a lot more expensive than it probably is, and there seems to be a hint of desperation in a lot of the furniture. It's perfectly nice, but I know John, and he would have wished the knockoff couch was a genuine Boca do Lobo and the coffee table a Koket.

Instead, he clearly had to settle for decorating his home with stuff that most people would be proud of, but that didn't quite cut it for him. I'll miss John.

Most of us are standing in the living room. The walls are covered in bookshelves that run up to the ceiling, and the only parts they don't occupy have framed diplomas and awards hanging up. Several upholstered leather chairs surround the coffee table, and someone must have brought in four or five other chairs from the kitchen at some stage. The older mourners sit sporadically around the room, drinking alcohol and whispering condolences to one another.

The whiskey is strong, and it burns as I sip it. It feels good, though. My nerves have been a bit shaky all morning, as funerals aren't really my thing. I always put my foot in my mouth and say something silly to the person I am talking to when all they want to hear are charming anecdotes about the deceased.

I am grateful that nobody here knows me. It helps me to go under the radar. I actually considered slipping away after the burial and going home but decided at the last minute to come to the gathering in John's old house. I owe him that much, at least.

I would have thought Lilith might have come today, but I understand why she didn't. All eyes would have been on her, especially if the man claiming to be Fletcher had come too. The story of his return is still big news in many circles.

I found out earlier today that the woman I saw crying a moment ago is John's only living relative. He married a long time ago but never had any kids. I guess the swinging bachelor persona he loved so much ran deep, and more power to him. John was a good man beneath all of the bravado and fancy suits. If he wasn't, he wouldn't have been so determined to bring down someone like Robert.

He did it for you, my subconscious sneers. *And he died for your cause.*

That might be true, but I never asked him to go to such lengths. He did it of his own accord, and if I could go back, I'd tell him to stop digging.

"Took his own life," a woman's voice whispers in my ear.

When I step back and turn around, I see Molly standing in front of me. I hadn't spotted her at the burial. She is wearing a black dress that stops just below her knees, and the material strains against her powerful thighs. It looks like she isn't wearing any makeup, but it's hard to tell because her brown skin is so flawless.

"What?" I ask.

"The priest at the funeral," Molly half-whispers. She looks around to make sure nobody is in earshot. "Telling us all that John took his own life."

That was one of the hardest things about being at the funeral: knowing something that everyone else didn't. According to the police, John committed suicide. Nobody else thinks any differently. Well, that's what I thought until now.

I try to think of something to say, something calm and collected that will give me time to figure out what Molly is driving at. The best I come up with is saying, "What?" again.

"Come on," Molly says, placing her half-empty glass on one of the bookshelves. "Let's talk outside."

I follow her through the crowd, surprised to find myself almost mesmerized by the swaying of her behind. There are a couple of smokers on the porch, and one of them holds his burning cigarette up and guiltily shrugs as we pass. Rows of cars line the street, but apart from the low hum of chatter from John's house, the neighborhood is silent.

Overhead, a gray sky threatens rain. It's almost three o'clock, but I feel like I've been going nonstop for days. I really don't like funerals.

Molly gives another one of those conspiratorial glances around, then leans into me to talk.

"He was killed, wasn't he?" she says, her tone as serious as I've ever heard it.

"I don't know what you're—"

"Cut the crap, Virginia," she says. In the grayness, her massive brown eyes look black. "I saw it in your face when the cops showed up."

"Molly, I—"

She cuts me off for a second time with the wave of a hand. "Look, I don't want to know the details, but I liked John. He was kind to me when my kid was sick."

"Okay?"

"John had a safety deposit box," Molly says, leaning in so close I can smell her perfume. "He kept the key under his desk. He showed me one day when he'd had a few too many at the building's Christmas party. If he had any information that he didn't want to keep at the office, that's where it would be."

"What are you telling me, Molly?"

Molly sighs and looks up at the sky. When she brings her gaze back down to mine, her eyes are wet. "As I said, John was good to me. Come by the office tomorrow, and I'll show you where the key is and where to find the safety deposit box."

Chapter 59: Lilith

"What's Fletcher doing today?" Astrid asks. She is sitting in the passenger seat of the SUV as we edge our way through the thin Sunday afternoon traffic.

I want to ask her why she can't refer to him as Dad, but I know I can't force something like that. As she said during our argument the other day, to her, he is just the man that left us twelve years ago.

Still, I think she needs to give Fletcher a chance. Does she still think he isn't who he says he is?

"I'm not sure," I tell her, then inwardly curse myself for answering so hastily. I know what she is thinking, but I can't ask Fletcher where he is twenty-four-seven. There has to be trust in a marriage.

"Is he home tonight?" Astrid asks.

"For dinner, yes."

A white Coupe pulls in behind us, and I shiver. Then a smile starts to form, and I chuckle at how silly I acted that night. Did I really think I was being followed through the fog? Wow, it's incredible what a rattled mind can do.

Astrid thought we should go to John Howerton's funeral this morning, but I felt it wasn't a good idea. Everyone there would be concentrating on us, as the whole Fletcher returning after twelve years thing is still the hot topic around town. It wouldn't have been fair to John's family. Anyway, I didn't really know him outside of a client-lawyer setting.

I notice Astrid hasn't followed up on her question. "It's okay if he comes over for dinner, right?"

She snorts a laugh, bringing her hand up to her mouth in a way that always makes me smile. It is a gesture I hope she never loses, as it instantly transports her back to being my baby girl.

"Of course," Astrid says, shaking her head as she grins at me. "I'm hardly going to say no, Ma."

The traffic that was thin a moment ago has filled out a little, and I have to bring the car to a slow stop. Then I turn to my daughter and remove any trace of a smile from my face. "Look, Astrid. I know this has been hard. I mean, it's such a crazy thing that's happened. But I want you to know that you'll always come first, okay."

Astrid chuckles again. When I don't reciprocate, she gets serious and places her hand on my arm. "I know, Ma. I've always known that."

Her expression changes for a moment, but I can't read it. It's like she is weighing something up internally—something heavy. Then she smiles again, and I push the car on at a crawl.

Since I woke up this morning, I've been replaying yesterday's conversation with Fletcher in my head. Astoundingly, it was followed by one of the most intimate moments we've ever had together. When he told me he loved me, I knew without a shadow of a doubt that he wholeheartedly meant it. I've never experienced that with him before, and it was overwhelming. But then there is the issue with whoever Kelley is and what he said to her on the phone.

It was only as we lay in bed afterward—my whole body satisfied in a way I've never known—that I realized we had never got to the bottom of it. I was no closer to knowing who Kelley was and what he was doing telling her that he loved her.

I asked him again as we lay there, our skin slick with sweat as our sides touched. With our gazes on the ceiling, he continued to deny it. He admitted that there were things he hadn't told me but would do so when he was ready. I understand that and want to be there for him, but I need to know the truth.

"I asked him about Kelley," I blurt.

Oh, well, it's out there now.

"Really?" Astrid asks. I'm glad I'm driving and can look straight ahead.

"Yes."

"And?"

"He says you must have misheard."

"Oh, Ma," Astrid hisses. "You don't really believ—"

I shush my daughter by bringing my free hand up in a defensive gesture. I don't mean it in an aggressive way, but I need her to settle herself before our conversation explodes like it did a couple of days ago.

"Slow down, honey," I say. "I believe you. But I also want to know all the facts before I react. If there is another woman, she's gone. Simple as that."

I risk taking a look to the side and see Astrid smiling as she nods.

"Okay, Ma," she says. "That's good. But what else can it have meant? He said he loved her."

"I don't know. It sounds bad, and I admit that. But he seems to be close to opening up on everything that's been secret between us. He's had it harder than us, Astrid. We have to remember that."

"I suppose," Astrid concedes, shrugging.

I turn the SUV into the shopping mall lot. The big green sign of Starbucks arches over us as we drive under it.

"Look," I say, easily finding a spot. "I know you and your grandmother are only looking out for me, but I wasn't born yesterday. I'm going into this with my eyes open. You just have to trust that I'll make the right decision."

Astrid nods and pats my arm. As she does, my phone buzzes, and I pull it out of my pocket. It's a message from Fletcher: *Can't make it tonight. Something came up. Lunch tomorrow?*

Sighing, I text back: *Okay*, and hit send.

"Everything okay?" Astrid asks.

"Yeah. Your father can't make it this evening."

"He's away all night?" she asks, that suspicious tone back in an instant.

"Yes."

Astrid grabs her own phone from her bag and types something. Then she replaces it and gives me a wide grin. "So, how about that coffee?"

Chapter 60: Virginia

John kept the small key taped to the underside of his desk. Molly showed me into his office first thing this morning, and we retrieved it, but the address she's given me for his "safety deposit box" is just a rundown train station on the southernmost point of town. I can see it now in the distance as I drive toward it, the morning sun reflecting off the old slate roof, the spattering of black square holes showing how many shingles are missing.

I know what I'll find will just be a locker on one of the platforms, and I should have known that's what it would be. It is one last glimpse into John Howerton's obsession with all things 1920s noir. I can imagine him choosing this relic of a station simply because it looks like something out of a Humphrey Bogart movie. I'm sure he liked to picture himself slipping a leather bag into the locker beside a fogged-up platform as a guy in a fedora with a card tucked into the brim snapped pictures with his giant camera while shouting, "What a scoop!"

The underground lot is packed already, even though it's only a quarter to eight. Of course, most of the inner city workers will already have loaded themselves into the train cars, as this station services some of the smaller towns and neighborhoods on the outskirts of Boston. The inside of the lot smells like oil and rubber, and I wrinkle my nose as I get out of the car.

A number was engraved onto John's hidden key: 26. I'm assuming it's the locker number, which kind of makes taping the thing to the underside of his desk a bit pointless. Then again, I think that deep down, John never thought he was in any actual danger. Even with the harassment that had come during his time with Enrico Suarez all those years ago, I think he felt like that was the worst it could get—just a little intimidation.

The stairs take me up onto one of the smaller platforms. Bainbridge Station is a mishmash of old spaces and slightly newer renovations all squished together. None of it seems to make sense, and getting lost is easy. Several kiosks pepper the open-plan area, with their owners selling newspapers, candy, and instant coffee in small paper cups. Most of the people I see are blue-collar workers and salt of the Earth type of folks. Only a few carry briefcases, but the majority are dressed in coveralls and baggy construction pants.

I'm wearing my black parka and navy jeans, and I zip the former up fully as I walk. I keep checking the people on the platform to see if any are watching me. If Robert has surveillance on me, now would be a terrible time for them to be watching me. What if I find something incriminating about Robert only to have it forcefully taken from me right after? Who would believe me?

Robert still holds all the cards. For some reason, he doesn't seem to have told Lilith about the restraining order. It doesn't surprise me, though. Why waste pocket aces by going all in before the flop? It makes more sense to keep such a powerful hand for later when he might be backed into a corner.

I wanted to tail Fletcher yesterday, but Astrid's text informing me he was canceling on Lilith again came through while I was still at John Howerton's house. Fletcher had already been out all morning by then, so I wouldn't have even known where to start looking for him. According to my granddaughter, Sunday seems to be one of his favorite days for vanishing.

Scanning the platform for shady characters or people watching me is pointless, I know. I'm here to check the locker, and nothing is going to stop me. Molly stuck her neck out by approaching me at the funeral yesterday, and I need to follow through.

A couple of men holding white paper cups walk past me, steam billowing out of the lids as they chat. They look like father and son, and the older one openly winks at me and smiles. I ignore him and keep walking. It would help if I knew what I was looking for, but I'm just going on a hunch that it's a locker. John told Molly that night at the Christmas party that his safety deposit box was at Bainbridge Station; he just didn't say where.

I could ask someone who works here where the lockers are, but a station this size probably has several sections for storage. Also, I want to arouse as little suspicion as possible until I know exactly what my next step is, and I can't do that until I've seen what's inside. Maybe it's nothing?

The first platform seems to be primarily kiosks, token machines, and benches, and I think this is more of a crossover area. A small entrance brings me out into a much larger space, and I see a couple of information desks appearing as two women in matching skirts and jackets roll up shutters. This platform runs so far down that I can't see the end, and the thick arches that crisscross along the ceiling are at least 100 feet above me. Several pigeons coo from the shadows up there, but I can't see them anywhere.

About halfway down the platform, I can see what looks like rows of lockers running along both sides. I put my head down and stuff my hands in my pockets as I walk. If the lockers are numbered, I should be fine. If the 26 on the key means something entirely different, I'm screwed.

There are more people on this platform, and that's good. I feel like I'm slipping into the crowd. The idea that Robert is having me followed at all times seems very extreme, and I still think that the pictures of me were taken by someone who he pays to watch *him*. It is the only thing that makes sense. A man like Robert needs a guardian angel, but not the Disney type.

The first set of lockers are numbered in the high one thousands. They are classic gray metal, with rusted edges and cigarette burns dotting the surface throughout. Most are secured with small brass padlocks that dangle below a clasp. A few people are kneeling or standing by them, stuffing their civilian clothes in as they readjust their construction gear or cautiously looking around as they hide their laptops or tablets inside before heading off to work for the day.

I walk past them quickly, all of the high numbers marking them making my heart drop. Still, at least I'm probably in the right area.

The next row is still in the thousands, but the numbers on each of the stickers are a bit lower. It seems I'm coming at this backward. Standing where I am for a moment with my hands still buried in my jacket pockets, I scan the platform again. Then I nod and cut through the crowd as I head toward the other side.

A man wearing a beige trench coat bumps into me as I walk, nearly knocking me off my feet. He stops for a moment and holds my gaze, then nods knowingly and strolls away into the crowd. Shaken but not deterred, I continue on my way.

Was that a knowing glance, or am I just being paranoid? Now that the moment has passed, I am leaning toward my paranoia playing a major role in what I think I saw in his expression. It has been in overdrive ever since the moment that rat-featured Officer Whitely slid those photographs across the table for me to see. That was when everything in my world seemed to get sucked out through the vents of that claustrophobic interview room, leaving me feeling exhausted and beaten.

The first locker I see has the number 42 on the door, and my heart rate doubles. With my finger in the air—the people around me are blurs now—I run it along as I count down through each one.

Suddenly, a wave of nausea washes over me, and my knees feel like they'll buckle. There is no way to tell from here if the locker I'm looking at is number 26, but I know it is without checking. The door is off to the side, hanging on one hinge. The rim is bent like someone hacked at it with a crowbar, and thick scrapes run along the parts of the surface I can see.

Knowing what I'll find, I slowly walk toward it anyway. My feet feel like my shoes have been stuffed with cotton balls, and my mouth is so dry that I think the insides might crack.

"Oh, no," I groan when I'm next to it.

There is nothing inside. Whatever John had kept in there is gone, and whoever took it did so by force.

Chapter 61: Lilith

"This is where the parking lot will be," Robert tells me, his voice booming in the early morning gloom. He is the only person I see—including me—who isn't wearing a yellow hard hat. Pleasure Bay is to our left, with City Point to our right. Robert points his finger toward the buildings and the city beyond. "And the mall will go here."

The area Robert DuBose is leading my eye to is the only greenery I can see for miles. In fact, it's the only greenery I can see, full stop. Why Pleasure Bay would need a mega-mall, I don't know. But apparently, one is coming, and DuBose Construction has been tasked with building it.

"Will you be a part of this project?" I ask Fletcher. He has been nervous all day, and I realize that he always is when he's around his father. Robert's presence used to put Fletcher on edge, but it was aggressive defiance I sensed in my husband back then. Not this shifty awkwardness.

"Eh, no, I don't think so," he says. "This will be afterward, I think."

Robert's eyes turn to slits at his son's bumbling answer. He has always prided himself on the DuBoses being strong and proud, not nervous and stuttering. I think Fletcher marrying me and giving me and my daughter their last name put a wrench in Robert's initial vision.

"After what?" I ask.

"What he means," Robert butts in, "is that he is working on something else." He brings his hand up and waves it over the groups of men in construction gear already laying out equipment and carrying scaffolding before continuing, "As you can see, we've already begun here. The foreman is one of my top guys."

"'Fore*man*?' I say. "Don't you mean supervisor or boss?"

"I mean foreman," Robert snarls. "I don't do all of that PC nonsense, girly."

I resist the urge to shiver, and then the feeling is replaced by anger. Robert DuBose is a neanderthal and a pig, but he is my husband's father. I need to handle his attitude with patience.

Robert starts walking again, and Fletcher and I fall into step behind him. When Fletcher texted last night after his no-show to ask me to meet him here before our lunch date, I didn't understand why. I still don't.

Is this just Robert's way of spending time with us? He is an extremely busy man; everyone knows that. If he is just trying to squeeze us into his hectic schedule, isn't there something almost admirable or even sweet about that?

"Astrid's birthday party," Robert says, his crystal blue eyes scanning the workers as he speaks. His tan looks extra dark today for some reason. "It's agreed that we'll have it at my home, right?"

I glare at Fletcher, and he drops his head. Then I turn back to his father. "What?"

"Yes," Robert chimes, still looking out across his construction site. "I told Fletcher to tell you."

"To *tell* me?"

Robert waves his hand a few times like he's wafting away an irritating odor. "You know what I mean, Lilith. I told him to offer my home for the festivities. I'll put on quite a show!"

I'll bet you will, you pompous ass.

"We barely discussed it," I tell him.

Robert turns to face me. "Well, let's discuss it now."

I nod. "Astrid doesn't like a fuss being made for her."

"Everyone likes a fuss made over them."

"Not Astrid."

Fletcher has remained silent. In fact, I see him trying to look everywhere but at the conversation between his father and me. It annoys me, as this is one time when he should stand up for me. If he has really changed as much as he claims, then he has to show it when it matters.

"Look," Robert says, sighing. His expensive suit looks preposterous in this setting of cement mixers and dusty tools. He runs a hand through his salt and pepper hair. "I will make it perfect for her."

"I'm not sure," I say. "Maybe Fletcher was right."

"Oh?" Robert exclaims, his eyebrows raised. When he looks at his son, Fletcher actually stuffs his hands in his pockets and kicks at a pebble.

"Yes. Fletcher thought we should leave it up to Astrid. It's her birthday, after all."

"Fletcher thought that, did he?" Robert growls. "Okay then. But you will miss our big news. Well, it will be *Fletcher's* big news, really."

Robert nudges his son, who smiles up at him. It's hard to tell if it's genuine or not. "Right, Fletcher?"

Fletcher nods and says, "Right."

Big news? Is Robert suggesting that Fletcher will announce something at the party—something big? The type of gesture that needs a grand setting?

"What big news?" I ask. I feel like a giddy schoolgirl all of a sudden, and I scold myself for it.

"Ah, that would ruin the surprise," Robert tells me, winking. The sight of it makes me cringe inwardly, even though the expression is made to promise an apparent nice surprise.

"I still don't see why the party needs to be at your house. Does it make a difference where it—"

"Okay, okay," Robert interrupts, a huge grin across his tanned face. "I know where this is coming from, Lilith."

"Oh?"

"Yes. You're afraid Virginia won't be able to go."

"That?" I say. "No, that's not an issue anymore. We made up recently."

"Sorry," Robert replies, chuckling. "You misunderstood. I meant because of the restraining order."

Chapter 62: Virginia

My joy at Lilith stopping by my apartment for the first time instantly turns to heartbreak when she hisses, "*A restraining order*! Really, Mom?"

"Come inside," I tell her, stepping away from the front door. When I buzzed her in moments ago, I didn't think this would be happening. I'm still a little shaken from my discovery at the train station, if I'm being honest. "Please."

Surprisingly, Lilith steps into the hallway, and I close the door behind her. She was never one for public displays, and I'm with her on that one. Only attention-seekers and drama queens air their dirty laundry for all to see.

"What the hell, Mom?" Lilith growls when I turn to face her. "What were you thinking?"

"It's not what it looks like," I say. Unfortunately, it kind of is, but I can't lead with that argument.

"Really? It seems pretty clear-cut to me. Robert says some photos are from nearly twenty years ago!"

"I told you the other day, Lilith. I suspected him of your father's murder. I couldn't just stand by and do nothing."

Lilith flicks a lock of her long black hair out of her eyes by blowing it away. "That's not the point."

"It's the *only* point," I snap.

"Stalking is never a solution, Mom."

"I was investigating."

"Oh?" Lilith scoffs, placing both hands on her hips. "And what did you find out in nearly two decades of *investigations*?"

"Please, Lilith. You know everything I do."

Really, Ginny? Everything?

"Do I?" she snaps, almost like she's reading my mind.

"Yes," I tell her. "Everything that needs to be known."

"You sound just like Fletcher," Lilith barks.

"What?"

"Nothing." She dismisses me with a flick of her wrist. "This restraining order is a step too far, Mom. I don't know how we move past this."

"You can't be serious!" I exclaim. We were so close to reconciling. So, so close. "Lilith, this is only fresh news to you. It's a lifetime for me."

"What's that supposed to mean?"

"Do you know how many times I wanted to bring you in on this? To tell you how I believed Robert had your father killed? If things hadn't worked out between you and Fletcher, that's exactly what I had planned to do. Then you got engaged. And then Astrid was born."

"So?" Lilith snaps, tapping her foot. Her hands are still firmly planted on her hips.

"So, I couldn't tell you by then," I say. We're still standing in the hallway, and I know I should try and edge her into the kitchen area. We're too close to the front door, and she could storm out at any moment. I have a feeling it will be extremely hard to bring her back again if she does.

I raise my hands in exasperation. "How could I tell you what I suspected when you were marrying Robert's son? When the man I suspected was your father-in-law?" Lilith motions to say something, then falls silent. I think I might be getting through to her, so I quickly push on. "Lilith, it would have torn us apart, and you didn't need that."

"What about after Fletcher's accident? Why didn't you tell me then?"

"Maybe I should have," I concede, shrugging. "But we were dealing with his death, and then time just got away from me. I had basically stopped checking on Robert by then, anyhow."

"Why?"

"Why, what?"

"Why did you stop?" Lilith asks.

"Because you and Astrid were in mourning. You had lost your husband—as much of a man as he was—and Astrid had lost her father. I wanted to be there for you both completely. Not chasing something that I'd probably never find."

Lilith shakes her head. "But you did start again, right?"

"Right."

"When Fletcher came back."

"Yes."

"Why?"

I let out a long sigh. We've been through this so many times, but it just never sticks with her. Regardless, I repeat it once more. "Because that's not Fletcher."

Lilith throws her arms up in the air. Her eyes are like saucers, and she is laughing as she shakes her head. There is absolutely no joy in the sound.

"Pathetic," she scoffs, pushing past me. When I grab her arm, she spins around and snatches it away with force. "*Don't touch me.*"

"Lilith, please," I manage before she snaps the front door open and steps out.

Lilith stops with the door half-closed and says, "Robert wants to host Astrid's party next week. I didn't think it was a good idea, but with this restraining order stopping you from going." She shrugs and says, "Maybe it's a good thing."

"Lilith, please don't—"

My pleas for her to listen to me are cut off by the door slamming shut. My back hits the wall with a low thud, and I slide to the floor until I'm sitting on it. Then I place my head between my knees and weep.

Chapter 63: Lilith

"You overreacted, Ma," Astrid tells me. She sounds angry, and I can't understand why. I mean, a restraining order! That sort of action is reserved for stalkers and—

Abusive partners?

—obsessive fans of movie stars.

"Nana isn't thinking straight anymore," I tell my daughter. The TV in our living room is off, and I can see her reflection on the screen when I turn away. She looks disgusted.

"Nana is trying to *protect* us," Astrid says, making me look at her again. "If anyone is acting strange, it's you."

"Astrid, you sound like a restraining order is nothing!" I exclaim. "You didn't even seem shocked when I told you just now."

"I already knew, Ma."

I snort once and shake my head. "Of course you did."

"You're not going to start that everyone-is-conspiring-against-me spiel again, are you?"

Astrid sits back in the chair and folds her arms over her stomach. The red Harvard University hoodie she is wearing makes her look younger than usual. The disapproving scowl on her face doesn't.

"That's right, Astrid," I scoff. "Your silly old mother is crazy."

"You need to grow up, Ma."

I don't know what to say anymore. It's clear that Astrid and my mother agree, and all the letters on it spell out that Robert and Fletcher are bad news. Nothing will change their minds, and if a restraining order isn't enough to make Astrid see sense, then I don't know what will.

Although, Mom's explanation made some sense, too, didn't it? Of course she would have done something to find evidence that my father was killed, whether or not it really happened that way. In her mind, it did. If I thought someone had caused Fletcher's death, wouldn't I have investigated? And my father was a better man than *that* Fletcher was, so Mom would have had even more reason not to let it go.

But the Fletcher that came out of that rafting accident is a changed man in so many ways. If Astrid and my mother won't give him a chance, then there isn't much I can do about it. At least for now. Astrid will surely come around if given the time. Until then, I'll just have to edge them both together over a longer period of time.

Astrid's recently arranged party plans come back to me like a slap in the face, and I grimace. A huge, elaborate event at Robert's grand estate is hardly edging father and daughter together slowly. Still, I have to tell her now. She deserves to know instead of me springing it on her on the day.

"About your birthday, Astrid," I say.

Astrid looks up at me with confusion on her face. "What?"

"Your party," I repeat.

"I don't want anything fancy, Ma," she tells me as she picks at her fingernails. Her tone is icy cold.

I suck air in through my teeth and put on my most apologetic smile. "I kind of agreed to have it at your grandfather's house."

"Robert's place?" Astrid asks, her mouth hanging open in a big O. "You couldn't get any fancier if you tried, Ma."

"Sorry, sweetie," I say. I nearly add that I didn't know she wanted it low-key, but I did. I was fully aware, yet I went and made plans I knew she wouldn't like anyway. And why? To rub my mother the wrong way. How petty of me! "Oh, wow. I really am so sorry."

"No, you're not," Astrid tells me flatly. When she stands up and looks down at me on the couch, I feel so small. I am, in a way. I'm a small, petty person.

"I wasn't thinking," I tell her. When was the last time we were this on edge around each other? The last few days have been horrible between us. In fact, I can't remember a time when we were at each other's throats as much.

"You were thinking *very* clearly," Astrid hisses. "All you wanted to do was hurt Nana, and having the party at Robert's house would do just the trick, right?"

"No," I plead. "I mean, yes, that crossed my mind. I-I, oh, no. I'm sorry, Astrid. I really don't know what to say."

Astrid shakes her head and grunts something indecipherable. I don't even think it was a word, just a snort of contempt, maybe.

"You know what the worst part is, Ma?" I shake my head in answer, and Astrid makes that noise again. Then she says, "Robert could possibly be the man who killed your own father, and you agreed to have my party there just to piss your mother off. Now, tell me," Astrid says, pointing her finger directly in my face, "who is it that isn't thinking straight?"

I watch as she marches out of the living room and into the kitchen. I follow her out just in time to see her slipping on her coat.

"Where are you going?" I ask, panic setting in. Everything feels like it is falling apart, and there is nothing I can do to stop it. "It's nearly eleven."

"I'm going to stay with Nana," Astrid almost spits. Then she turns on her heels and storms out of the house.

With the sound of the front door slamming still echoing in my ears, I walk on legs that don't feel like my own to the kitchen table and flop down into one of the chairs.

When the heavy sobs suddenly wrack my body, I let them take me. There is nothing else I can do.

Chapter 64: Virginia

Astrid has been staying with me for the last few days. As it stands, she has no intention of going to her eighteenth birthday party at Robert's, despite the endless texts and calls from Lilith. I've tried to convince her to go, and sometimes I even feel like I'm getting through to her. Then she gives me one of her firm head shakes, and I know she has her mind made up. I don't know why Robert wants to host her party so much; I just know it will have a purpose behind it.

More than that, it's important that Astrid celebrates with her mother. My granddaughter might be a strong, passionate—and yes, stubborn—young woman, but she's not spiteful. Not going to the party to prove a point should be beneath her.

"How's your soup, Nana?" Astrid asks.

She is sitting across from me on one of the two chairs in the living room area of my apartment. Her hair is down tonight, her arching bangs framing her painfully cutesy features. Astrid is one of those women who will only get better looking as she ages, and she is already stunning. I dread to think how many unwanted advances she'll have to fight off in her adult life.

"It's good," I tell her, smiling over my spoon. It really is tasty, and culinary skills seem to be another skill we can add to Astrid's ever-growing repertoire. "Have you talked to your mother today?"

"I called her this morning just to let her know I'm doing okay," Astrid says, and I inwardly applaud her maturity. I know plenty of women a lot older than her who would dig their heels in and drag out the silent treatment just to hammer home their point.

"Good. How is she? I tried calling her myself, but..." I shrug, letting Astrid fill in the rest of the sentence.

Lilith has blanked me since she came to my apartment and let me have it. Part of me doesn't blame her, but I mostly think she is cutting off her nose to spite her face at this stage. Yes, a restraining order sounds terrible out of context. But when it is viewed from a neutral perspective, it can surely be seen for what it really is: a mother trying to protect her daughter and grandchild.

"She is stubborn," Astrid says.

"I'd call it proud."

"Maybe."

We eat in silence as we watch TV. On the screen, some nobody is being voted off a show by a panel of other nobodies. I watch as the woman who just got told she can't sing bursts into tears, and my mind drifts back to how I was in the hallway after Lilith stormed out. If Astrid hadn't shown up at my door later that night asking to stay, I don't know how I would have got myself together.

She filled me in on how her conversation with her mother went as we sat at the kitchen table sipping tea last night. I told her to at least text Lilith and say that she was safe and well, and Astrid informed me she already had. We went to bed soon after, and the last five days have been nice, even though I feel terrible for Lilith.

"Why are you so sure, Nana?" Astrid asks, breaking my train of thought.

"What?"

"About Fletcher," Astrid says. "You've been so sure it's not him from the beginning. Why?"

I clear my throat and readjust my sitting position. Astrid's question is a lot more loaded than it probably seems to her. Even so, I still don't know if I can give her a satisfactory answer. Not because of the things I know but because I'm not even sure if they're real anymore.

"I don't know," I say. "I don't think I could explain it if I tried."

I remember the day after Fletcher left for his rafting trip on the Gauley River. How Lilith had collapsed in tears as the police officer told us what had happened. *He couldn't have surviv*ed, the man in the navy uniform had said. *The raft was completely destroyed, and blood was all over what was left.*

Lilith had cried for hours after the police had left, and I always felt like she was shedding mainly tears of relief. But maybe that's just what I wanted to think. Perhaps that made it easier for me.

"The DNA test, though," Astrid says, shaking her head. "Those things can't be wrong."

"I know," I concede, shrugging. That part confused me from the moment I heard it.

Maybe he survived, Ginny? You can never be sure that he died.

"I would like to have seen the results myself," Astrid says. "Not that I don't trust Mom, because I do. It might help put my mind at ease."

"Well, if she says she saw them, then they're real."

"Right. Only..." Astrid says, then trails off. She shakes her head like she's trying to get rid of a thought that keeps clinging to her mind.

"What, Astrid? What is it?"

Astrid places her empty bowl down by her feet and dabs at her mouth with a napkin. "Fletcher only *showed* her the results. It's not like she went to the hospital and had them confirmed."

I think I actually flinch, but I can't be sure. Lilith told me she saw the DNA results, but I never questioned their validity. My daughter is no fool, and she would have been able to tell the difference between real and fake documents. But she is prone to moments of irrational actions. Not often, but whenever Fletcher was involved in proceedings, she had a tendency to act in ways that weren't reflective of her strength and intelligence.

"She must have checked," I say after a moment. I chuckle a little at how my mind just went in such a dramatic direction. "Your mother is a smart woman. She would have checked."

"I suppose you're right."

"And anyway," I say, a thought suddenly occurring to me. "The cops confirmed it to me when I was at the station. They had one of their guys check everything out during our interview."

All of this is fact, but medical records can still be faked. And if this is all the work of Robert DuBose, there is no other man in Boston who would have the sway to do such a thing. Now that I think about it, Robert was very keen to have us all over for lunch that day when he nearly caught me snooping around his office. That was around the time that the DNA results were first mentioned.

If Robert is pulling the strings in all of this—and I know he is—then DNA records, files on a man being found wandering in Hagerstown, and all the rest would be things he would have sorted out long before he put his plan into action. But the man that showed up at Lilith's door really looks like Fletcher, so how the hell could Robert pull that little trick off?

I consider discussing these thoughts with Astrid, then decide against it. Right now, they're just a bunch of crazy theories that wouldn't make much sense when said out loud.

There *is* an answer in them somewhere, though. I just know there is.

Chapter 65: Lilith

Mom has agreed to meet me today, and I hate how nervous I am. Only a month ago, we were so close, but everything has changed so quickly. Now, my daughter has been staying with her for over a week, and I feel like I'm losing everything that ever meant anything to me. I have Fletcher back, but at what cost?

"Hey," Mom says as she comes up next to me. After leaning down and kissing me on the cheek, she sits on the other side of the picnic bench.

The park is pretty quiet this morning, but the kids are in school, so that's often the case. A few rays of sunshine have fought their way through the thick white clouds, but there is still a chill in the air. Across the way, a man walks hand-in-hand with his daughter. She must be no older than three, and I can feel the love she has for him from here.

"Hi, Mom," I say, folding my arms over my stomach and smiling.

"You look good," Mom tells me, nodding at my hair. "Did you get a trim?"

I instinctively bring my hand up to my head, like I have to check to see if I've been to the salon recently when I know I haven't. "No, I just tied it up differently, I think."

"Well, it looks nice," she says. Her cheeks are red from the cold, and small clouds of condensation puff out of her mouth as she speaks. "Astrid says hi."

I feel my eyes stinging, but I hold back the tears. Not having my daughter around the house is killing me. Fletcher has tried to fill the void, but he is around less and less lately. Robert has him working on something big, apparently.

"I miss her," I say.

"I know. She just needs some time."

"I miss *you*, Mom." This time, the tears come. "I miss *us*. It was always the three of us against the world."

Mom stands up and comes around to my side of the bench. When she sits down beside me and takes me in her arms, I sink into them. A heavy weight is instantly lifted from my chest, and I let go of all that I can. It comes out in big, heaving sobs, but I don't care. When I feel a warm droplet hit the back of my neck, I know Mom is crying too.

After what seems like a very long time, I sit up and wipe my eyes. Both of us smile at each other, and Mom lets out a small chuckle.

"We're a couple of idiots, huh?" she says, dabbing at her cheeks with the sleeve of her parka.

"Yeah, we are."

Mom laughs again and pulls out a pack of cigarettes from the inside pocket of her jacket. When she sees my shocked expression, she grimaces and says, "Oh, sorry. Force of habit. I forgot you didn't know I was smoking again."

"Really, Mom?" I ask. "Smoking?"

I watch her as she examines the cigarettes like she is seeing them for the first time. Then she shakes her head, walks over to the trash can next to the bench, and tosses the pack into it.

"I don't need them anymore," she declares, giving an over-the-top dismissive wave. "I've got my baby back."

She sits on the other side of the bench as I laugh at her bad acting.

"How's work?"

"Good," I tell her. "I'm working there full time now."

"That's great!"

"Yes, I'm happy with it."

Mom nods, then her face gets serious. "Lilith, I want you to know that I'll support you no matter what, okay?"

"Mom, we don't have to talk about that stuff right now."

"We do, Lilith," Mom says. "Well, I do, anyway."

"Okay."

"My thoughts on Fletcher or whether it's him or not are irrelevant," Mom continues. "If you love him, and more importantly, if he loves you, then I'll be there for you."

"Thanks, Mom," I say. Butterflies flutter in my belly, but the tears stay at bay this time.

"No problem," she says, nodding. "As for Robert, I can't say the same. I'm sorry, sweetie, that's just how it's going to have to be."

I want everything to be perfect, but life never is. Mom thanks me for understanding when I tell her this. Then I say, "You really think he killed Dad, don't you?"

"I do."

"Is it okay if I don't?"

I know this is a horrible thing to say, but Mom has always based her claims on a hunch. I can't throw away my second chance at my relationship with Fletcher on a hunch.

"Yes, it is," Mom says, nodding again.

"Robert's an asshole."

"Yes, he is."

Both of us burst out laughing, and Mom actually starts banging the picnic bench as she howls. When my eyes start to water this time, it's for a whole other reason. This is how we always used to be—Mom, Astrid, and me. We were inseparable. We *are* inseparable.

"But he *is* Fletcher's father," I say breathlessly after a few minutes, a few chuckles still lingering in my belly. "So until something changes, I have to give him the benefit of the doubt."

"Better you than me," Mom says, shrugging.

"Amen to that."

Mom's phone buzzes and she pulls it out of her pocket. Holding up a finger as she puts the phone to her ear, she says, "Sorry, Lilith, but I have to take this."

As she wanders away from the bench, mumbling her conversation, I marvel at how this meeting has gone. In my wildest dreams, I couldn't have imagined it going this well. We even came to some sort of truce on Fletcher and Robert! But most importantly, we comforted each other. That has always been the spine of our relationship, and it feels as strong as ever.

When I look up, Mom is standing over me. Her phone is nowhere to be seen, but she has a serious expression on her face.

"Everything okay, Mom?"

"Yeah, all good," she says. "But I have to go, I'm afraid. Something has come up."

Chapter 66: Virginia

I walked out of the police station yesterday in a daze. That's the only way I can explain it. It felt like I was cocooned in wool, and everything I touched was softer than it should be. As a matter of fact, it still feels a little like that today. That's how weird my meeting with Officer Demarco went.

"Your coffee, ma'am," a young gentleman wearing a gray apron says.

I blink twice. "Huh?"

A row of cars drift by next to me, and a jerk in a suit behind me says, "C'mon, lady. I haven't got all day."

I turn back to the vendor holding out my coffee and smile. "Sorry. I drifted off."

The guy who runs the coffee stand is young—maybe early twenties—with curly brown hair and dark eyes. His stubble is expertly trimmed, and his teeth are pure white. He looks embarrassed about the rude man behind me.

"That's okay," he says, passing the coffee to me. "We all have those days."

"Not me," the asshole in the suit grunts.

When I go to reach for some cash to pay for my beverage, the vendor shakes his hand in the air.

"Hey, it's on me." He nods at the guy behind me. "To help ease the strain of *one of those days*."

I return his smile and thank him, then continue my aimless wandering through downtown Boston.

I'm still trying to process what happened yesterday. My meeting with Lilith was amazing. We connected on so many levels, and it felt like it used to be between us. That alone would have been a cause for the strange otherworldliness that has taken over me, but my phone call and the chat with Officer Demarco that followed blew me away.

The things he told me were in strict confidence, and I knew he would be in a lot of trouble if they got out. But he seemed to want to stick his neck out for me. That reassuring smile of his; I could look at that all day. His wife—

Did you notice a ring?

—is a lucky woman.

I pass a store with the latest fashions in the window. I resist the urge to go buy a gift for Astrid's birthday. It's not that I won't be getting her something special; it's just that I never buy clothes for other people. Style is something so personal, and it is extremely difficult to get what the person actually likes. Her birthday is in a couple of days, though, so I'll need to get cracking.

I don't need to get her much more, as I'm already giving her the locket Wally gave me when we first started dating. Ever since Astrid was a little girl, she's had her eye on it. I know she will be delighted to have it, and I'll be even happier to give it to her. She is a special girl and deserves everything the world has to offer. Not that she has ever demanded anything more than the bare minimum.

"Nothing is certain yet," Officer Demarco told me yesterday as we walked back out of the Boston Police Department's parking lot. "So don't get your hopes up. Our guy could flip-flop. He has done it once already."

I nodded and promised to keep it to myself, but I had seen the sudden dread in his expression. If nothing came out of his lead, then telling me was certainly breaking protocol. Why had he told me then? He explained it away yesterday as merely putting my mind at ease, but that would only make sense if his information were solid. The way he told it, his lead could go either way.

Whatever the case may be, things are better now than I could have imagined they would be. I talked to Astrid when I got home yesterday evening, and she agreed to suck it up and go to Robert's undoubtedly obnoxious lavish party. As we discussed, if the three of us are going to make this work, we will all have to swallow our pride at different stages.

Things have changed now, and the happy little life we had created together is gone. Lilith loves Fletcher, whether it's really him or not, so we have to be happy for her. He hasn't laid a hand on her this time so far as we know, so we can only hope that it remains that way and that he really has changed.

I sip my coffee and push my doubt away. No family is perfect, and we're no different. Millions of relatives across the world miss out on parties, weddings, and all sorts of events because of family feuds and grievances. If I have to skip the odd one because Robert is there, then so be it. There is nothing I can do but be there for my daughter and grandchild in the moments when we are together.

The coffee tastes good, and I notice that I've come to the entrance of the park. In fact, I can see the bench I sat on yesterday as I hugged my daughter and cried right along with her.

Smiling in the early morning gloom, I pass through the small metal gates and walk along the winding path.

When my phone rings, I slip it out and check the screen. My mood darkens instantly when I see a number I don't recognize. Scanning the park to see if there is anyone watching me who shouldn't be, I answer.

Chapter 67: Lilith

"You look beautiful," I tell Astrid, my throat closing up as I fight back tears of joy.

Her hair is braided, showing her beautiful features off to the world, and the red dress she is wearing hugs her perfect frame without being too tight. Her bare shoulders look as smooth as silk, and when she stands next to me and is an inch taller, my throat closes again.

"You okay, Ma?" Astrid asks through a chuckle.

"Yes, I am, sweetie," I tell her. "You just look so grown up."

"I am grown up, Ma!" she chimes, rubbing my arm as she grins at me.

"I know, I know. But can you just be my little girl for one more day?"

"I'll try."

We embrace, and then I step back and take another look at her. How I haven't had problems dealing with any boy trouble, I don't know. Yes, there have been a few brief relationships with guys at her high school, but nothing that has caused heartbreak. It seems odd, as I thought every teenage girl went through that sort of thing as a rite of passage.

Maybe she did? Maybe she went through it on her own?

Astrid's bedroom door opens behind us, and we both turn around. Mom is standing there in a cream skirt and a slightly lighter jacket. Underneath is a white shirt that makes her glow. Her hair is loose and full, seeming to balance on her shoulders.

"Wow," she says as she walks toward Astrid. "You look amazing."

"Aw, shucks," Astrid says mockingly.

Mom playfully punches her on the arm like a jock in a locker room. She is only short of snapping her behind with a wet towel!

I'm still a little shocked that Robert dropped the restraining order so Mom could go to Astrid's party. When she arrived here earlier in the week and told me he had called to invite her to the party, I felt on edge instead of relieved. Sure, I was happy he made the gesture, but it still worried me.

It killed me to tell her that I had to make an effort with him when we met at the park. Of course, what I said was true, but I wish I could take her side completely. I'll never know if what Mom says about Robert and my father is true, but I have to give my relationship with Fletcher a chance. The fact that Robert makes my skin crawl is just one of the less pleasant sides of it, I suppose.

"You look stunning," Mom tells me, looking me up and down.

I was quite happy that my old little black dress still fit, even if the thighs were a bit snug. Fletcher actually likes my ass with a bit of jiggle in it, or so he tells me. The old Fletcher was only short of making me take weekly weigh-ins, so the seemingly endless compliments I get from him now are a welcome surprise. At first, I thought he was just being nice, but every time I reach down and take him in my hand, the proof that he likes me the way I am is there.

"You look great, too, Mom," I say. She really does.

"The three of us turning heads together again!" Mom chimes.

I laugh out loud and see that Astrid is doing the same. Instead of helping my nerves, I get a wave of that uneasiness again. This whole day will be rough, I feel. Robert has acted like he is trying to do what's best ever since Fletcher showed up, but there is always that undercurrent of doubt that he is up to something.

"Is Fletcher meeting us there?" Mom asks, and I have to resist the urge to hug her for using his real name. No more of that Michael Foster stuff.

"Yeah," I say, stepping forward and straightening the lapel on her jacket.

I want to tell them what Robert said about the "big news" that we would be getting at the party, but I don't want to worry them. They are still untrusting of him—and rightly so—and I don't want to spoil the mood. Anyway, it could be nothing more than another arrogant announcement about a DuBose Construction merger or some other such nonsense.

"Okay, shall we go then?" Astrid asks, picking up her purse. Then she looks out the window at the unseasonable sunshine. "I don't think we'll need coats?"

"Maybe just in case," I say. "We can keep them in the car."

When I turn to Mom, she is checking her phone. She looks up and then stuffs it back into her bag. I remember the call she got at the park when she suddenly had to leave. Could I have ever imagined that morning that the three of us would be standing here in my daughter's bedroom a week later, all dressed up and ready to go to her party? Not in a million years.

"I'm so happy we're all here," I tell them both.

"Don't, Ma," Astrid says, her voice wavering. "If I cry, I'll ruin my makeup."

Mom smiles and holds out both of her arms. Wordlessly, Astrid and I step forward and let her embrace the two of us. The mixture of perfumes should be overpowering, but it's not. It is the scent of three strong women returning to the people they once were. We were only gone for a while, but everything seems to be falling into place again.

Chapter 68: Virginia

Robert's home has been decked out to look like something from *Goodfellas*. Every room downstairs is shining, and the long tables stacked with food will be mostly full by the time we leave. Astrid is a popular girl, yet I only spot three or four people her age here. The rest of the partygoers seem to be the men who work for Robert or other business acquaintances. Even with that, there must be less than a hundred people milling aimlessly about. There is food for a thousand, easy.

At the end of the main table—the one that wasn't just set up for today—is a small, makeshift podium. A microphone sits on top of it, and there are several speakers set up around the rooms downstairs. When I first saw it, I nudged Astrid and said, "I hope you have a speech prepared?"

She had nudged me back—a little more firmly than I had for good measure—laughed and said, "Maybe it's for you, Nana? Although, is it two hundred yards away from Robert?"

As I stand off to one side nibbling hor d'oeuvres in the enormous dining room, I idly wonder if anyone else here knows about the restraining order. Then I realize that I don't really care if they do or not. It may be lifted now, but I have no intention of ever being within two hundred yards of Robert DuBose after today.

I place the porcelain plate with my half-eaten crab puff down on the end table next to me and slip my phone out of my bag. Relentlessly checking it is starting to stress me out, but I haven't heard from Officer Demarco since he met me in the parking lot a week ago. Was he just trying to put my mind at ease, or did he genuinely have something?

"There is a trash can over there," a smarmy voice says beside me. As I slip my phone back into my bag, I look up into the dead blue eyes of Robert DuBose.

"Excuse me?"

He nods at the crab puff on the end table, then over at one of the many pop-up trash cans the caterers must have set up.

"I'm not finished yet," I tell him, trying everything I have not to be the first to drop our gaze.

"Ah, I see," he says, nodding slowly. "You're talking about the hor d'oeuvres, right?"

"What else would I be talking about?"

Robert shrugs, and I realize how much taller and wider he is than me. Why this thought should suddenly come to me now, I don't know. But all I can think about is how easily he could wrap his hands around my throat and squeeze the life out of me.

Don't look away, Ginny. Don't show him any weakness.

"Well?" I ask. "What else would I be talking about?"

Robert chuckles. "Who knows, Virginia? Who knows."

Someone in a tuxedo waltzes up to us, holding a tray of drinks over his shoulder. Robert takes one of them from him, and I do the same. The scotch is strong, and I try not to grimace as I swallow it.

Robert continues to look down at me. Then he taps his breast pocket, and I see the tip of a large cigar.

"Will you join me outside?" he asks.

"No, thank you."

His tanned brow creases up. "Oh? You're not smoking?"

"I don't smoke," I tell him firmly.

"Really? I could have sworn you did."

"No, sorry. I don't."

"Huh," Robert says dismissively. Then he grins so widely that it looks like the top of his head might separate. "Well, I'm sure you know where to find me."

He minces off through the small crowd before I can answer. I know he is just playing silly games, but even standing next to him is agony. I'll probably never be able to prove what he did to Wally, and that's heartbreaking.

The next hour is spent wandering around the dining room and living room, chatting with people I don't know for a minute before running out of things to say. Astrid seems to be a lot better at this sort of thing than I ever will be. Whenever I see her, she is effortlessly conversing with whoever wants to talk.

I see Fletcher and Lilith together a few times. She looks beautiful, if a little on edge, and he seems awkward and scared. I don't think I've ever seen Fletcher show fear before now. Well, that's not entirely true. But still, it doesn't suit him. I probably should feel sorry for him having a father like Robert. But whenever I do, I remember my daughter's bruises, and it goes away.

Suddenly, there is a sharp ringing noise, then the unmistakable sound through the speakers of a microphone being tapped. When I look to the end of the room, Robert stands next to the podium. I scan the room for Astrid, but I can't see her. I spot Lilith and Fletcher standing together off to the side, the latter of them looking terrified now.

"Ladies and gentlemen," Robert's voice booms. "Welcome to my granddaughter Astrid's eighteenth birthday party."

Robert is grinning like a shark. It makes the one he gave me an hour ago seem like a twitch of his lips. It's at this moment that I know he is about to bring the axe down. I just don't know how.

Chapter 69: Lilith

Robert looks as smug as I've ever seen him as he stands at the makeshift podium. I couldn't believe my eyes when we arrived earlier and saw it constructed at the head of the long table. Who has a podium at an eighteenth birthday party? Fletcher just shrugged when I asked him and said, "You know him."

The hour since then has been spent mingling with people I can only describe as DuBose Construction employees. There is a spattering of other men and women in evening wear that I don't know. I think they are Robert's business associates. The handful of Astrid's friends—I think I counted four—seem to have been randomly selected from her phonebook.

Robert pauses after addressing the room. I see him scanning the crowd until his eyes land on me.

"Ah," he says, his already booming voice ten times more intrusive through the speakers. "There she is. My one-time daughter-in-law."

Fletcher squirms beside me, and I lean in and whisper, "What is going on?"

Fletcher shrugs and looks at his feet.

"I say one-time daughter-in-law for a reason," Robert continues. "Because when we all thought my wonderful son was dead, their marriage was technically dissolved. But I think dear old Lilith was hoping Fletcher would ask her to marry him again, wasn't she?"

Robert looks down at me as he speaks these words, and I try not to look away. I don't know what game he's playing, but I suddenly regret ever having agreed to this. He hasn't changed, and he never will.

I break his childish game of locking gazes and scan the room for Mom. We are too close to the front, and the rows of people who have gathered around the dining room table make it impossible for me to see far. Everyone is standing facing Robert, looking awkward.

Robert chuckles into the microphone, and I look back up.

"Don't mind me," he declares, still laughing a little. "I'm just messing with her. No, we are here to celebrate my granddaughter's eighteenth birthday, a big day in anyone's life." The crowd seems to breathe a universal sigh of relief, and Robert presses on. "Yes, a very important day in *any* person's life. A day when they become an adult, and a day when they get ready to go out into the world and find their own path."

A man somewhere in the crowd slurs the words, "Here, here," and a few others join in.

Robert brings a hand up to silence them. "But this could have been an even bigger day for our little Astrid, couldn't it?"

That awkward feeling seems to press down on the room again. I'm scanning the crowd for my daughter, but she is nowhere to be seen. My heart is beating too fast, and every time I look at Fletcher for support, he drops his eyes. Does he know what his father is doing up there? Is there some big, mean punchline coming?

"Yes," Robert says. "Until the miraculous return of my son, Astrid was due to get 10 percent of any future earnings made by one of my firms in City Point. Fletcher, in his disdain toward me, had signed it away in his will before his tragic trip to the Gauley River. It was his little way of saying, 'screw you, Dad.'"

"Come on, Robert," a man I can't see in the crowd says. "There is no need for this."

"SHUT YOUR MOUTH!" Robert roars, making me jump. A couple of people gasp, and I see Fletcher cringing. "This is my house, and I'll say whatever I goddamned like."

Robert readjusts his dickie-bow and grins again just as Astrid comes up beside me.

"Come on, Mom," she says into my ear. "We should go."

"I couldn't agree more," I tell her through clenched teeth.

"Ah, there she is now!" Robert calls from the podium. "You know what happens today, Astrid?"

"I don't care, Robert," Astrid tells him, her eyes locked onto mine.

"Your shitty little inheritance becomes null and void," Robert declares, ignoring her. "Now that you're eighteen and never claimed what your father left you, the will Fletcher made means nothing!"

I can't believe Robert is doing this over 10 percent of future earnings in one of his firms. What would that even amount to? John told me years ago that it might mean as much as a new car each year, but not much more than that. Robert must have spent ten grand on this party alone. Is he really so petty to want to screw his own granddaughter out of what must amount to a pittance to him?

Astrid has me by the hand as she leads me across the room, and I can feel Fletcher following behind me. As we pass by the podium—close enough that I can smell Robert's cologne—he leans into the microphone again and says, "Do you hear me, Lilith? Your scrounging family is done stealing from me!"

I want to tell him where he can stuff his 10 percent, but Astrid has already turned on him.

"I never wanted your money, Robert," she hisses. Beside me, Fletcher looks like a deer caught in headlights. Astrid points her finger at the podium. "Understand this. I don't care about it."

"YOU'LL CARE!" Robert roars. "YOU'LL CARE BECAUSE I SAID YOU'LL CARE!"

It's then that the side door Astrid is leading me toward opens. What seems like a sea of people in navy flak jackets with BPD printed on the back in yellow come streaming in. They are holding pistols, and I suddenly feel like I'm dreaming.

One of them—a strangely handsome older man with a blond crew cut—steps up to the podium holding a piece of paper. He says, "Robert DuBose, I'm arresting you on suspicion of the murders of Henry Lakes and Donald Piaza. Anything you say can and will…"

The rest fades into a stream of words I can't really hear. I turn to see if Fletcher is still behind me, but he's gone. I keep looking for him as Astrid leads me from the dining room, but he has slipped out somewhere and disappeared.

Chapter 70: Virginia

The weeks following Astrid's birthday party were tough. The public showing of Robert's arrest and the media storm that came after it was not something we were prepared for. Honestly, who could be ready for something like that?

Surprisingly, I was pretty sad leaving my apartment. Of course, I was happy to be moving back into my old place next to Lilith's, but I had grown attached to my little nest in the city. But my daughter's welfare will always come first.

Months have passed now since Robert's arrest, and the media interest has died down. It will spike for a while again when the trial starts, but there is nothing we can do about that except be there for each other. When the time comes, we'll be more prepared, as we've dealt with it once already.

"Your move," Tony says, nodding at the chessboard.

We are sitting at the kitchen table of his one-bedroom place on Northampton Street. Outside, the last of the summer's beautiful weather continues to hold on to its glory before spring takes over. I think of Astrid starting her time at Harvard and smile, knowing she will succeed there as she has in every other aspect of her life.

She has tried to explain what molecular biology is to me on many occasions, but the things she says all sound like white noise to me.

I take my pawn and move it one space up. Tony looks at me with those deep, blue eyes and smiles.

"That's it?" he asks, chuckling. "All that time just to move a pawn?"

"This shit is chess, not checkers," I tell him, imitating Denzel Washington in his pièce de résistance, *Training Day*.

Tony Demarco laughs loudly, the sound booming around the room. His boyish features—the ones that had me putting him in his early forties when I first met him and not his actual fifty-one—crease up as he bangs his knee with a meaty fist.

"Yeah," he says when he's finally gathered himself. "I suppose you're right."

Getting involved romantically with Robert DuBose's arresting officer was never in my plans. How could it be, as it is just so ridiculous? For one thing, I never thought Robert would *have* an arresting officer. The charges they got him on were from eight years ago, and Tony had only informed me when we met in the BPD parking lot that the police had a man who claimed to have something incriminating on Robert. What it was or how they came to have such a man in custody was confidential.

Even now, I only know what is available to the public, which is actually most of the story.

Robert DuBose had ordered the slaying of two of his competitors—Henry Lakes and Donald Piaza—eight years prior. At the time of their deaths, police didn't even investigate it as a murder case. It was seen as a basic DUI, as the two men had copious amounts of narcotics in their systems and had been driving at high speed when their car hit a wall. Of course, no one seemed to question why two competing construction company owners were supposedly taking a friendly ride together. *Or* the fact that Robert DuBose's company had become the largest one in the whole of Massachusetts overnight.

As it turned out, the man whose testimony would lead to the arrest of Robert DuBose at his granddaughter's eighteenth birthday party had been arrested on a completely separate charge. After a night of heavy drinking, Faustino Cole got involved in a high-stakes poker game downtown. This had led to an argument with a fellow player who had accused him of cheating, and the forty-eight-year-old Faustino had pulled a gun on him and shot him through the heart.

Following his arrest, Mr. Cole supposedly sang like a canary, promising dirt on one of the biggest crime bosses in Boston. He then proceeded to explain that he had been a witness to an order being given by one Robert DuBose to have his two main competitors die in a—finger quotes at the ready—car crash. His resulting testimony, coupled with some shrewd negotiations from Cole's lawyer, got him a short sentence in an unknown prison while Robert DuBose was dragged out of his home in cuffs.

"How's Lilith doing?" Tony asks as I consider my next move. He has shown a big interest in my daughter's well-being, which is just another wonderful side to the man.

"Better," I tell him. "She's getting there."

Losing her husband for a second time was another part of this whole thing that was unforeseen. Fletcher or Michael Foster, or whoever he was, slipped out of the party the moment the police came through the door. I've asked Tony if they had anything on him, and he swears they didn't. Then he went on to add that even if they did, he couldn't tell me.

I think Lilith is waiting for Fletcher to come back. I see it on her face every day. This isn't like twelve years ago when I always sensed some relief in her that he was gone. No, this time, she has lost a man that was kind and loving to her. It breaks my heart to see her suffer, and I know she is putting on a brave face for Astrid's sake.

I take my rook and move it halfway across the board, making Tony lift his eyebrows.

"That's either a nothing move, or it's a genius one," he says.

Smiling, I reply, "Maybe it's both!"

"Is that possible?"

"Anything is possible."

"Damn, you're hot," he chimes, leaning in and kissing my lips.

When his hand comes up and cups my face, I forget about the game. And when he scoops me off my feet and carries me into the bedroom, everything else slips away too.

Chapter 71: Lilith

The Noanet Woodlands is a long way to drive just to go for a walk, but the trees and the air are so nice that it's always worth it in the end. I come here with Mom at least twice a year, and we always seem to leave with our minds and our relationship in a better place. There is something about walking through a wooded area that brings great calmness to any conversation. Maybe it's the constant, pleasant distractions of everything buzzing, swaying, and growing. There is always something amazing to look at.

"How are things with Tony?" I ask. I'm so happy for Mom to have found someone, and Tony Demarco seems like a nice man.

"Good," Mom replies, and I notice she's blushing. We are both wearing sweats, but her radiant mood seems to make hers look like a lavish evening gown.

"Seems like a little more than good to me," I tell her through heavy breaths. We've been walking for nearly two hours, and we're close to having done the full circuit. The gravel parking lot at the northern side should come into view at any moment.

Mom shrugs and sniffs in some of the country air. As she does, her eyes close, and she looks so happy. Again, I'm filled with gratitude that she has found someone to make her feel that way.

I thought I had, but it turns out that the new Fletcher was still just the old one when the chips were down. When things got tough, he ran. Even through my bitterness, I can't help feeling that I'm wrong about that part. Or am I hoping? He had changed so much, and it wasn't just an act. I know that with all my heart, but then why did he leave me again? Sometimes I wish he really had died that day on the river instead of coming back and giving me a glimpse of how it could have been.

"Are you okay?" Mom asks, and I instantly feel guilty for having turned the attention to me.

"I'm good," I tell her, and it's almost true. It will take a while to get over this, but I know I will. I have my two best girls on my side, so anything is possible.

"And the job?" Mom asks. "A fresh year as a full-time teacher and all that!"

"It's great. I forgot how rewarding it could be knowing that what I start with the kids, I'll be able to see out."

"You're a good person, Lilith," Mom says. "I hope you know that."

"Thanks, Mom."

In the trees all around us, unseen critters and birds go about their day. Bars of sunlight cut down through the lush foliage, casting thick rays of dusty light before us. The winding pathway weaves through the undergrowth, cutting a trail for us to follow. I can smell soil and berries, and the earthy sweetness is soothing.

After the circus that followed Robert's arrest, calm days like this are a blessing that I refuse to waste by fretting. Still, it's hard to shake such negative thoughts when there is no closure. It's almost a certainty that Robert will be sent down; it's only a matter of for how long. Rumor has it that he will never see the light of day, and that's good. But not knowing where Fletcher is and why he left will be a door that I'll probably never be able to shut.

Mom has her own unanswered questions, too, and I need to remember that she has been dealing with the main one for twenty years. Whether or not Robert killed my father is still unknown, and I don't believe we will ever find the answer. Do I think he did it now? You bet your life I do. I just wish I had stood by Mom when she first suggested it.

"I'm sorry, Mom," I say, keeping my eyes firmly ahead of me.

"What?" she almost snorts. "What are you talking about?"

"I should have believed you when you told me about Dad's murder."

"Hey," Mom says, stopping me with her hand. When I look into her eyes, they show only love. "I shouldn't have pushed it on you. You had enough to deal with, and it was my issue."

I smile at her, but I still feel bad.

We only walk for another five minutes before I see the parking lot ahead. There are five or six cars there besides my SUV. A man is getting out of one in the distance, and I can see that he is holding a picnic basket. A small child climbs out of the back seat and runs around to him, her hands in the air as she presumably asks to carry some of the stuff he is holding. It reminds me of Astrid when she was little and how she always wanted to be seen as one of the grown-ups.

Mom must be thinking the same, as she says, "So cute. There is no way she is carrying that basket!"

Smiling, we both walk through the small wooden arch with the sign dangling from it announcing where we are. The man with the picnic basket has his back to us as he unloads more stuff out of the trunk. It looks like he is alone with the girl, and I get the feeling he is a single dad bringing his little one out for the day. There is something in the way he moves.

As we pass his car, he turns around, and I almost scream. I hear Mom gasp beside me, and I have to blink a few times before I can accept what I'm seeing.

"Fletcher?" I somehow say after a moment.

"Daddy, who's that?" the little girl says, looking up at her pop. "Daddy, who's Fletcher?"

"Hi, Lilith," Fletcher says sheepishly. "Listen, I can explain."

Chapter 72: Virginia

The little girl, who we've discovered is named Lucy, is playing on one of the wooden climbing frames near the entrance of the Noanet Woodlands. Her father is sitting on the opposite side of a picnic bench, facing Lilith and me. To her credit, my daughter has remained amazingly calm. I don't think she would be if a little girl weren't in such close proximity.

"Sorry, Ms. Townsend," Fletcher says. God, is it really him? It can't be. I'm more confused than I've ever been. "Can I speak with Lilith alone?"

"Whatever you have to say, you can say in front of my mother," Lilith snaps. I can see that she is trying very hard to keep her voice down.

"That's fair," he says. "Well, I suppose I should properly introduce myself."

I swallow hard, completely unprepared for whatever is about to happen. With the way things have gone this year, I wouldn't be overly shocked if he peeled his skin off to reveal a metal face before telling us he is an android sent back from the future to wreak havoc on unsuspecting families.

Instead, he inhales deeply and lets it out in one long breath.

"My real name is Charlie Bowles," he begins. "That girl behind us," he turns around and points at her as she hangs from the monkey bars, "is my daughter. Her mother and I broke up not long after she was born."

"I don't know what this has to do with you pretending to be my goddamned dead husband," Lilith hisses. I can hear her teeth grinding together, and I reach across and place my hand on hers. She grips it tightly.

Charlie—it's going to take a while to get used to that—lifts a hand in surrender. He looks like he's about to burst into tears, and I can see him shaking from here.

"I'll get there, Loly—"

"Don't you *dare* call me that," Lilith spits.

"I'm sorry. Lilith." He looks over his shoulder again to check on his daughter, then turns back to us. "My wife left me because of my gambling. It was bad... really bad. But I got better. It was too late for us for things to work, and by then, I was too deep into Robert's pocket to ever get out." For some reason, he brings his hand up to the scar on the side of his head. "Well, there was one way he would allow me to get out."

"By pretending to be my husband?" Lilith says.

Fletcher nods once. "I said no. It was just too twisted." A single tear rolls down his cheek as he leans across the table. His voice is no more than a hoarse whisper. "They showed me pictures of Lucy—on her way to school, playing in the park, even one through the curtains of her at home with her mom. They said that she wouldn't live to see her eighth birthday if I didn't do what they wanted."

Lilith groans beside me, and I feel my hatred for Robert DuBose rising. If this man is telling the truth—and I see no benefit to him lying at this stage—then Robert is even more twisted than I ever imagined.

"Why would he be so devious?" I say, making them both look at me. "Just for the 10 percent?"

Charlie shrugs. "So far as I know. He never really spoke to me outside of the times when all of us were all together. I usually got a call from a man I don't know when they needed me to say or do something."

"*Do* something?" Lilith growls. "*Do* something. So all the times we were..." She looks at me for a moment like she is weighing up whether she can say what she needs to or not, then turns back to him. "All the time we were intimate, you were just *doing* something?"

"Oh, God," Charlie groans, looking away. "No, Lilith, those moments were real. That's why I had to get away. I was going to leave after Astrid's party anyway. Run away and never come back. I couldn't keep playing his game when I was falling for you."

"Oh, drop the act," Lilith spits. "Robert is locked up, and your debt is paid. You can stop stringing me along."

"I wasn't," Charlie says in a low voice, more to himself than us, I feel. "I love you."

Lilith shakes her head, but I can see some of what he is saying getting through to her. It is seeping into me too. The poor man seems genuine, and if someone like Robert threatened to harm my daughter, I'd certainly do whatever he asked.

"But you look so much like Fletcher," I say.

"Apparently Robert had waited a long time for *that* opportunity," Charlie says, pure venom in his voice. I can see that he loathes Robert DuBose as much as I do, maybe even more. "He almost did a little jig when his guys brought me to him. Said I was a dead ringer."

"And the scar?" I say, pointing at it. "Bit of a coincidence, huh?"

"This," he says, pointing at it himself. "Courtesy of a crowbar swung by one of Robert's goons. He wanted it to look authentic, as he put it. Watched the whole thing being done and even waved at me as his guys loaded me into a car and brought me to one of his shady doctors to have it stitched up again.

"That was months before I even met you, Lilith. Robert wanted the scar to heal fully before his plan went into action. He kept pressing me to get closer to Astrid, but I just couldn't drag her into it. At least, no more than my cowardly actions already had."

Charlie's head drops so low that I can see the back of his shirt collar. When I look at Lilith, she is stone-faced. This is almost too much for me to take in, so I can only imagine how hard it must be for her. Through it all, I can sense her feelings for the broken man before her, and I can almost see her physically trying to fight them.

"The DNA, hospital records, all that stuff?" Lilith asks. Has her voice softened just a little? It's hard to tell.

Charlie brings his gaze back up to hers. "All forged, I reckon. He didn't really fill me in on the details, but he knows a lot of powerful people. Something like that would be nothing to him."

"Son of a bitch," I snap.

"Agreed," Charlie says. When he smiles, I think I hear Lilith let out another one of those low, pained groans.

"Well," Lilith suddenly says, standing. "I think we've heard enough."

I go to protest, but Lilith grabs my hand and pulls me up. I can see how much she cares for this man, regardless of the lies he told. From the sounds of it, his feelings—and hers—were real. Lilith's hand is holding mine so tightly as we walk toward her car that I wince. I see her look back over her shoulder once, and then we're getting into the car, the silence almost tangible.

Lilith starts the SUV up and spins it around so that Charlie Bowles is in the rearview mirror. With tears streaming down her face, she drives out through the main entrance, leaving the man I know that she loves broken on a picnic bench.

Epilogue: Virginia

Robert DuBose was given two life sentences to run back-to-back. In his desperate attempts to save his own bacon, he gave testimonies that brought down several of his main men and a few of his enemies. Being a rat did him no good, and the judge informed him that he was one of the most evil men he'd ever seen before slamming his gavel down and telling the bailiff to take him away.

Much like the time he was arrested, the media feeding frenzy was intense. It was easier to handle, as we were a lot more prepared. Of course, one of their biggest stories was how Robert's daughter-in-law was being spotted at restaurants or out shopping for groceries with the handsome man he had blackmailed on her arm.

I like to think that it was this bit of information that hurt Robert the most. And if I know the man as well as I think I do, I'm certain that it would have.

Charlie is everything that Fletcher wasn't: caring, loving, and a good man. Now that he has opened up to Astrid, they have become quite close over the last year. Lucy has slotted into our family like a proverbial pea in a pod, and her lovable determination instantly cemented her as one of the girls. We are now four strong instead of three.

"Are you ready?" I ask my daughter as I adjust her veil. She looks radiant, and I couldn't be happier for her.

Behind her, Astrid scans the ground with a comical grin across her face.

"What's up with you?" Lilith asks, turning around.

"No twenty-foot hem this time?" Astrid mocks.

"Shut up!" Lilith says, laughing. "That wasn't my choice."

The wedding dress Lilith got to pick herself this time is simple yet elegant, which is a lot like her. Her bare shoulders shine in the lights of her living room, and the brown eyes looking back at me seem happy. In fact, I know she is happy.

Astrid picks her phone up off the coffee table as it buzzes, reads something, and says, "That's a text from Tony. Charlie is at the church. We should get going."

Lilith takes a deep breath, smiling nervously as she lets it out.

"No need to be worried," I tell her. "Charlie was worth the wait."

Astrid nods in agreement, and Lilith's smile broadens. My girl has been through so much, but things are finally looking up for her.

The sound of a small, tapping foot makes us spin around. Lucy is standing in the doorway between the living room and kitchen, holding a basket of flowers. Her dress is just a miniature version of Lilith's, and she looks adorable.

Pointing at an invisible watch on her wrist, she says, "Are we going, or what?"

The three of us laugh, making Lucy scrunch her face up. Then we all gather up our things and head out into the morning sunshine.

A man in top and tails is standing beside an old, classic car that gives me déjà vu. Then the sensation passes, and the four of us load into the back. As we begin our journey to the church, I look at my daughter as she begins her new adventure. Her last one ended badly, but I see it going a lot differently this time.

Although the memory is still dark, I can't stop my mind from drifting back to that night thirteen years ago when Lilith called me in tears. Seeing her face as white as a sheet as she told me what Fletcher had done had almost broken me. I'd know what he had been doing to her before then, but this was different. It was confirmation.

As I drove through the night toward the Gauley River, I kept waiting for some part of my conscience to make me stop. Had I known the entire trip what I would do when I caught up with him? Yes, I had, and I don't think there was anything that could have stopped me. There is only so much a person can take, and that feeling is endlessly multiplied when someone's child is the one being harmed.

Seeing Fletcher's smug face the next morning as he prepared his raft had pushed me over the edge. Watching him standing at the water's edge without a care in the world after what he had done. How could he be so nonchalant after battering my daughter for the umpteenth time? Even now, on this happy day, my anger is at boiling point.

He's long gone now, I tell myself as I blow out air. *You made sure of that.*

I did. And I'll never apologize for it. The sound the rock made as it came down on the side of his face will stay with me forever, as will the panic I felt as I smashed his raft apart right after. If he hadn't set out so early that morning, there might have been other people around. If someone had come upon the scene, I'd be the one behind bars right now. But they didn't, and I rolled him into the water with the bits of his raft and watched as the current dragged it all away.

Robert got lucky with the spot he picked on Charlie's head. The scar was so close to where I struck Fletcher that it was one thing that nearly convinced me I hadn't finished the job. That, and how much he looked like him.

I never fully believed it was Fletcher, though. I couldn't. I'd felt how lifeless his body was as I pushed him into the river. I saw the blood as it spilled onto the raft by his feet. Sure, I was sleep deprived from the overnight drive, but I knew what I had experienced had been real. Nobody could have survived that.

By the time I had driven back to Lilith's house, the police would have been pulling bits of his bloodstained raft from the water.

"Nana," Astrid says, clicking her fingers in my face. "Hey, old woman!"

"Old!" I exclaim. "You cheeky little pup!" I try to clip her hand away, but she whips it back before I can. Lucy giggles into her palm, and Lilith laughs. "I'm sixty years young!"

"You're only as old as the man you're feeling, right, Nana," Astrid says, raising her eyebrows up and down a few times.

This time, it's Lilith who covers her mouth when she laughs, and I take another half-swing at my granddaughter.

"You're just jealous that I have a boy toy," I tell her. "Although technically, can a fifty-two-year-old man be a boy toy?"

"I hate boys," Lucy informs us. "But I looove toys."

When the three adults in the back of the stately car erupt in laughter, Lucy looks startled. Then she joins in, slapping her knee for emphasis. When we've all calmed down, I see the steeple of the church appearing in the morning sun.

When the car comes to a stop, the four of us get out and stand there for a moment. Tony appears through the crowd of sharply dressed wedding guests and comes up beside me.

"You look beautiful," he tells me. Then he turns to the bride, "And you look angelic, Lilith."

After that, he gives Astrid a big hug and a peck on the cheek.

"Can I have a moment with Mom?" Lilith says to the others. As they nod and wander off toward the front of the church, she looks at me and smiles through her veil.

"Tony is right," I tell her. "You do look angelic."

"Thanks, Mom," she says. "For everything."

We hug, and I feel that pinch of guilt that has been with me for thirteen years. Everything I did, I did to keep my family safe. Seeing my daughter now, about to marry a man who loves her more than life itself, I know I made the right decision. I guess some bad things that happen end up being good things, and I'm sure it can work the other way too.

"Your father would have loved to be here," I tell her. "To walk you down the aisle."

"I know," Lilith says, nodding slowly. Then she smiles again, her entire face lighting up. "But I have you here, and that's enough for me."

I link my arm around my daughter's, feeling her warmth against my skin. Our bond will never be broken, especially not by a hidden memory of the Gauley River. What happened in the past can stay there, and as I walk my daughter toward her future, I know everything has worked out the way it should.

Did you enjoy The Univited Caller? If so, be sure to check out The Chambermaid!

Also By Ramona Light

Sign up to my mailing list for a free e-book:

What's Yours Is Mine

Available on Amazon:

The Lost Son

Red Below Deck

The Chambermaid

No Place Safe

The Uninvited Caller

Made in the USA
Middletown, DE
01 May 2023

29838479R00215